The Repulse Chronicles
Book One

Onslaught

by
Chris James

www.chrisjamesauthor.com

Also by Chris James

Science fiction novels:
Repulse: Europe at War 2062–2064
Time Is the Only God
Dystopia Descending
The Repulse Chronicles, Book Two: Invasion
The Repulse Chronicles, Book Three: The Battle for Europe
The Repulse Chronicles, Book Four: The Endgame
The Repulse Chronicles, Book Five: The Race against Time

Available as Kindle e-books and paperbacks from Amazon

ISBN: 9798654531063

Chapter 1

10.07 Monday 19 December 2061

With only moments left to live, Kaliq Zayan crouched by the hot, hard metal container and shivered despite the heat. Terror chilled his body as the port city of Jeddah receded and the vast ship on which he stowed away proceeded towards open sea. He'd heard the rumours; he knew the risk. He felt the pulse in his right temple pound against the small data-pod sewn into the *agal* that held the traditional *keffiyeh* headdress on his head.

All of his life, Kaliq had wanted to know why. His memory replayed childhood recollections of his exasperated mother and confused father. Kaliq was different from his siblings, but only his parents grasped this. After problematic schooling, an uncle secured a place for the young Kaliq at the leading Tehran technical university, and from there he'd been 'spotted' by a lecturer who was also a covert member of the *alkhidmat alssrriat al'uwlaa*, the near-mythical department of the Third Caliph's personal secret service. This service covertly monitored Kaliq for months until, a few days before his

1

matriculation, the lecturer had called him into his office. Two other men flanked the lecturer.

Thereafter, Kaliq regarded that day as The Day: the last day he saw his family, his friends, his fellow students. The day his life changed irrevocably in the service of the Third Caliph. His relentless inquisitiveness, and chance that his lecturer was a member of the secret service, had altered the direction of his life to ensure it would end much sooner than it should have. The men took him from Tehran along the new network of highways which crisscrossed the entire terrain of the Caliphate. On the way, they explained the vast honour Kaliq had been fortunate enough to receive: he would be set to work with the most sophisticated artificial intelligence yet created, for the glory of the Caliph. At that time, Kaliq relished his good luck.

They took him to Tazirbu, an oasis deep in the Sahara desert. Rumours of such places had abounded at his university, unconfirmed secrets whispered late in the evening, but the shock Kaliq felt when he arrived at the sprawling weapons' production facility equalled his confusion at being removed from his studies mere days before he would complete them. The men from the *alkhidmat alssrriat al'uwlaa* handed him over to another man who, Kaliq later found out, was the director of the entire complex.

Kaliq's speciality meant his responsibility would be to monitor and interrogate the super AI tasked with overseeing construction. On the second day, he underwent a medical examination which included the doctor warning him that he should not question his orders, and should know that if he ever left Tazirbu, he would not be the only one to suffer. This veiled threat unnerved the young man, but a voice deeper in his mind whispered that the threat was empty, because the benevolent Caliph would not stoop to such measures.

A few weeks after his arrival, the facility began producing hundreds of autonomous combat aircraft. Through the super AI, he found out that this facility was one of a number spread throughout Caliphate territory, and in tandem with manufacturing arms on an immense scale, millions of warriors were also being trained, and a vast army would be created to invade and fight the infidels wherever the Third Caliph decided. In combination, super AI, Chinese raw materials and modern production techniques would be used to create a martial force greater than any the world had previously seen.

As the days turned into weeks, Kaliq met others like him and formed fleeting friendships with young men who had also been removed from towns and cities across the Caliphate. These friendships cut through Kaliq's naivety like a butcher's knife through lamb. Soon, he understood that the veiled threats carried more than a grain of truth. His faith in the Third Caliph's benevolence wilted before finally dying when all of them concluded that their lives were indeed in the severest danger.

Denied contact with their families and friends, they realised that what was happening at Tazirbu had to remain absolutely secret; so secret, in fact, that very soon an air of fatality settled over the young men. Conjecture became rumour which became believed as fact. They knew the Caliph himself regarded Tazirbu as one of the first and most important steps on a journey which would make him the most powerful global ruler in history. Against such a destiny, these young men thought, and then talked themselves into believing, they played an important yet ultimately terminal role in the Third Caliph's designs.

One hundred and twenty-three days after The Day, Kaliq decided he would see his family again, whatever the risk. The volume of ACA production increased as a second and then a third production line were added to the mass of weapons being manufactured, and Kaliq sensed the governing super AI required less and less interrogation. Among his colleagues, recent rumours of their likely fate once their work was complete included everything from benevolent removal to distant mountain villages to summary execution.

Through some small subterfuge, he managed to acquire a cleaner's uniform to aid his escape. In retrospect, he would come to see his attempt as the most futile act of his short life, but at the time he considered the four-and-a-half-thousand kilometre journey via Cairo, Damascus and Baghdad, to be achievable. Before he left, he elected to load data regarding current ACA stockpiles and the production rate, along with a few restricted reports he'd accessed concerning the extent of warrior training programs at other facilities, into a small data-pod. He sewed this into the *agal* which held the *keffiyeh* on his head. He wanted to prove to his family all in which he had been involved.

He left after the roll call at sundown to give himself as much of a head start as possible. He hoped they wouldn't investigate his sudden absence too keenly, and he'd have time to reach his home province. However, Kaliq's problems began before sunrise the following day as the transport approached the Siwa Oasis, still some seven hundred kilometres southwest of Cairo. Inspectors from the Transport Ministry boarded the multi-carriage autonomous vehicle and began checking identifications and questioning passengers on the purpose of their journeys. Kaliq had anticipated this, but when the moment came he doubted they would believe him, and he panicked. He overrode a lock between two of the spacious carriages, clung on to the outside grips, and pulled himself up onto the roof. He stayed there for the hour for which the transport remained at the oasis, breaking back in just as it accelerated towards its next destination.

The journey to Cairo saw the panic inside Kaliq grow like bacteria in a culture. He caught casual glances from

4

strangers which made him think they were watching him. As the transport approached Cairo, his dread solidified, hardening into a perception that danger lurked around every partition. He walked back and forth along the length of the transport, from carriage to carriage, becoming more terrified at what awaited him. He realised the futility of his decision to leave Tazirbu, and briefly entertained the idea of returning. But in his panicked state, Kaliq only saw the potential for disaster in each of his limited choices. The belief that he would see his family again faded with the hot sunlight.

The transport arrived at the Cairo terminus, at which point fate intervened. Spotted and then chased by two *Mutaween* agents, Kaliq ended up hiding in the toilet of a transport bound for the port city of Jeddah. During the four-hour trip along the coast, Kaliq formulated a new and radical plan: to escape the Caliphate altogether, and warn the rest of the world of the vastness of the armaments and armies the Third Caliph had in hand. This was a novel idea in the young Kaliq's head, but his relentless inquisitiveness had led him along other, far less safe paths of thought. For in his childhood he'd even questioned the existence of Allah, and of everything that everyone around him believed without question.

In his hour of panicked flight, he understood what he had to do, what he'd always had to do. The billions of souls in the rest of the world could not all be infidels and unbelievers. They could not all be contemptible. They had to have lives and loves and passions and dreams and families and friends and a desire to live in peace. If the Third Caliph wanted to become the most powerful ruler on Earth, millions would have to die at the hands of all those ACAs and warriors.

When the transport arrived in Jeddah, Kaliq hurried to the port by following road signs and dodging autonomous vehicles, their occupants taking no notice of him. He felt better as soon as he vaulted a chain-link fence and landed on the hard, dusty concrete among endless rows of giant metal containers. He stared at the enormous cargo ships as he walked around the docks and wharfs, his cleaner's uniform now giving him a strange sense of anonymity.

Three hours later, Kaliq Zayan crouched by the hard metal container and shivered despite the heat. He looked out past the aft rails at the port as it receded, and felt exhilaration and terror and disbelief at what he'd done. He also felt a strange kind of freedom: he didn't know the ship's destination, although he guessed it would probably be a port in China, but his spirit exulted at being outside Caliphate territory. He had no concept of what he might do when he got to his destination, and he did not even know how he would survive the voyage undetected.

For several hours, Kaliq's heart had been beating very hard in his chest, and he wondered why it should continue to do so as the immediate danger faded with the coastline. Abruptly, his heart stopped and he fell onto his back. Kaliq's final thoughts revolved around the single word that had defined his life: why? He didn't understand why he could no longer breathe or why he could no longer move. He stared at the deep blue sky above him as the word 'why?' remained at the centre of his fading mind. The blue deepened to black, and at the last, Kaliq understood his life had reached its end.

Unknown to Kaliq Zayan, Caliphate authorities had followed his progress from the moment he stepped outside the facility at Tazirbu. They tried to apprehend him on the transport to Cairo, but both of the agents declined to follow him onto the roof, their controllers deciding that since the bulk of Zayan's work had been done and he was scheduled for liquidation shortly in any case, it would not have mattered if he fell to his death. A further attempt to capture and liquidate him was made at Cairo, but when he escaped on the transport to Jeddah, the authorities realised he intended to make a foolhardy attempt to leave Caliphate territory, and stopped all attempts to apprehend him. Everyone involved in the operation knew that as soon as the Chinese container ship left Caliphate territorial waters, the nano-bots injected into his body during the medical on his second day at the facility would shred his heart.

Chapter 2

00.33 Friday 13 January 2062

The Englishman curled up in the bed and smiled to himself. He knew Marshal Zhou had finished for the night, for in the darkness he could hear his lover's breathing slow as Zhou's body relaxed. In a few moments, that familiar growling snore on the inhalation of each breath would begin, and the small yet heavily built form of Marshal Zhou would sleep soundly until it was time for his 4.00 am pee.

The Englishman pulled the sheet up to partially cover his face and chewed on part of the seam, a habit which had comforted him since childhood. He glanced out at the polished wood floor and at his and his lover's clothes strewn over it, dimly lit by broken silver moonlight. The Englishman knew they were safe here in Zhou's private quarters in the compound, and the faintest exhilaration gripped his heart when he thought again how far he'd come in the few short months since his diplomatic posting to Beijing.

He and Zhou had been lovers for six weeks, and the Englishman worked hard to maintain for Zhou the elation that a married, middle-aged family man felt when, after a lifetime of lying to himself, he finally released his deepest, truest feelings for the first time. For the Englishman, too, pleasure reigned as the last few weeks had seen so many nights dissolve in a whirlwind of sweat and desire. Zhou's passionate enthusiasm still left the Englishman taken aback, and he wondered if, when he would be Zhou's age in twenty years' time, he might find a similarly young stallion who would yield to allow him to reach such plateaus of ecstasy.

Unfortunately, Zhou did not know the Englishman's secondary role inside the English diplomatic mission, although, he reflected, it shouldn't have been difficult to guess. China was the richest and most powerful country in the world. It had the largest and best equipped armed forces, and its social prosperity was held up as a beacon of progress in lesser countries around the globe. In addition, the Chinese government maintained the most widespread network of covert operatives of any nation state—and every other nation state knew it. Thus, other countries wanted very much to keep an eye on China, and so Beijing was a hotbed of covert surveillance and spies masquerading as business people and diplomats.

In this environment, the Englishman's success in seducing Marshal Zhou could objectively be considered an outstanding achievement, but this night had given him something far more satisfying than the marshal's semen, which had begun to escape from the Englishman in a slick dribble. One night during the previous week, Zhou had mentioned the shocking news in military circles that the New Persian Caliphate had created a vast army, despite the Caliph's constant declarations of peaceful intent. The captain of a container ship transporting goods from the Caliphate to China had discovered a data-pod in the clothes of a suddenly deceased stowaway, and transmitted the contents to his masters. Zhou told the Englishman the data contained in it had caused a shockwave in the Chinese military. According to his lover, the Caliphate was secretly constructing an army of ACAs and warriors to rival that of India's. But while China might not consider this a potential threat, the Englishman realised that London needed to know about this unwelcome development in international affairs.

This evening, after their ritual drinking and drug-taking, the marshal had given the Englishman a present: the contents of the data-pod. The two men had shared a glance, and the Englishman felt certain that Zhou must have realised he was a spy. Zhou had kissed him and declared his love. This gave the Englishman a twinge of guilt, for he felt no emotion for the marshal beyond enjoyment of their shared physical pleasure.

Now, as he lay facing away the moonlight and Zhou snored behind him, the Englishman closed his eyes and twitched a small muscle in his left eye. This activated the lens and displayed the data he'd waited all evening to see. The contents of the mysterious data-pod splayed out as an overview menu, in Farsi. The Englishman breathed slowly while the Persian characters were overwritten with Roman ones, and he could read the menu headings. With more subtle movements of the six tiny muscles around his left eye, he explored the sub-categories. Over the next twenty minutes, his heartbeat slowed to a cadence almost in time with the marshal's snoring. He read about armies and battle groups and ground transports and air transports. He read about vast ACA manufacturing plants in transformed desert oases which, the data insisted, were producing up to three thousand ACAs a week. He read about orders of battle and a new, super-AI produced military doctrine which obviated the need for heavy artillery. But none of the items gave any hint of planned deployment or future use. At length, the Englishman considered that such a force could not have been created if it were not to be used, but no matter how thoroughly he searched the data, he could find no clue as to how the Third Caliph would employ this army.

Finally, the Englishman collapsed the files and deactivated the lens, so he saw only darkness when he closed his eyes. Of all the titbits of information and gossip he'd gleaned here, in the capital city of the most powerful nation on Earth, the contents of the data-pod made him feel as though he'd won the espionage jackpot. First thing in the morning, he would encrypt it and send it to London.

Chapter 3

General Sir Terry Tidbury stared at the data in the screen on his desk, fighting an overwhelming sense of disbelief. He stroked his right hand over his bald head as he exhaled, and glanced up at Simms, his adjutant, whose stern, angular face retained its passive indifference.

"Did MI5 say where they got this from?" Sir Terry asked.

"A deep-cover agent in Beijing, Sir Terry; apparently reliable."

The General looked back at the screen and shook his head. "And Squonk's probability?"

The adjutant shrugged: "Slightly less than eight percent."

"What's your opinion?"

"The obvious reaction is to agree with Squonk. The Caliphate is certainly a brutal society, but—"

"We don't know that. It's only what our intel surmises."

13

"Absolutely, Sir Terry. But since the cuts a few years ago which saw MI6 folded into MI5, for intel we've had to rely much more on our super AI's forecasts and other estimates. And Squonk ascribes higher probabilities to many other scenarios: civil war, economic collapse, rampant internal repression. The Caliphate was built on—"

"But supposing it's true?" Sir Terry broke in. "What if the Sunnis and Shias aren't at each other's throats as we've always thought? What if the last two Caliphs have somehow unified enough of their domain to produce those kinds of armaments and that great an army?"

Simms nodded in acceptance and replied: "Then Squonk would factor it in and increase the threat probabilities accordingly, which it has—" Simms broke off as his face twitched. "Ah, ten minutes to today's COBRA meeting, Sir Terry. Your transport will arrive downstairs in three minutes."

"Very well. You're excused."

Simms nodded and left the room.

Sir Terry glanced back at the screen. His dislike of the department's super artificial intelligence added to his sense of foreboding. The English government, in keeping with all governments and corporations the world over, employed super artificial intelligence in supposedly advisory roles. But over the years, Sir Terry had noticed a growing tendency at all levels of authority to trust super AI until it progressed from an advisory to a primary role.

"Squonk," Sir Terry said as he rose from his chair and walked towards the vast, ornate windows which looked out across the slate-grey Westminster rooftops, "assume the figures in the data-pod are accurate and estimate what such forces might be used for."

The gender-neutral voice replied, seemingly from the middle of the room: "The highest probability would be for the

Caliphate to assimilate the Muslims in the Asian Caucuses closest to its bor—"

"Yes, but what about Europe?" Sir Terry interrupted with impatience. "What is the probability of the Caliphate using these forces to attack Europe?"

Squonk answered: "Negligible. Given the Third Caliph's actions to date and the historical and behavioural patterns, the likelihood of an assault on Europe is less than eight percent."

Sir Terry watched the vehicles on the streets between the buildings scurry and buzz and weave, each one controlled by intelligences like Squonk. "Let's assume that this eight percent is enough. If the contents of the data-pod are accurate and the Caliphate attacked Europe with that volume of armaments and warriors, how long would it take NATO to defeat them?"

"With such overwhelming numerical superiority, defeat would be all but impossible. The most frequent range of forecasts project total defeat for NATO from within two weeks to four months. However, all available data insists that such an attack is highly unlikely."

Sir Terry stared through the window, lost in thought. An inexplicable suspicion preyed on his mind. He considered yet again how NATO's position in global affairs had become less relevant over recent decades. On one level, this made Europe marginally safer: the world's military flashpoints all involved China and India and Russia and a myriad of fault lines in Asia, Africa and South America. On another level, however, Sir Terry felt the sidelining of Europe's significance on the global stage might work against it.

Rationality insisted that Squonk and the other NATO super AIs must be correct in their assessments. When he looked at the facts presented so starkly in the data-pod, common sense pointed out that there were two almost insurmountable barriers to believing that Europe could be in even the remotest danger. Firstly, the data-pod's contents could merely be an elaborate hoax: for the Persian Caliphate to have produced such vast stockpiles of ordinance as well as the described six armies totalling three million warriors, defied belief given what the rest of the world suspected of life inside the Caliphate. Secondly, if true this information would be of far more interest to the states closer to the Caliphate's borders, especially India, but also those countries adjoining the Caspian Sea, including Turkmenistan and Kazakhstan. Russia would not appreciate the Caliphate expanding towards its soft underbelly, and such a manoeuvre would raise serious concerns in Delhi as well as Beijing. Still, Terry reflected as the midday sun glinted from one of the skyscrapers on the south bank of the river, an eight percent possibility should not be entirely discounted.

"Squonk," he said, "will the PM be at the COBRA meeting?"

"Affirmative. She is en route."

"Connect me with her."

Chapter 4

C rispin Webb, Director of Communications to the prime minister, scratched the stubble on his cheek and looked through the window as the vehicle in which he sat glided over Westminster Bridge. He didn't see the buildings on the north bank of the Thames because in his vision four separate threads splayed down, each one informing him of who was doing what to whom in his boss's government. Raised foremost was the media thread: the latest unemployment figures were due to be announced at any moment, and Webb needed to be ready to respond and refute without delay. On the occasion of any important government data going public, Webb had to direct his team to counter media criticism immediately, lest the media control the narrative in a disagreeable fashion. Such events were one of the key parts of his job of protecting the prime minister, Dahra Napier. He would have mere moments to influence the slant on the story and keep it in the government's favour. If he failed, it meant a bad day for his boss, which meant a bad day for him.

Abruptly, a communication icon flashed and expanded. Webb groaned aloud to see it was a redirect from General Sir Terry Tidbury, trying to reach Napier. Of all the problems he had to deal with, this relic of an old soldier was absolutely the one he could most easily do without, especially given that the COBRA meeting was due to begin in a few minutes. But the super AI had sent the redirect to him as the most senior person available, rather than to one of his subordinates. Webb twitched his eyelid to select audio only.

"Yes, Sir Terry?"

"Mr Webb, I wanted to have a word with the PM before the meeting to make sure we're all on the same page. I assume she's been briefed on the new intel we've received?"

At that moment, the new unemployment figures went live, showing a steep climb in the number of registered jobless in England. "Ah," Webb stuttered, "I think we can discuss this at the COBRA meeting, General—"

"But the new intel suggests the Caliph—"

"Yes, I'm sure it does," Webb snapped. "But, with respect, the PM is rather wrapped up in getting the gaming legislation through its second reading. See you in a few moments, Sir Terry." Webb ended the connection with another twitch of his eye. Then, a slight movement of another muscle under his eye brought up the six top news feeds, and he groaned.

"Sylvia?" he called, and the connection went through.

"Yes, Sir?" inquired the bright round face which appeared in a thumbnail in the top-left of Webb's vision.

"Refute, why aren't you refuting?"

The girl's face frowned, "We are. Doug has—"

"And *The Mail?*"

"They're next."

"I thought I told you they should've been first?"

Sylvia's face creased into anger and she said: "We know, but a four percent increase is pretty stark, Sir, and we're getting follow-up to our initial expla—"

The thumbnail disappeared as frustration made Webb twitch his eye to terminate the connection. With another blink the other data feeds dissolved from his vision and he could look outside the vehicle. As usual, the super AI controlling the Westminster traffic flow halted the east- and west-bound vehicles so Webb's Rolls could cruise into Whitehall unhindered. Webb used to get a flash of pleasure from enjoying these super-AI benefits that came with real political power, but now he appreciated the problems that such power also attracted. His boss's government had more than enough issues to deal with, and few demanded greater attention than the reason for this COBRA meeting. Taking precedence over and delaying thousands of Londoners on their travels was scant compensation.

Chapter 5

Cabinet Briefing Room A must have seen better days, Webb thought as he shuffled along the oblong conference table to take his seat. Polish could only soften the aged scratches in the oak surface, not make them invisible, and a fine splinter protruded from the edge where he sat. Six other people filed into the room as he tapped at a small panel in the desk in front of him to link the lens in his eye with the huge screens in the walls around the table.

After much shuffling and a volley of coughs, Prime Minister Dahra Napier gave a flick of her head and addressed the large, pugnacious mayor of London, Jack Stone. "What exactly happened yesterday?"

The man's blank eyes stared back at her, set back in his fleshy face. "The New Thames Barrier was raised successfully half an hour before high tide," he replied in a goading voice.

Napier nodded to Webb and he took her cue to reply: "We know that, Jack," he began, giving the mayor a sardonic smile. "Because the Medway floodplains are currently under an extra two metres of water. What the PM would like to

21

know is why you delayed okaying the raise order until it was almost too late. You've seen the media this morning, haven't you? The most popular story in *The Mail* is 'Fifteen minutes from disaster'. Why is that, Jack?"

The mayor sneered and replied: "I told you: as far as I was concerned, I'd given my authorisation to raise in the morning when we knew how high the water would be. The idiot shift manager should have—"

"That 'idiot shift manager' was following the correct procedure," Webb broke in.

Napier continued: "David Perkins here, from MI5, has passed on to me some worrying information, Jack."

The mayor's chin jutted as he glanced at the slim form of the government's master spy. Then he looked at the others around the conference table and the façade of arrogant indifference began to crack. He blustered: "It was a miscommunication, that's all. It doesn't change anything. I was reached, and I responded in time. You can't possibly think—"

Napier leaned forward and hissed at the mayor: "If you don't, quite literally, stop fucking around, Jack, the party will find a way to replace you. Spring is on the way, Jack. There'll be more high tides, so we'd all be very grateful if you could treat the responsibilities with which the voters of London entrusted you with just a tad more use of your brain than your penis. Now, get out."

Webb failed to suppress a smile of satisfaction when he saw the mayor's hand tremble as he got out of the chair. Stone looked down at Napier and opened his mouth to speak, but the PM put her hand up and said: "No, just go. And be very, very careful what you say to the media." She added: "And do give my regards to your wife when you get home, Jack."

The door closed behind the mayor and Napier said to the others: "Well, having come to within a whisker of tens of thousands of Londoners drowning, I think it's time we moved on to consider the rest of the country. Linda?"

The thin, angular face of the Minister for Coastal Defence, Linda Wright, her skin the colour of beige dusted with cinnamon, creased in a slight frown. She blinked twice, then swore. "Damn, hang on... New lens fitted yesterday. Sorry."

The screens on the walls of the conference room flickered before coming to life with a map of the east coast of England. Red markers and other signs littered the inland areas, and Wright explained: "Er, right, so... Yesterday's high tide breached defences at the points on the coast you can see there." She nodded to Sir Terry Tidbury sitting opposite her as she went on: "Local army relief units reported the surge at Wisbech to be a full metre higher than anticipated—probably aggravated by ground saturation—and army AAs are evacuating the last 50 residents of the villages of Wimblington and Doddington, which are now believed to be permanently cut off."

Napier asked: "What about the defences at Slip—" and was interrupted by Wright.

"Sorry, Dahra, I've got Steve in Norwich, ready to report."

"Put him on," the prime minister replied.

On the screens appeared an earnest young face showing concern and frustration. "COBRA?" his coarse voice queried. Then: "Good. Thanks for letting me join in."

"What's the situation like there today, Steve?" Wright asked.

"In a word: crap," came the reply. "Nothing changes. We need either more or preferably better construction replicators to protect the city centre. The high tide yesterday just about did it for the Mid-Yare reserve downriver."

Napier asked: "But funds were made available for sufficient replicators to defend the city. They should have been enough. Why aren't they?"

Webb rolled his eyes as Steve replied with naked sarcasm: "Er, because this shit is second hand Chinese crap? They load themselves up with too much raw material and break down. The super AI spends half of the day shutting individual units down because of diagnostic issues, and then can't get them back in place again. Worse, three days ago we had an ultra-Graphene ribbon breakdown on a northern buttress. By the time the army fitted a replacement, and the super AI got things going again, there wasn't enough time for the limbs to initialise. So, yesterday that section collapsed and the city authority is going to get its arse sued off for compensation."

"No doubt making greater demands on the government-backed compensation scheme," Napier noted dryly.

Wright's right eyelid flickered and Steve's image faded, to be replaced with a picture of a windswept bearded face holding a hand aloft in a high wind. "COBRA? Alfie says I'm on, can ye hear me?"

"Yes, Finley," Wright confirmed. "Looks a bit choppy up there. Go ahead."

"We got the Humber mostly under control, but we're in a running battle with leaks on the north side at Broomfleet."

"How are your replicators holding up?" Wright asked.

Finley scrunched his face against a more powerful gust and shouted: "Our super AI, Alfie, keeps chopping and changing, but she can't help a breakage. She sends the request for a replacement but these things take time to get here. The flanges have a habit of getting bent out of shape after three million tonnes, and we can end up waiting days for new ones because we don't have more modern replicators. We get many

24

more tides much higher like this and we could be in big trouble."

"Thanks, Finley. Go and get out of that wind now."

Finley vanished to be replaced by the map detailing the breaches of the defences along England's eastern coastline.

Napier looked over to Wright: "Casualty update?"

The data appeared on the screen and Wright read out numbers the people at the conference table could see anyway. "Twenty-eight dead, fifty-three missing. These are low numbers all things considered. People in the affected areas had plenty of time to get prepared."

Napier let out a sigh and looked at Webb. "Would a quick tour of some of the more badly hit places help?"

Webb replied, shaking his head: "Your schedule is too busy. Let me see if we can't organise a short tour of the affected areas from a minor royal. One of the King's grandchildren, perhaps?"

"Good idea. Sir Terry, how are the rescue AAs performing?"

"They're at one hundred percent," Sir Terry replied.

"Everyone's grateful for the army's help," Linda Wright said to the whole table. "But as Steve said, all of our super AIs repeatedly note the growing need either for better or more construction replicators."

A slight woman with long, straight black hair, who had yet to speak, looked at Wright and spoke in a soft voice: "The Treasury says there are no more funds available. They claim that what was allocated in the Autumn Statement will have to suffice."

"Thanks, Pam," Wright said with a trace of sarcasm. She glanced at Napier and asked: "Are they aware of the increased ice melt that's been forecast for the spring?"

The prime minister held out a calming hand: "Linda, the Treasury has limited resources, and increased ice melt will also keep weakening the Gulf Stream, which will lead to harsher winters, for which we also need to keep reserves available. I don't want to go running back to the IMF for yet another loan, not at least until we really do have no choice."

An awkward silence descended over the table. Crispin Webb considered how he and Napier were familiar with the English government's financial limitations, but explaining the issue to those not fully aware of just how tight those limits were often led to understandable consternation in other departments.

Napier looked at Sir Terry Tidbury and said: "Sir Terry, you wished to discuss another potential threat, yes?"

"Yes, thank you," Terry replied. He stabbed at a pad embedded in the table in front of him and Webb wondered if the General knew he was a relic. To Webb, it was a mystery how anyone could function without a lens in their eye. The General and Head of the British Armed Forces made his case by describing his concerns. The contents of Zayan's data-pod replaced the graphics of compromised coastal defences. Crispin Webb sensed the other attendees give due consideration out of politeness more than actual interest—Sir Terry was after all an experienced soldier whose key role in the twilight of his career was the defence of the British Isles. The British Armed Forces remained the last reminder of times past: decades after the union had been dissolved, the Home Nations of England, Scotland and Wales still maintained joint armed forces, with a fudge whereby the English king remained nominal head of the British Armed Forces, but the Scottish and Welsh presidents enjoyed 'privileged commander' status.

Sir Terry concluded his presentation: "I would like to make an official request to increase autonomous combat aircraft production in the event this threat materialises."

His remark elicited scoffs and headshakes around the table. Pamela Sutherland muttered, "Not going to happen."

Napier spoke: "Sir Terry, while I appreciate your concern and accept your arguments, numerous independent super AIs have confirmed that our current ACA coverage is suffice—"

Sir Terry broke in: "We ran a war game on this and—"

And was interrupted by the head of MI5, David Perkins: "But that's never going to come about. All forecasts insist the Caliphate doesn't have any designs on Europe."

Sir Terry dropped his voice: "Perhaps we shouldn't rely so much on this technology, which does no more than tell us what we want to hear. If this data is accurate, it places a vast and powerful army at the disposal of a dictator—"

"That's a massive 'if', Sir Terry," Perkins shot back, throwing his hands out on the table. "All super-AI units in Europe and America are more than capable of extrapolating the probabilities of millions of scenarios, and any risk of a military confrontation with the Persian Caliphate is pretty far down the list."

"The key word here is 'artificial', Mr Perkins. I don't trust these things to take account of human unpredictability."

"Really?" Perkins replied. "Those 'things' as you call them know us better than we know ourselves. They can predict what choices we will make. Do you know that the super AI in the Health and Safety department last year had an accident-prediction accuracy rate of one hundred percent? It forecast how many people would die in domestic accidents—everything from falling down the stairs, falling off ladders, to kitchen fires—and got the number exactly right for a country of forty million people. With respect, General, if the super AI says the risk of a military confrontation with the Persian Caliphate is less than eight percent, that's because it simply isn't going to happen. Unless you think you know better than the most sophisticated artificial intelligence yet created?"

Sir Terry didn't respond.

Perkins turned to Napier and said: "I believe we should accept the super-AI position: that there is actually a far greater probability that this data-pod is in fact planted information designed to raise tensions with either India or Russia, or to scare Europe, and the data it contains is simply false."

Crispin Webb hadn't enjoyed a COBRA meeting this much in a long time. He sat next to Perkins and could feel the heat coming from him. Sir Terry sat at the opposite corner and stared at his antagonist with unblinking eyes.

Napier spoke in a level voice: "Thank you, David. Sir Terry, for the time being we have little choice regarding our military defences against a supposed Caliphate threat, given the funds we need to support our civil defences against nature. Perhaps you could approach the Americans and enquire about the possibility of extending our current autonomous combat aircraft leasing arrangements with them?"

Sir Terry glanced at the prime minister and nodded.

Napier said: "Okay, then. Thanks everyone for coming along. Hopefully there'll be no more high tides for a while and we'll meet next in a week's time, as usual."

Chairs slid back on the wooden floor as the attendees stood. Wright and Sutherland left first, and then Napier looked at Webb and said: "Wait outside would you, Crispin? I'd like to have a word with the General."

Webb replied, "Of course," and caught a frown fade on Perkins' face as the men left the room. Webb saw Perkins glance back and throw Sir Terry a half-smile of nonchalance before he pulled the door closed.

Chapter 6

10.08 Tuesday 17 January 2062

Once Webb and the others had left the room, Napier turned to Terry and asked: "Why are you really so worried, General?"

Terry sat back in his chair and replied: "I'm not sure I can explain, PM. A hunch? A feeling?"

"But a hunch or a feeling is hardly evidence, is it?" Napier respected her most senior general, but military issues were almost inconsequential compared to the very real damage rising sea levels were doing to the English coastline. The thirty thousand British Army soldiers whom the country could afford were mostly employed in coastal defence.

"Maybe I'm getting too long in the tooth for this job?" he replied. "Perhaps you should replace me? I can recommend a few lieutenant-generals who would likely find it a lot easier to get along with Squonk and the other super AIs than I do." He paused and fixed Napier with a hard stare. "You can have my formal resignation within an hour."

Napier smiled back at him and decided to be honest: "I've always wondered about you Forces people. You join the

Army or the Navy or the RAF knowing that there hasn't been war in Europe in over a century, and I often speculate what you expect to get out of it. How many of you truly have some ancient, martial desire to fight, when you know you'll probably spend your careers training for an eventuality which will not come to pass, and helping out with natural disasters and such-like?

"But that data-pod has piqued my interest, General, although even if true I don't expect for a moment Europe could be a target. And you are correct: we rely too much on artificial intelligence, to a degree. So, for the foreseeable future I have absolutely no intention of accepting your resignation. If there's one thing I have come to rely on, Sir Terry, it is your reliability, which I need especially in peacetime. I haven't forgotten that AI malfunction three years ago and how you managed the Army's emergency response so well. How many lives did you save that day? Five thousand?"

Sir Terry's left eyebrow dipped. "I didn't save any lives; the men under my command did the work, PM."

Napier smiled and said: "The King decided to bestow his gratitude on *you*, Sir Terry." Then, her smile faded and her tone hardened. "But today, I have enough problems in my inbox, and I value you far too much to let you go. Keep being suspicious, General. Keep distrusting our artificial intelligence. I'll be honest with you: as I said, I don't see any real risk and agree with Perkins that the data-pod is most probably planted to scare us or someone else. Can you believe, with their centuries of mutual hatred, that Sunnis and Shias could ever work together to construct what the data-pod claims?"

"We don't have enough data on what life is actually like inside the Caliphate. And we shouldn't believe a word that does come out through official channels."

"Agreed, although I don't think it will matter. These islands face far greater challenges, which are very real." Napier paused, wondering if Sir Terry's concerns really had any basis in reality. Her thin eyebrows rose and she said: "I think I'll have Crispin leak this data-pod business to the media. In addition to the coastal defence problems, unemployment is up again, and the legislation to restrict those bloody gaming companies is, I strongly suspect, going to get beaten to within an inch of its life in the debate this evening. The government's also under huge media pressure to increase the Universal Basic Income, for which there is also no money. This little potential threat might give the media something else to talk about."

"Very well, PM."

"If they approach you for a quote, stick to what you told us today and feel free to be as controversial as you like. That might get them all riled up."

Sir Terry smiled and said: "I'll see what I can do."

Chapter 7

Sir Terry Tidbury stood and watched Lieutenant General Studs Stevens of the USAF picking at the buffet food on the table in front of them. He recalled their first meeting eighteen years previously, on a NATO training exercise during a bitterly cold February in Germany. They had been captains then: Stevens had commanded the last exercise ever to involve piloted combat aircraft, supporting Captain Tidbury's ground assault to take a hill occupied by the forces of a fictitious enemy which employed tactics strikingly similar to the Russian military. They'd stayed in touch as their careers advanced and as their families grew, and now they both shared the same concerns.

Stevens glanced up and responded to Terry's stare. "Not eating, Earl?"

Sir Terry shook his head, "Not hungry, Suds," and smiled despite the joke being so old. Their friendship formed during the debrief after that first exercise, when Captain Tidbury looked askance at Captain Stevens and told him that no one in the world with the forename of 'Studs' could

33

possibly be taken seriously, and declared that in future he would call him 'Suds' as it was a less-embarrassing word for him to enunciate. At once, Studs fired back that someone with such a high forehead and even teeth had no business being a soldier in the British Army, and should in fact be playing fusion jazz in New Orleans, so Studs would call him Earl, after his favourite jazz player, Earl Klugh.

The two men moved closer among the other attendees that milled around the buffet tables. Sir Terry held a paper plate with two sausage rolls and a small collection of various cheeses, meats and fruits speared by cocktail sticks, while Stevens sipped from a coffee cup.

"C'mon," Stevens said, indicating a free cocktail table next to one of the large conference room walls.

The two men made their way through the politicians and military personnel, nodding acknowledgments and swapping hellos.

Studs looked down at Sir Terry and said: "Hell of a decision for the council to take."

Sir Terry grunted his agreement. "Not really a surprise though, is it? They follow what the artificial intelligence tells them, because it tells them what they want to hear."

Studs eyed Sir Terry. "Earl, do you think it's actually possible that you and I are so outdated that we've become relics? That artificial intelligence is the smartest thing ever created. It's got access to every goddamn bit of information ever, and here we are treating it like some dumbass piece of junk."

"Yes, it is *probably* right, Suds. And that's what I detest about it: its bloody probabilities. Eight percent? One in fourteen? Seriously? And these people think that makes them safe?"

Studs nodded and said: "There are too many 'ifs'. The Caliph keeps on insisting that he only wants peace, but—guess what?—on the other hand, he may or may not have this vast armada of ACAs and warriors—"

"Listen to the pair of you," said a new voice.

Stevens turned around, shook the outstretched hand, and gave its owner a warm smile. "Hey, Bill."

Admiral William Rutherford of the Royal Navy, tall, upright and severe, gave a short nod back and his defined cheek bones rose in a restricted smile.

Next to him, as though the other half of a comedy double act, stood the squat form of Air Chief Marshal Raymond Thomas. "Hello, Lieutenant General," the airman growled, shaking Stevens' hand.

Sir Terry also shook Admiral Rutherford's hand and then Air Marshal Thomas's. Sir Terry said: "Oh, look. A sailor, soldier and an airman walk into a bar, and the barman says—"

But the Admiral interrupted him, his expression stiffening: "You two still think that planted evidence could actually be real? You heard what Hasselman said, and all the chiefs agree, the 'what-ifs' are far too improbable. What are you going to get—"

"Bill," Terry said, "it's not about 'getting' anything. Do you seriously believe I can't see how everyone thinks I must be mad? You can be certain I hope I'm wrong, but—"

"The vast majority say that you are wrong, TT," the Admiral broke in again, and Sir Terry saw Suds catch the underlying tension.

"We should be producing more arms, Bill," Sir Terry said flatly. "A lot more."

"Yes, indeed we should, especially ACAs," the Air Chief Marshal said in support.

"You know how that would play politically," Rutherford replied. "Floods everywhere as sea levels rise; unemployment going through the roof thanks to the vulture gaming companies and those godforsaken replicators, and the government starts throwing what little spare money it has into weapons' production? Besides, if—and it is a very vast and implacable 'if'—the Caliphate has managed to produce a force of that size, our role would be purely as spectators to a potentially entertaining set-to between the Caliphate and India, or the Caliphate and Russia."

Stevens said: "Ample Annie regards Russia as a greater threat to NATO than any other potential belligerent."

The Admiral replied: "And she's right."

Sir Terry sighed, sensing how strongly the American and the Admiral thought him mistaken. "I disagree. I think we could find ourselves in a tricky situation. It's a feeling I can't shake, and I'm not overly concerned what others think of me for voicing my concerns."

Air Chief Marshal Thomas said: "I agree with TT. We should be increasing ACA production as much as possible, in the event he is right."

Terry looked at the airman with irritated sympathy. Like most air forces in the world, the RAF had been reduced to little more than an appendage to the British Army. It no longer employed any pilots as all air transport, from combat ACAs to troop transportation to medical evacuation, was managed entirely by super artificial intelligence. Thomas enjoyed the rank of Air Chief Marshal only as a sop to tradition. If the RAF were completely subsumed into the British Army, the size of the force would entitle Thomas to the rank of Lieutenant Colonel at the most.

Admiral Rutherford nodded to Terry and said: "It's only intel, TT. Information in a data-pod which might very well be false, designed to panic either us or, more likely, those countries closer to Caliphate territory. According to our best research, taking together everything we've been able to find out, we already have an idea of the Caliphate's likely armaments. And we have two naval battle groups—the *Ronald Reagan* carrier group in the Mediterranean and the *Roosevelt* carrier group in the Arabian—ready to respond at once if the Third Caliph gets any silly ideas."

Stevens looked at Terry and said: "You know what, Earl? I think the Admiral's got a point. With all those SkyWatchers and PeaceMakers backing the navy up, Europe ain't in any real danger."

"Exactly," the Admiral concurred.

"I disagree," Thomas said, the flesh around his face wobbling like jelly.

Terry looked at each of his antagonists in turn and said: "You are right, *probably*... I don't know. Let's wait until next week's North Atlantic Council meeting. Perhaps we'll know more then. I'd be delighted to have confirmation that the data-pod was planted. Honestly, nothing would make me happier than to have everyone here laughing at me for overreacting."

The Admiral said: "You're going to look absolutely ridiculous, *Sir* Terry, as the NAC meets week after week, and nothing whatsoever transpires from that damnable data-pod."

Chapter 8

Maria Phillips forced the anger down as her father repeated: "I've told you, they're just stupid rumours. Ain't nothing going to happen. The whole country's skint, NATO's skint, and this is the only way the military can bleed a bit more cash out of the government. Gets right on my bloody nerves, the constant whinging—"

Her older brother, Martin, broke in: "But it says here the navies report more ACA activity than usual off the North Afri—"

"Don't mean nothing," their father insisted, continuing to shuffle the deck of cards. "What's the Caliphate got to do with us, eh? It hasn't bothered anyone else in years, and what it does in its own backyard ain't no-one else's business. You shouldn't listen to those right-wing hawks, young fella. The Caliphate is the best thing that ever happened in that part of the world, and if you want to know what it used to be like, just ask your Gran."

Martin shrugged his shoulders in indifference and picked up another jelly baby from the bowl on the table. The jelly baby lost its head first. "The report just says—"

"Isolationism works very well for all concerned, lad," his father interrupted again, stopping shuffling and wagging a knowledgeable finger. "But you see how the hawks operate? First, one of the generals is all over the place saying we need to find the money to manufacture more weapons. Then, when that falls on deaf ears because we've heard it all before, suddenly up pops reports of our supposed 'enemies' showing 'potentially aggressive' behaviour." Anthony Phillips started throwing cards down in front of them, one at a time, face up. "That's the way it's always been, lad. First jack deals."

"Don't you think you're being just a bit cynical, Dad?" Maria asked as she finished drawing the scoring grid on the paper in front of her.

"What cynicism?" Anthony replied.

A jack landed in front of Maria. She collected the face-up cards and took the pack from her father. She shuffled, began dealing, and said: "Some people are worried there might actually be a war."

"Yeah, to take people's minds off the real problems, like the failing sea defences, the worthless U-Bee, the—"

"The U-Bee's not worthless, Dad, come on," Martin said.

"It's all Mark gets because he's addicted to his gaming and won't get a job. And I've told you before: a five-grand-a-month handout from the government is barely enough to keep him fed," her father said.

Maria knew that her brother's constant immersion in online gaming worlds hurt their father. While she and Martin had jobs and bought in reasonable salaries, the middle child, Mark, had what they euphemistically referred to as 'issues' which saw him reject the real world for other artificial and very violent ones. The only money Mark bought in was the Universal Basic Income to which every citizen was entitled.

She looked at her cards, picked up the pencil, and said: "Forecast whist, first round, hearts are trumps. Your first call and lead, Dad."

Anthony replied: "I reckon I'll get four."

Martin looked at her and said with certainty: "One."

"So, I can't have two. Thanks a bunch, guys... I'll have one, so we've got one spare. Your lead, Dad."

Anthony put down the king of spades as Martin said: "I read the government will put the U-Bee up by five percent in the next Budget."

"With inflation at eight percent, that'll make all the difference," Anthony replied as Martin laid the ten of spades.

"First trick is yours, Dad," Maria said, throwing down the six of spades.

Anthony collected the trick and looked at the cards in his hand. "I remember when they introduced that, years ago. All of us thought it was the first step to some kind of utopia: everyone would be able to afford the basics because so many more things were being done by those new, clever robots. But if you knew anything about economics, you'd've known right off the bat that the U-Bee would be next to worthless as soon as it was paid out. All the prices would just go up, and they did. Right, let's see the colour of your money." Anthony threw down the six of hearts.

His children groaned on seeing a trump card so soon, but each put down a lower trump so their father won the trick.

He then laid the queen of hearts as Martin said: "You're such a relic, Dad. The U-Bee is still the mark of an advanced society, even if it is worthless." Martin nodded at the card, "That's a beast," he said, and threw down the jack of hearts.

Maria said: "That's yours as well, and it was my 'one'," as she put down the ten of hearts.

Anthony laid the ace of clubs as Martin said to Maria: "Get ready, here comes the speech: 'When I were a lad, you could go to a nice restaurant, see a play at the theatre, get a taxi home and still have change out of five hundred'."

Maria smiled: "And Dad remembers when the taxis were driven by real, actual people."

"Hey," Anthony chided, "I ain't that old, cheeky."

Maria looked at her father with warmth. "Dad, what I mean is that you shouldn't be so cynical. The military are there to defend us, and if they say we should be concerned, I don't think we should just dismiss it."

"But you have to look at the history of it, sweetheart," her father stressed. "The Second Caliph kept his word for years and years. When I were—" Anthony broke off at the sound of a guffaw from Martin, before continuing with more precise enunciation: "When I was significantly younger, a lot of people thought it would be madness to allow the New Caliphate to be so isolated, and things got quite nerve-wracking a couple of times. But that old bastard stuck to his guns. He traded only with China and Russia, and he closed his domain off to everyone else. When you look at what had gone on before when it was called the Middle East, it really was the best for everyone. Now, we've had this Third Caliph for a few years and—"

"And he's a crook, Dad," Martin broke in, as he followed Anthony's ace of clubs with the seven, and Maria, shaking her head as the game progressed, tossed out the nine of diamonds.

"Right," Anthony said, "that's my four tricks. Now I'll show you how to lose the lead," and he threw down the five of clubs.

"Not unless Maz can help you, Dad," Martin said with a smile as he tucked the three of clubs under his father's card.

Maria produced her sweetest smile and said: "Sorry, Daddy," as she put down the five of diamonds.

"You two kids, you've stitched me up again. What's up? Do I look like a kipper to you?"

All three smiled, and Maria enjoyed the familial warmth around the table. "It's your fault for being so hopelessly out of date," she said with warm affection.

Anthony shook his head, taking mock offence. "That's what I admire in you youngsters: ambition. Now I'm going to put the both of you wrong." He threw out the four of hearts.

Martin began to play his card but his arm stopped in midair and he said: "Uh-oh," while his gaze drifted into the middle distance.

"Something happened?" Maria asked.

"I dunno. Eye in the Sky just went dark."

"What? All of it?" Maria said, suddenly aghast.

"Yup."

"Put your card down, lad," Anthony instructed. "And what's 'Eye in the Sky', anyway?"

Maria answered, her eyes on her brother's, as she watched him follow whatever his lens told him. "Dad, I showed you a couple of months ago, remember? You wanted to see cousin Bernie's ship? I showed you how to use the feature so you could actually see *HMS Argent* out in the Atlantic."

"Ah, yeah, you're right."

Martin placed the five of hearts down slowly while still staring into the middle distance.

Maria said: "I'm out of trumps so that's yours," as she laid the seven of spades.

"Come on, Martin, switch your damn lens off and concentrate on the game," Anthony said.

"Just a minute, Dad. I'm trying to find out what happened."

"Anything on the media?" Maria asked.

"Difficult to be sure, Maz. The authorities are refusing to say what's going on, but snitches say it's that the Caliphate has sent up more ACAs than usual, again."

"So it's nothing to worry about," Anthony said. "Martin, your lead."

Martin twitched his eye and came back to the game. "Yeah, right," he said, and laid the king of spades.

"Sod it," Maria said as she threw down the queen of spades, "that was also my 'one'."

Anthony smiled as he put down the two of hearts to win the trick. "Said I'd put both of you wrong." He looked at each of his children and smiled, "Now, have either of you kept the right suit?"

"As long as I lose this, I'm going to get my bonus—" Martin stopped when he saw the two of diamonds his father threw down. "You're joking," he said as his own six of diamonds landed on top of it. He implored his younger sister: "Please tell me you've got a higher diamond."

Maria shrugged, "Sorry, all of my diamonds have gone, but I've got a little spade," she said, and laid the four of spades.

Anthony let out a light-hearted chuckle, collected the cards and shuffled them. He glanced at his eldest son, whose eyes once again had glazed over.

"This is a precedent, really," Martin said.

"Oh yeah, how?" Anthony asked with a hint of sarcasm.

"Eye in the Sky has never gone down, not in its twenty years of existence. It's almost as if someone doesn't want people to know what's going on."

"There's a first time for everything. Let's keep fingers crossed it'll be back soon," Maria said.

Anthony shook his head, smiling, and dealt each of them six cards. "Except for you kiddie-winkies beating your old Dad at forecast whist. There'll never be a first time for that."

Chapter 9

02.43 Tuesday 7 February 2062

Able Seaman Bernard Rowley stared at the screens in front of him and imagined once again how it must have been in the past, when Royal Navy sailors could walk about the decks of an elegant, glorious battleship in the wind and spray and savour the brutality of the ocean and facing the enemy in the open. Now, all he and his shipmates had to look at were screens, banks of which hung from the walls that surrounded the central combat station, an island command table which projected three-dimensional holographs of the world outside. Apart from the air deck and the 'garage' at the rear of HMS *Argent*, the ship offered no other possibility to get outside, its hard yet sleek angles designed to defeat enemy detection. His best mate, Rigger, said that in another ten years, all military ships would be unmanned because people wouldn't be needed anymore.

"Sensor tolerances?" called the first officer from the command table.

"Minus-one acceptable, sir," Bernard replied, confirming that the systems for which he was responsible were behaving as expected.

From behind Bernard, the captain called out: "Navigation, adjust heading to bring us to within three thousand yards of *Hyperion*. How far is she from the *Ronald Reagan*?"

"Twenty thousand yards and closing," a navigator on the opposite side of the bridge area answered.

Another voice spoke with urgency: "Multiple contacts coming into range, captain. Sig confirms hostile signatures."

Bernard scratched a sudden itch under his left ear as he monitored the readouts in front of him. Inside, he felt a new kind of thrill. They had drilled and trained so many times for this moment: a genuine attack by a real enemy. Now, it was down to the fleet commander, Captain Burgess on the *USS Ronald Reagan*, to decide whether all of the ships would go dark in an attempt to avoid detection, or whether they would stand and fight. Bernard sensed everyone else on the bridge holding their breaths in the silence.

"Sig," called an operator on the other side of the bridge. "The order is: light up."

At once, the captain called: "Battle stations," and a klaxon rang out in a two-tone blare which Bernard considered unnecessary. Throughout the frigate, the three-hundred crew members would be informed in numerous ways that the ship was now on a war footing, and the klaxon struck him as a needless nod to a bygone age.

"Ops," the captain called, "accept Horatio's recommendations and switch to automatic targeting."

"Aye, sir."

The klaxon stopped. Bernard kept his eyes on his screens but listened as the captain and first officer talked.

"How many d'you think they'll field, number one?"

"A few hundred, I expect, sir, certainly no more."

"Curious that they've decided to have a go now. So much for the Caliph's years of peaceful intentions, eh?"

"Perhaps it's some kind of malfunction, or a rogue element within the Caliphate?"

"Questions to be answered later, number one."

The operations officer spoke: "Automatic targeting engaged. Horatio linked to other vessels."

"The computers are relaying the required course adjustments," the warfare officer said. Bernard stole an insubordinate glance behind him, at the command console. On it, a forest of bright lights glowed as the hostile targets approached the image of the fleet at the centre.

The captain spoke in a tone which, to Bernard, differed little from a training exercise: "What does Horatio say about other threats? Have they deployed any submarines or surface vessels?"

The warfare officer responded: "Improbable, sir, at less than five percent."

"Shan't be much of a fight if the Caliph is so slack as to have neglected to build a decent navy. But let's keep our eyes sharp in any case. Weapons?"

"All green, captain."

"What the devil are those machines, anyway?"

"Something we haven't seen before, that much is certain," the first officer replied.

In the holographic image above the command table, the lines of light denoting the approaching enemy machines gained on the fleet of fifteen NATO ships at the centre.

The first officer said dismissively: "There's no way they'll be able to breach our defences. This will make a good live training exercise for the crews."

The captain grunted his agreement.

The warfare officer announced: "The *Jarvis* and *Mississippi* have engaged at ten thousand yards."

Bernard kept staring at his screens, monitoring the *Argent's* power flows and diagnostics, but inside him an excited child's voice cried out that this was the real thing, it was not an exercise or a drill.

"The *Ronald Reagan* has also engaged… Hostiles within range, captain."

The captain ordered: "Weapons free. Fire to automatic."

Bernard's heart-rate increased as he visualised the Sea Striker laser canons firing their invisible shots at the incoming enemy ACAs.

Suddenly, the warfare officer muttered: "That can't be right," and the captain asked him to explain. He replied: "Sir, the incoming enemy ACAs appear to have more resilient shielding than we anticipated."

"Meaning?"

"Meaning that the Americans' Pulsar Mk IIIs and RIMs are not performing as effectively as expected, and nor are our Sea Strikers."

The captain scoffed. "And just how bad can it be? Horatio and all of the other computers told us that the Caliphate cannot have shielding any better than ours."

"I'm afraid theirs is, sir."

In the holographic image, the enemy ACAs kept advancing towards the fleet. Suddenly, there came a bright flash in the display.

"Finally," muttered the warfare officer.

"Analysis," the captain ordered, peering at the image with a more concentrated expression.

"Sir, the device absorbed nearly three times the expected number of laser shots before its shielding burned through, which is impossible. Or, rather, it should be impossible."

"We have to react. If they have so much stronger shielding than we expect—" the captain broke off when more flashes erupted in the display. He watched this, then said: "Get me Captain Wexley."

"Aye, Sir," the comms officer replied. A moment later, he nodded.

The captain said: "Mike, I think we're going to need better tactical options. We should—"

The voice of Wexley, captain of HMS *Hyperion* and Commander of the Royal Navy fleet in the Mediterranean, broke in: "There's no material threat at this time. We've got sixty hostiles inbound, and while they have far stronger shielding than they should have—wait, new data to all ships. Hold your station, for now."

The *Argent*'s captain looked over to the other side of the bridge. "Weapons?" he called out.

The warfare officer answered: "Port side all in, green. Fleet PeaceMaker launches in progress."

Bernard glanced at the readouts on his screens and adjusted the settings to see, among the array of data, a curious statistic: the first enemy machine the *Hyperion* had brought down required seventy-eight Sea Striker laser shots to burn through its shielding, and a further ten to destroy it. He knew that NATO ACAs were able to withstand no more than twenty-five laser shots, and everyone assumed it would be a few years at least before the next generation of ACAs would have stronger shielding. In addition, Bernard had researched the issue himself and had to agree with the warfare officer: current shielding tech, especially the way the shielding was generated, simply should not be able to withstand that much punishment from NATO's lasers. The overlapping problems of shielding generation, ACA weight, firepower and manoeuvrability were well understood, and Bernard realised that these machines should not be able to perform to this level. He breathed a word of thanks that there were only sixty of them, all of which would shortly be destroyed.

51

Then the captain said, "Well, that's interesting," in a fatalistic tone.

Bernard turned around in his chair to see what had made the captain speak, and the first officer noticed, glared at him, and spat: "Continue to man your station, Able Seaman Rowley."

Without thinking, Bernard spun back at once to face his own screen and almost shouted, "Yes, sir!" before the idea entered his head that he'd be in serious trouble for such insubordination. His imagination began inventing excuses for his lapse, but the shock of seeing the strength of the enemy's shielding, he hoped, would be sufficient at the hearing.

"Multiple new contacts detected," the officer at Comms said.

"Tactical analysis," the captain ordered.

"Sir," the warfare officer began, his voice wavering, "Horatio is constantly reassessing the probabilities as more contacts are detected... Assuming surrender is not an option—"

"Indeed it is not," the captain replied testily. "Time to contact?"

"Four minutes for the first wave."

"Very well." The captain pressed a small light on the command table, and when he spoke his voice boomed throughout the *Argent*. "Attention, all hands. We are tracking hundreds of hostile ACAs emerging from Caliphate territory. From what we have learned thus far in this engagement, the next half an hour might be a little... tricky. Nevertheless, I have the utmost faith in the ability of this ship and her remarkable crew, with whom it has been a pleasure to serve. Let us do our great ship and our Senior Service proud."

A lump formed in Bernard's throat. Since joining the Royal Navy four years earlier, he'd never doubted it was his role in life to be a mariner. He sensed his plans for the future recede as the hostile ACAs approached the ships. He'd hoped to get on a first officer or even a captain promotion track, if he could pass the exams. But now, with the captain's admission that they were suddenly outnumbered and outgunned, his memory threw up details of all the heroic naval stories he'd read as a boy, of the *Repulse* and the *Prince of Wales* in World War Two, of the Battle of Jutland, all the way back to Henry the VIII's *Mary Rose*. He thought of the disasters like the *Hood*, which in 1941 sank in six minutes after a direct hit on her magazine, from which only three men escaped out of a crew of fourteen hundred, and all the other innumerable thousands whom the sea had swallowed. Bernard realised that he and his shipmates would shortly join them.

He'd never considered that something like this might happen. The modern Royal Navy had never really been about war. It was about rescuing people and helping with international relief efforts as sea levels rose. A feeling of profound strangeness pervaded him as he understood that a vast, new war was starting here, tonight, in the Mediterranean Sea, and this fleet and its crews were to be its first casualties.

The comms officer spoke loudly: "Naples is launching ninety-six PeaceMakers which will be in theatre in three minutes."

"Total number of approaching hostiles?" the first officer asked.

The warfare officer replied: "Over three thousand now, but the SkyWatchers are picking up new waves emerging from Caliphate territory at the rate of five hundred a minute."

"The reinforcements from Naples should help, a little," the first officer said, with no hint of understatement.

"Yes, sir. Two hundred and fifty-six enemy machines are breaking formation to converge with the reinforcements," the warfare officer said.

The captain said: "The situation is not yet hopeless. If the ship can maintain power, the lasers can continue firing indefinitely."

The warfare officer announced: "The Americans have engaged the second wave. Hostiles will be in range in thirty seconds."

The captain answered: "Very well. Fire to automatic when ready."

Bernard monitored the power flows and diagnostics in the ship's systems as it began firing the Sea Striker laser canons on the port side. His heart rate crept upwards when he realised that the Caliphate's ACAs were getting very close to all of the ships, and the thousands more of them piling in could only lead to one conclusion.

Comms called out: "Sir, the *Jarvis*'s defences have been breached."

"So what happens when one of those things does get through?"

After a pause, the comms officer said: "The *Jarvis* has foundered. She's gone."

"So quickly? How?" the captain demanded.

"Wait... Two of the ACAs got through... And expelled multiple smaller devices which appear to be some kind of mobile bomblet. New data is being fed into Horatio."

Bernard heard the captain scoff, "I don't need a computer to tell me—" and stopped abruptly as something outside crashed against the hull and the *Argent* creaked. The captain shouted: "Damage?"

Bernard felt the ship roll a little from the impact, but saw at once from the data on his screens that the cause was debris rather than ordinance. Nevertheless, the unnatural movement strengthened the fear in him that worse was to come. He heaved in a breath, trying, wanting, to remain professional and composed, just as Royal Navy sailors had been through the centuries when facing such a 'tricky' battle. He pushed thoughts of his family and friends back in England to one side, determined to meet his and his ship's fate with a decorum of which the Senior Service could be proud.

"Two Sea Striker canons disabled—"

"Helm, bring us about. We need to bring the starboard canons to bear."

"Aye, sir," the weapons officer answered, before adding, "The *Mississippi* and *Ronald Reagan* have gone, sir."

"Our own PeaceMakers are lasting mere seconds; they're completely outgunned," the first officer said, horrified.

"Sir, Captain Wexley is on Comms."

The voice of the *Hyperion*'s captain filled the bridge: "Attention, all ships. It looks like the Americans have bought it. But there is a chance. I've set our AI to vary the Sea Striker shot coherence length. If we adjust—even fractionally—this value, it reduces the number of shots required to burn through these bloody things' shielding. Each captain must instruct his ship's super-AI system to make this adjustment, and keep at it so as not to give their AI a chance to catch up. Good luck!"

"Do it," the captain of the *Argent* shouted at his warfare officer.

Bernard analysed the operational data running across his screen and saw the number of laser shots required to knock an enemy machine out decrease by more than ten percent. A flash of desperate hope rose within him before vanishing when he realised it would make no difference given the thousands of hostiles gathering above the rapidly sinking NATO fleet.

The warfare officer spoke: "Captain, Horatio is predicting that our Sea Strikers will be overwhelmed with targets in five, four, three, two, one—"

Bernard jumped when loud clangs came from outside the ship. Unnerving click-clacking sounds followed. The captain shouted, "Abandon sh—" which ended in a vast popping explosion. Bernard felt his head go forward into the screen in front of him.

He blinked and gasped, realising he'd been unconscious for several seconds. Warm liquid ran down his face and his ears hurt. Flames crackled around him. Voices shouted, some in pain, some extolling escape, but the pressure damage to his eardrums added to his confusion, creating a sense of numbed distance. He pulled himself out of his chair and peered at the smoke and steam and fractured lights. His training told him to leave the ship via the aft section, so he took a step forward but fell over.

Pain came to him with his senses, and again he heard the strange click-clacking of metal on metal. The sound faded, there came another vast popping noise, and the deck beneath him seemed to first move away, then instantly return to smash him hard in the face. The other voices stopped. Bernard pulled himself upright again. He knew he had eighty metres to cover to reach the 'garage' aft of the ship, but the pain screaming from his head and his leg told him this would not be possible. The ship listed to port, and surfaces which should have been vertical or horizontal now leaned to port disconcertingly. He limped and pulled himself out of the bridge area and into a corridor which led to the sleeping quarters and mess deck. After struggling for ten metres, he had to step over a crumpled body that he did not recognise. Then he heard the gentle sigh of seawater inside the ship. Bernard turned back and stared in fascination as the water came towards him in a leisurely, almost comforting, surge. The ship groaned acceptance of its fate, and from the bridge area he heard hisses, crackles and metal shearing as the *Argent* sank.

In an instinctive reaction, Bernard glanced above him and saw an access tube which, he recalled from his training, also led to an escape hatch, topside. The water swirled around his legs and chilled them.

It brought the body of the captain into the corridor, where his arm snagged on a bent flange, and the swirl made his legs appear to paddle as though he were swimming instead of dead.

Bernard caught his breath when the water reached his waist, and he suddenly felt intense stinging from the injuries to his leg. The ship continued to list and the power went out, plunging Bernard into darkness. When this happened, part of his spirit rose up in a refusal to simply lie back and drown for England. His head stung and the bones in his face felt as though they were burning, but he told himself to count his blessings. He switched on the bright torch in his life vest and grabbed hold of a pipe among the dancing blue shadows. The *Argent* listed a few more degrees and the power of the surging water threatened to pull him away from the access tube. He dragged himself into it as the corridor filled with water.

Bernard abruptly realised that the ship would soon turn turtle and his escape route would point downwards, towards the seabed. Ignoring the increasing pain from his injuries, he pulled himself along the tube, which had now come almost horizontal. The water gurgled and rushed and swirled around and submerged him. He flipped open the mouthpiece of the tube he held and bit down a second before the sea engulfed his head. As long as he kept water out of his own respiratory system, the tube contained sufficient oxygen for thirty minutes under water.

After what seemed like minutes instead of seconds, Bernard reached the escape hatch. His light led him to the lever. He broke the seal, slid the glass panel back, and pulled the lever with all his strength. The equalisation of water pressure when the hatch opened surprised him, and he chided himself for not realising the different pressures between the water flooding into the ship from above, and the water outside. He hung on to the lever for a moment, then when he judged it safe enough, with his one good leg he kicked himself outside the *Argent*.

Bernard rolled into the cold blackness of the open sea as his ship finally turned over and began its last twisting journey to the seabed, some two thousand metres below. His light penetrated the water to create little more than a shimmer of deep blue around him. He could not establish which way was up, nor how far away the surface might be. He pulled the cord to inflate his life vest, and felt himself moving in a direction which he decided must be up. At the same time, he also felt the pull of his ship, and of his shipmates. There were five thousand other souls who this night had been dragged unwilling to a death they neither expected nor felt they deserved, merely due to the foibles and eccentricities of their political masters. For a few brief moments, as the *Argent* continued in one direction and he travelled in the opposite, he could almost touch the sense of a terrible, unjust sacrifice.

Suddenly, he broke the surface. The swell was slight but enough initially to obscure his view of any fellow survivors. Bangs and explosions and the shrieks of ACAs filled the night as the waves tossed him hither and thither. He spat the breather from his mouth and it bobbed in the water on its lanyard. He gulped in breaths of real, fresh air for the first time in days, dazed that he should be on the surface of the Mediterranean Sea when so many of his shipmates had perished. His view changed as the swell lifted and lowered him, and at the high point, he saw orange fires on the horizon. In the sky, numerous streaks of light zoomed and flashed overhead, and he marvelled at the technology, lost in amazement first that he should have survived, and second that there could be ACAs with shielding capable of absorbing so much energy.

Soon Bernard picked out cries and salutations from other survivors in the water, both near and far. Elation sparked inside him that he would live, to be first crushed by guilt, and then by the abrupt realisation that he might not survive after all. A flare burst overhead some distance away, above a life raft. It shone orange over the black and blue of the ocean, and when the swell lifted him, he saw a black shape swoop out from the sky and down to the life raft. There came an explosion and a truncated scream, and a gout of water leapt upwards. The life raft and its broken occupants fell and hit the water with loud slaps.

Bernard saw more black shapes in the glow from the flare and realised that the Caliphate machines intended to leave no survivors. As quickly as he could, he pulled on the lanyard and bit down on the breathing device. With his other hand, he searched under his life vest and found the release valve. He twisted it and the air hissed out from the vest. He ducked underwater and silently thanked god that his arms were not injured. Despite the pain from the cracked bones in his face and the shredded skin on his leg, under the surface Able Seaman Bernard Rowley pulled himself down through the water and swam for his life.

Chapter 10

03.35 Tuesday 7 February 2062

Turkish engineering student Berat Kartal woke with a start when bright colours exploded in the darkness of sleep. He'd programmed the lens in his eye to alert him to a number of potential events, all of which were highly unlikely but each of which he had to know about at once if they actually happened.

These events included natural disasters such as volcanic eruptions, earthquakes and excessive flooding, and manmade catastrophes ranging from lost contact with the joint Chinese/US colony on Mars to noteworthy accidents which involved multiple deaths. Regarding Mars, speculation abounded as to what had happened to an unmanned supply ship with which contact had been lost the previous Thursday. Regarding accidents, Berat and many of his student friends speculated that the Boeing 828–600, the newest sub-orbital passenger aircraft used by several operators, was overdue for some kind of drama, as it still boasted an unblemished record after seven years of service, and even the Chinese A17 didn't have that.

Now, however, his lens told him that something violent and involving many deaths had happened in the Mediterranean. Groggy from the interrupted sleep, at first he couldn't see the reason. With hard blinks of his eye, he nevertheless traced the cause back to a 'What if?' game he and his fellow students had played the previous year, concerning an imaginary surprise attack on India by the New Persian Caliphate. Such an attack, military strategy insisted, would first require the subjugation of Turkey. He wondered how the lens could be right. If true, this would completely upend the accepted world order.

The Caliphate had existed for nearly all of Berat's young life. The earliest recollections of his parents talking about the Second Caliph leapt from his memory. He recalled the tension when the New Persian Caliphate was still forming, and then his parents' relief as the violence headed southwards, not north, and their conviction that Turkey would be safe. He remembered all the fuss at home and in school when China announced to the world that the establishment of the Caliphate had finally brought peace to a vast area that had suffered strife and bloodshed for decades.

But in the last few years, local stresses and tensions had returned anew with the election of Yagiz Demir and his *Allah Her Yerdedir* party. Berat's parents warned him to be careful to whom he voiced his opinions, and the previous semester at university had seen many arguments between lecturers and students concerning the direction in which Demir planned to take the country. Rumour of a referendum to accede to the Caliphate had gained much currency, and until this moment, represented the single issue of stress in Berat's otherwise ordinary, mundane life.

He got out of bed and padded to the bathroom. He looked past the data that the lens in his left eye scrolled at the front of his vision, to the mirror on the bathroom wall. The night's stubble shadowed his small, round face. He would normally shave now, before going for a run. Then he would shower, eat a breakfast of bread and honey washed down with black tea, and spend ten or more hours researching for and writing his thesis. How could he keep to his normal routine now, after this news? Brown eyes stared back at him, doubting the data's accuracy, questioning reality, suggesting he'd woken inside a dream and should now awake for real.

He refocused back to the data and twitched small muscles around his eye to control the flow. One of the data feeds came from a clandestine bot which could listen in on government channels. This piece of software rarely worked well, and often not at all, but for fourth-year engineering students, Berat and his best friend Omer were proud of their little forbidden bot, even if it wasn't very good. Now, however, Berat felt his heart slow as he willed the software to work properly. He read written fragments in English which mentioned a massive assault on the NATO naval battle group stationed in the Mediterranean, and then that thread faded for a few seconds before another came up which carried Turkish Army icons, but whose text was encrypted.

He swore, left the bathroom and went to the small desk by the window of the living area. He tapped a screen in the surface of the desk. When the link went through, the data from the lens transferred to the screen, which gave Berat more options for investigation. It was a minor source of frustration that the human eye was managed by a mere six muscles, which with various blinking options limited how effectively data in the lens could be manipulated.

He tapped and swiped at the screen, trying to expand the volume of feeds, trying to search for encryption key codes. But the bot's performance became more erratic, and Berat's heart rate increased. He licked his lips and the metallic saliva in his mouth tasted the way the fear in the pit of his stomach felt.

Abruptly, the bot grabbed an unencrypted data packet and splashed the contents over the screen.

"*Sikme,*" he swore as the translation software transformed a report from an Italian Reuters stringer in Rome. Berat saw the raw statistics of the Caliphate's attack on the NATO ships and shivered. He looked at the time in the corner of the screen, and the digits read '03.44'. He told himself it must be a nightmare, he was in bed, sleeping in peace, and this was one of those very realistic dreams he sometimes had. But as hard as he tried to wake up, too many other senses told him that he was already awake.

Then, something more frightening happened: the bot latched on to local police force comms close to the demilitarised zone, the buffer between Turkey and the Caliphate. From the ancient Mesopotamian city of Mardin, local police reported thousands of machines descending from the sky, and then the comms ceased. Berat's eyes widened as he watched the bot report similar urgent calls from towns and cities spanning a line almost four hundred kilometres from Mardin in the east to Iskenderun in the west. He deduced that the Caliphate must be attacking his country with a massive wave of thousands of machines, to subdue it and protect the Caliphate's northern flank before it invaded India. And their leading machines had one very important job: to disable Turkey's communications.

Berat withdrew the image on the screen to an overview map of the demilitarised zone and Turkey's eastern rump. The pattern of disruption to comms took the form of a surge; a fractured, broken wave, as the bot struggled to track and collect the sudden explosion of data. Seconds later, a definitive undulation emerged from the east and swept across the land. Berat's heart almost stopped. The mass of machines rode behind a leading edge of microwave disruption. To subdue his country, its electronic infrastructure must first be obliterated by powerful, precisely targeted microwave bursts to burn out the physical equipment on which so much of the virtual universe relied.

With a deft flick of his left index finger, Berat removed the lens from his eye, understanding that it would soon be useless. He looked down at the screen in the desk and waited. A voice in his head urged him to use the last few seconds to contact and warn his parents in Istanbul and his university friends, scattered around the country on the winter study break. His left finger dabbed a comms icon. A blank message resolved and he began loading contacts. He dared to hope he was wrong, that he still slept in his bed and was dreaming these unthinkable things. As he entered his parents' address, the screen went blank. Berat swore aloud again. Suddenly, the screen came back to life with: 'No connection—use offline services?' and Berat let out a scoff of frustration. He stepped back from the small desk and his throat constricted. He knew with certainty that the microwave pulses with which Caliphate forces blasted his country were burning through the very physical components that carried so much virtual traffic. These node burnouts would cripple infrastructure, render civic functions inoperable, and remove from the population the ability to know or find out what was happening.

He dabbed at the screen and replayed the data which the bot had collected before the burnout. "There must be a pattern..." he mumbled to himself as he scanned the numbers and maps and other data. He opened his mouth to ask the apartment block's managing super AI to analyse the data and draw conclusions, until he realised that it would no longer answer him.

A few moments later, he stood and walked to the window. He pulled the curtain aside and looked down the street. Few street lights shone through the darkness, but he could make out the endless rows of low-rise apartment blocks similar to the one in which he stood. In Usak, most buildings had up to ten floors, seldom more, and in this southern residential part of the city, their delicate pink and yellow exteriors were dulled by the weak light.

He wondered how many of the thousands of other people would be aware of what was happening. He could not refute the conclusion to which the scarce data he had gleaned pointed: a full-scale military invasion of his country had begun, without warning and in the middle of the night. His young, logical mind provided a further sequence of inescapable conclusions: millions of people would run before the advancing Caliphate forces; little help would be forthcoming; and the only option he had now was to escape the country.

He glanced around the room, understanding that his life and the lives of millions of people had changed irrevocably in the last thirty minutes, although most of them did not yet realise this. He went to the small storage space in an enclosure above the narrow hall. He stood on a one-step stool, reached in and pulled out a large rucksack he used for summer climbing in the Western and Central Taurus Mountains.

As he cleared detritus out from the last trip, he spoke to himself: "Right, think. All digital connections burned out, so nothing works. No super AI, no integrated systems management. No vehicles running anywhere, hospitals in the dark, airports too."

He returned to the desk and opened a bureau next to it. "Can't contact anyone, so everyone's on their own… Okay, where is it? Got you." He took out an elegant, leather-bound desk journal which fitted snugly into the rucksack. He rummaged through the rest of his possessions to take what practical things he could find, and blessed the course he'd chosen at university, in particular the map-reading module. He took out a detailed topographic atlas of Europe and leafed through the pages. He recalled how badly he and his fellow students had reacted on being presented with this appalling relic of a long-gone era, but the lecturer had insisted they spend an afternoon learning what the contours and other indicators meant. In addition, their course professor maintained that the old skills remained a key ability of any proper engineer. Berat shook his head at the memory of how he'd laughed then. He didn't laugh now.

Ten minutes later, he began his flight from danger. He left the apartment and padded down the three floors of concrete stairs, unsurprised that the super-AI-controlled lift no longer worked. He collected his bicycle from the secure area at the rear of the block, and after some rudimentary checks of its mechanical condition, he pedalled off in the direction of Izmir, two hundred kilometres distant and the best hope he had of getting a ship out of the country.

Berat realised that no one outside Turkey would—or could—know of the disaster befalling his country. Unlike President Demir, Berat regarded the Caliphate's secrecy with suspicion, and its public displays of the satisfaction, wealth and the happiness of its peoples to be manufactured. As he cycled through the darkness, scarf and bobble hat protecting his head but not stopping the numbing winter chill on his face, he wondered what would happen next. A voice inside him questioned this night-time flight and suggested that, perhaps, he should've simply gone back to bed and slept off the worry and bad thoughts. All would become plain in the bright, fresh light of the morning. But the failed attempt to contact his family and friends acted as the sledgehammer of realisation that the immense danger was all too real.

He pedalled out of Usak with grim determination, armed with his journal and atlas, some biscuits and a bottle of water. The Caliphate would burn out all modern equipment, but the world would still know how it treated Turkey. By the time the sky paled, the sun rose, and the chill breeze on his face eased a little, a grim, granite determination had formed inside Berat Kartal, a determination that the Caliphate would not enjoy free rein as it overran his country.

Chapter 11

Geneneral Sir Terry Tidbury stared at the impenetrable black night outside his kitchen window, his hands clenched around a mug of steaming tea. The pane reflected the harsh glare of the overhead light, but behind it, outside, there existed only blackness. To Terry, the news he'd been woken to receive took a similar outline: the sudden, painfully bright light with only an empty void beyond it. In the next few moments, hours, days and weeks, the veil of uncertainty, so abruptly thrown, would lift to reveal a future which in this instant remained unfathomable.

He glanced at the screen to his left, in the wall next to the cooker, and read the text scrolling past. Some deeper level of consciousness inside him wondered if he'd slipped into an alternate reality, where—

The screen chimed and broke his line of thought. "Yes," he said.

The broad African-American face of General Joseph E. Jones, Supreme Allied Commander Europe, resolved on the screen, the low-slung jaw set in a grimace. "Sorry to wake you, General."

Terry shook his head in dismissal. "What news of the Arabian fleet?" he asked.

"Also totally destroyed."

"No survivors?" Terry asked, sipping his tea.

"None at all. We picked up two in the Mediterranean: an Able Seaman Tech from the *Argent* and an ordinance jack from the *Ronald Reagan*, but they're both pretty beat up."

"How can I help you at this stage, sir?"

Air whistled through Jones's teeth, then: "The obvious, to begin with: talk to your people, get the politicians briefed and onside. We need to respond damn quick."

"Satellites report increasing jamming over Turkish airspace."

The American nodded, "Yup, we believe they've already invaded—"

"Are we going to invoke article five immediately?"

"Nope. Turkey left NATO two years ago, so she's on her own."

"Christ, the Caliphate forces will steamroller right over the Turks."

Jones's face creased in confusion. "Steamroller?"

"Not important. How long do you think Turkey will be able to hold out?"

"That depends what the Caliphate hits them with—"

"Do we assume that the contents of that data-pod are accurate now?"

The American stroked his chin. "I guess that's the initial step, till we can get any more reliable data."

"Sir, I believe we should proceed on the assumption that tonight's attack is the prelude to a full-scale invasion of Europe."

"I agree, although it's too early to be certain. All war-game scenarios state that subjugation of Turkey would be a prelude to any invasion of a larger, more powerful state. I can't wait to hear what that piece of shit in Tehran is gonna say about tonight."

"I wouldn't expect him to admit his long-term plans in public, sir. Not yet, at any rate. Turkey's been drifting towards autocracy for a while now, and I wonder if Demir had planned acceding to the Caliphate all along."

"We need to formulate a response if Turkey asks for assistance."

"Indeed. What are the computers saying now?"

A wry smile crossed Jones's face. "Ample Annie is starting to sound like a goddamn politician with all the dumbass excuses she's coming out with. She keeps reassessing probabilities and claiming she needs more data to decide if the next target—assuming there is a next target—is gonna be India or the Asian Caucuses."

"Very well. I'll start making sure the right people understand what's at stake. One important thing does worry me."

"What's that?"

"We're talking about a part of the world which hasn't experienced war for more than one hundred and twenty years. If the Caliphate's main target is Europe, we'll have a mountain to climb to raise sufficiently strong armies."

General Jones shook his head. "No, we don't know that it'll come to that, yet. This could be no more than an attempt to assimilate Turkey. Besides, nearly all conventional warfare is conducted by machine now. One step at a time, General. I want you at the NAC meeting we're putting together for nine this morning CEE time, eight GMT. Patch in with your super AI."

"Sir."

The instant Jones's face vanished, Terry instructed: "Squonk, connect me with PM Napier."

As he expected, the face that appeared in the screen belonged to Napier's aide, Crispin Webb. The PM's aide frowned and said: "Ah, Sir Terry. Are you up to date?"

"Yes, is the PM?"

Webb hesitated. "We are about to wake her and brief her, but we thought we'd wait for more data."

Terry's mouth fell open. He said: "Half of His Majesty's Royal Navy has been sent to the bottom of the sea this night and the prime minister of England and first lord of the treasury still hasn't been told?"

Webb paused and scratched his stubble before his familiar arrogance returned. "I decided it would not be appropriate to wake the PM until we can brief her properly regarding re—"

"The fleet was sunk over two hours ago," Terry exclaimed.

Webb's red eyes narrowed, and Terry took a sliver of pleasure from Webb's own shock at the sudden turn of events. "Yes, but there's no point waking her with incomplete information and a badly organised brief—"

"And are you clever youngsters sufficiently organised to get transport from my house to Number Ten in fifteen minutes?"

"Yes, of course. If you think you can help."

Terry ordered: "Do it," and ended the connection before Webb's petulance riled him further. He drank a mouthful of hot, malty tea and heard footsteps padding closer behind him. He smiled when he felt the long, slender fingers of his wife Maureen caress his shoulder.

"What's happening, Terry?" she asked.

He laid his fingers over hers and said: "I think these shocked youngsters need some help... And I'm going to show them that, today, I'm their best friend."

Chapter 12

Prime Minister Dahra Napier tucked a strand of auburn hair behind an ear, pulled her mauve shawl closer around her, and asked Terry: "But what happens next? They can't just sink our ships, kill thousands of our sailors, and expect to get away with it," in a voice that managed to sound both plaintive and authoritative. Her tone unnerved Terry as he sat opposite the kitchen table on the third floor of 10 Downing Street. Through the windows, the morning winter sky shone blue and fresh and cold.

Terry looked at Napier's hazel eyes and saw the fear and concern in them, almost all authority stripped away, like acid strips paint, by an event which was proceeding to shatter everyone's nerves. He tried to reassure her: "No, they can't, PM. But the situation is very fluid, and we need—"

"What we need," Crispin Webb broke in, "is to hit these bastards as hard as we can as soon as we can. Show them we won't accept this."

Terry smiled and said: "With what?"

"Our own ACAs, of course," Webb said as though Terry didn't know. "We should arm them with nuclear warheads and destroy the Caliphate."

"And you believe the enemy hasn't considered that?"

Webb blustered, "What? I don't know, probably, but... We have to attack them—"

Napier broke in: "Crispin, they would like nothing more than for us to do that, because then they could nuke us back."

"And what you don't seem to realise, Mr Webb," Terry added, "is that they might stop our nuclear attack in its tracks with their overwhelming air superiority, while we would not be able to stop theirs."

"But, but," Webb stuttered, "we have too many other things to deal with. There can't be a war, now, surely? What about the flood defences? The army is wrapped up with that. What about the polls? The anti-gaming legislation is supposed to be the defining achievement of the PM's premiership—"

"Yes, well, it seems our priorities have changed somewhat in the last few hours, Crispin," Napier chided.

"The press are going mad for a reaction. They won't stop—"

"So go and do your job," the PM suddenly said. "Go and write a press release for me, now."

Webb blinked in shock, and then mumbled his agreement and stalked out of the kitchen.

When the door closed behind the aide, Napier looked at Terry for a moment before admitting: "I have no idea what to do next, Sir Terry."

"Firstly, please drop the 'Sir'. Secondly, you have vast military experience at your disposal, PM. We've run simulations and war games and trained for potential confrontations—"

"But this is different, isn't it? They attacked our ships with many more ACAs than we thought they had, and do you know what's happening in Turkey?"

Terry wanted to show Napier the respect in which he held her, but he admitted to himself that he would've preferred to be dealing with another man. Women in positions of power performed well in times of peace, when measured restraint was required and the most significant threat to the status quo remained the relentless rise of the seas. Now, with an abruptness which defied belief, Europe faced a storm of violence the like of which its peoples had not seen in over a hundred years.

He decided to be blunt: "Things are probably going to get a little worse before they get better," he said.

Napier let out a scoff and replied, "A choice understatement, Terry. But what on earth happens next?"

"Containment, PM. We absolutely cannot react offensively until we understand fully how better equipped they are than us." Terry nodded to the door through which Webb had exited. "Reactions like that can't be allowed to guide what we do in the coming days and weeks, or I think it could all be over for us very soon."

"Crispin is not suited—"

"At the same time, we also need stability. People like him, I assume, know some history; they're aware of the potential situations they could find themselves having to deal with."

"Perhaps, but this is unprecedented, it's—"

"Not so much, PM. It's happened before and will likely happen again. What might catch us out now is the speed—" Terry stopped as the prime minister's eye twitched and she glanced down.

"Hello, Maddie," she said with a tight smile, then: "Of course, but I have my military advisor here so I'll put you on a screen." Napier pulled her shawl closer around her shoulders, got up and walked over to a wall on the far side of the spacious room. Terry followed, looking at the puffs of bright winter cloud through the high Edwardian windows and shuddering again at the prospect of what the future held.

The screen came to life with the oval head of Madelyn Coll, President of the United States. The artificial light in the Oval Office shone down from overhead, accentuating the shadows under Coll's eyes. The President squinted and said without preamble: "Obviously we've gone to DEFCON 1 now and we'll submit a condemnation motion at the UN, but I'd like you to make your special forces available for immediate deployment—"

Terry broke in: "I think we should wait for the emergency NAC meeting before we make any hard-and-fast military decis—"

And was himself interrupted: "Dahra, we're going to have to move against the Caliphate very soon, and all NATO allies need to be onboard."

Terry saw Napier's chin jut as the PM replied: "We are, Maddie, but don't you think—"

Anger flashed across the President's face: "I've got a military complex here straining at the leash. In the last few hours, the Third Caliph has wiped out two naval battle groups in an entirely unprovoked attack. It must be made to pay. We're readying our PeaceMakers for a full-scale nuclear assault on Caliphate territory."

Terry and Napier swapped a glance and Terry saw the prime minister's anxiety betrayed by a nervous lick of dry lips.

"Maddie," she pleaded, "please reconsider and wait, just a few hours. It seems reasonable to assume the Third Caliph would not have attacked in this manner without considering our response, and I believe a full nuclear attack is not only what he's waiting for, but what he's actually expecting. And that means it must be bound to fail."

President Coll's eyes narrowed as she appeared to consider the point. She said: "Our super AI suggests there is a moderate probability that could be what might happen."

"So does ours," Napier replied.

"But after what they've done, totally unprovoked, emotions are running kinda high."

"It's the same here, Maddie, but we can't let ourselves be goaded into a trap."

The President leaned off to the left, and despite her lifting a hand to cover her mouth, Terry heard her query, "Goaded?" and a lightly spoken reply came from out of view, "Led into."

The President looked back into the screen. "Okay, we'll wait for the NAC meeting and the official triggering of article five. But Ample Annie got it wrong big time, and I've a mind that she might be wrong again."

Chapter 13

After terminating the connection with President Coll, Terry and Napier returned to the table in the middle of the room. A maid came in and provided them with fresh tea and coffee, and gave Terry and Napier each a pair of VR glasses.

When he put the glasses on, Terry entered the North Atlantic Council meeting in Brussels. He turned his head left and right to take in the attendees and noted many familiar faces among the throng of over a hundred people. He sat at the England position at the long, curved horseshoe table which extended to his left and right. On his right sat the PM, even though in reality she was opposite him in the room in Downing Street. Terry looked down at the very real mug of steaming tea in his hand, and made a mental note not to try to put it down on the illusory table in front of him. He swallowed back the discomfort such arrangements caused him given the drama of the night's events.

Despite mere virtual attendance, Terry sensed the fear and panic; he saw it in the unnatural postures, in the nervous tics, in the fidgeting. As he scanned the area, more figures resolved, sitting or standing at the horseshoe table. Between the ends of the large conference table stood a podium on which leaned the imposing, broad-shouldered form of Bjarne Hasselman, the Secretary General. Hasselman's eyes peered out through lines of concern on his face, and he nodded as Terry made eye-contact with him. Next to Hasselman resolved the Deputy Secretary General, Wolfgang Eide, and his slighter, slim body leaned to the left and then the right to take in the attendees. On the large wall behind them, a screen shone with the words 'Emergency NAC Meeting, Monday 6 February 2062: 09.00 CEE'. Terry glanced at the chrono in the lower left of his view and noted that the time was already 09.03.

Abruptly, Eide coughed and tapped the podium. "Good morning," he began blandly, and Terry wondered what on earth could be good about it. Terry shook his head in mild bemusement at listening again to people for whom English was a second language. Eide went on: "Thank you all for attending, er, this unusual meeting. I will, er, bring us up to date with our latest intel..."

The Secretary General flashed his subordinate a look of mild frustration. On the screen behind them appeared an image composed of indistinct dark masses. Terry declined the option to 'step up' and enter whatever the image was, which the VR glasses offered him. Eide explained: "A few hours ago, two NATO carrier groups were sunk; one in the Mediterranean, the other, er, in the Arabian Sea. We know they were overwhelmed by ACAs which came from Caliphate territory. What appears to have been a, er, important factor in the defeat is the, er, strength of the ACAs shielding as well as their aerial dexterity."

Hasselman spoke: "The carrier groups were destroyed by weapons which we have never seen before, and whose performance exceeded those of our own by a significant margin. The ships did not have a chance, as well the Third Caliph knew—"

"We must attack!" shouted a new voice. Terry looked to his left to see the Lithuanian Defence Minister slap his palm on the table in front of him, confirming his actual presence at the meeting in addition to the strength of his feelings. Those around nodded in agreement, and Terry had his first inkling of the potential for disaster if this meeting were not managed appropriately.

Hasselman ignored the outburst and continued with the briefing: "If you look at the screen behind me, this is the scene from a camera on board the *USS Jarvis*, the first American ship to be sunk, some six hours ago."

Hasselman leaned over the podium and spoke while dabbing a finger at what Terry assumed was a screen. "This is an image of the ship's hull. Now, at this point in the battle, the Caliphate's new ACA had got to within sufficient range to deploy a new and particularly effective autonomous bomb."

A darkened shadow in the lower part of the image suddenly enlarged. The pixilation redefined the silver blur which shone more brightly than its darkened surroundings.

"The naming committee has assigned the reporting name 'Spider' to this new weapon. Ladies and gentlemen, watch carefully." The blur moved in and merged with the central dark mass. "This is the moment the Spider impacted the Jarvis's hull."

The image zoomed and enhanced again. Terry saw what looked like part of a silver egg protruding from the smooth metal of the hull. Suddenly, the smooth surface of the egg split open. Articulated appendages snapped apart silently, and the device strode away along the ship's hull.

Hasselman said: "The ship's other sensors recorded this... thing moving to the thinnest hull plating below the waterline before detonating." The Secretary General paused and scanned the room. "Just four of these Spiders caused the *Jarvis* to sink in less than three minutes. Compared to the Equaliser bomblets carried by our PeaceMakers, the Spider appears to represent an advancement in munitions' tech of several years."

Terry glanced around the horseshoe table and noted the mixed reactions: disbelief, sneering contempt, and shaking heads. When he looked right, he saw that Crispin Webb had joined the meeting, sitting on the other side of Napier. Terry hoped the PM's aide might gain an inkling of the gravity of Europe's new predicament.

The image on the large screen changed to a satellite view of the battle area. Streaks of light and a cluster of alphanumeric codes in various bright colours denoted the NATO ships in the Mediterranean fleet and the routes taken by the Caliphate's ACAs as they attacked. Hasselman went on: "Initial findings suggest that the Caliphate's new battle ACA out-performs the PeaceMaker by at least twenty percent on all axes. The naming committee has assigned the reporting name 'Blackswan' to this autonomous combat aircraft. Records of the battle show that each one carries fifty Spiders. The Spiders appear to jointly generate the Blackswan's shielding. I need hardly point out to you all that, whatever the naval battle groups' strengths, they could not have withstood this onslaught."

With some relief, Terry sensed the belligerence in the room wilt under the raw, devastating statistics which laid out plainly how the two carrier groups had met their fate. The screen changed again to a list of each ship, a summary of what it had faced, and how it had been sunk. Hasselman said: "Given the overwhelming evidence of from where this attack originated, the NAC recommends all NATO member states agree to the invocation of article five of the NATO treaty, immediately."

The recommendation was a formality, of course, and Hasselman seemed to acknowledge this as he continued: "In addition, a land invasion of former NATO member Turkey appears to be under way. As you might recall, there was a great deal of speculation that the Turkish President had been planning a referendum on whether the country should accede to the Caliphate, and it now appears the Third Caliph has made the decision for him."

A voice shouted out: "So where will he stop?" and Terry saw the Estonian Defence Minister gesticulate, pudgy arms straining against the tight material of his suit. The agitated, bald man continued, his accented and badly broken English echoing in an auditorium which was real enough, even if many of the attendees were present only virtually: "We have constant spectre of the Russia, always looking for opportunity, yes? Now, what does this Caliph mean? Is he wanting only Turkey? Or is he looking at the all continent? Is he to invade India? All his machines now invade Turkey, so Caliphate is defenceless, yes? We must attack! Everyone here know this already."

Hasselman extended a placating hand, although Terry thought he saw more subtle signs of frustration. Hasselman said: "Please, Mr Valk, with article five invoked, we begin a prearranged sequence of building up our resources to meet any thr—"

And was interrupted by the Chief of Staff of the Italian Army: "The Estonian minister is right. These are the most modern weapons and we must react quickly. If the Caliphate has committed all of its forces to this invasion, then we have a chance to strike a blow. We should get—"

Another voice shouted from behind Terry: "The Caliphate must be contained! We need containment, containment, containment!"

Others took up the chant of "Containment," and many of them slapped the wood in front of them on the second syllable. Terry eyed the podium. The Deputy Secretary General's pasty forehead glistened with sweat and his slight chest heaved in and out, but the taller Secretary General stood motionless apart from a sneer which formed on his otherwise calm, Nordic face. Terry made eye-contact with him and the two men shared a knowing nod. Then Terry glanced at Napier and Webb, and wondered what they thought of all the noise.

Napier gave him the answer when she leaned over and said in his ear: "The last thing we need now is a lot of braying donkeys."

Terry smiled as he looked at the Secretary General. Hasselman remained still, staring down each attendee in turn. At length, the noise died down, to be replaced with a sense of awkward embarrassment.

Hasselman said with diplomacy: "While I appreciate emotions are running high, I believe this is a time for cooler heads. Our super AIs have all been making recalculations, and although the invasion of Turkey may have left the Caliphate exposed, on the other hand, our computers could be wrong—again—and the Caliphate could still be well defended or even preparing for a further invasion. We should be concentrating on ensuring the defence of our lands and our homes. I call on General Sir Terry Tidbury, as the most senior soldier in attendance, to give us his expert opinion."

Terry sipped his tea and waited for the VR glasses to indicate that his voice would be amplified. He addressed the meeting: "The fact is that we have insufficient forces to take any kind of offensive action, for today at least. All of our countries have maintained standing armies on the assumption that they would be a sufficient deterrent to any other regional powers. And if we're honest," he said, trying to look at as many individuals as possible, "most of us have seen the funds available to our militaries drop due to more tangible threats to our lands than an enemy that might never have materialised."

A voice shouted out: "Well it's fucking materialised now."

Terry glanced down and suppressed a smile before looking up and replying: "Yes, it does appear to have done so. But how NATO responds in the next hours and days could decide the very future of our continent, and I do not say that lightly."

Terry paused and scanned the attentive faces with more patience. He recognised several of them, and memories of joint exercises in inclement weather surfaced briefly. But many of the politicians he knew to be inexperienced in military matters. His adjutant, Simms, had briefed him on which defence ministers should be watched with care as they had no knowledge of their portfolios, being merely career politicians, but Terry struggled to remember them. He decided to treat all of them with suspicious circumspection.

He continued: "Initial conclusions based on the events of the last few hours suggest that our computers have underestimated the true military strength of the Persian Caliphate by at least a factor of five, possibly more. If we attack now, the range of potential outcomes leaves us too potentially exposed, if our computers have got it wrong again. As the Secretary General said, of course we are all feeling deeply disturbed by the remarkable storm that has erupted today, but patience and prudence are what is required now. The Third Caliph, it is reasonable to assume, has the same tech which we have, and absolutely cannot have taken this path without forecasting what responses we have at our disposal, and subsequently being prepared for th—"

"Nuke the bastards!" a voice shouted, followed by quieter wave of agreement from a number of others.

The Secretary General pointed an accusatory finger at the transgressor: "Have you not listened to a word Sir Terry has said?"

Terry looked over at the politician who'd made the demand, and raised his voice: "Which is *exactly* what the Third Caliph wants us to try to do. It is more than reasonable to assume the Caliphate knows we do not have the conventional means to repel the invasion of Turkey even if she requested it; the only response we have to the destruction of our naval battle groups is a full nuclear assault. Who in their right mind would undertake such a course? The Caliphate employs comprehensive jamming over its entire territory—and today we've found out why. In my opinion, any immediate attempt to attack it must absolutely result in failure, whatever percentage figures our super AI is producing now. And when it does, the Third Caliph will claim every right to obliterate Europe in response—"

"But we're not even sure the Caliphate has nuclear weapons," said the Czech Defence Minister.

Terry saw the audience divide into those who thought the statement asinine, and those who appeared to give it credit. He surmised the former were mostly military people, while the latter were politicians. He answered: "Are you really willing to gamble on such a fact after last night's events?"

Silence followed. The Czech Defence Minister looked down at his shoes. Terry prepared to explain further when he sensed a ripple of excitement go through the room. In the lower right of his view, the words 'Breaking Priority' resolved.

At the podium, the Secretary General instructed his Deputy: "Put it on the screen. Use the Reuters feed."

Behind them, the data reporting the destruction of the naval battle groups disappeared, to be replaced by the image of a handsome, dark-skinned young man. He sat at a typical news-reading desk and the official crest of the Third Caliph appeared over the man's right shoulder. He spoke, and Terry recognised a few of the words of modern standard Arabic. An English translation scrolled along the bottom of the image. It read: 'The illustrious Third Caliph, leader and protector of the Persian Caliphate, announces the assimilation of the nation state formerly known as Turkey. The government of that territory had requested its accession for later this year; however, it has been necessary to act now due to pre-emptive steps taken by the war-like, infidel states of Europe and America. The Caliphate regrets having been forced to neutralise the aggressor infidel, which he brought upon himself. Nevertheless, the Caliphate reiterates its commitment to regional and global peace, and will continue to expand only to those Muslim states who freely request to join. God is great.'

The image froze and then disappeared, replaced with the NATO logo. The silence was broken by a female voice Terry heard from somewhere behind him: "That bastard really knows how to take the piss."

Standing at the podium, Hasselman said: "I think that empty, meaningless statement tells us only that the invocation of article five is, thus far, the most prudent step to take. We will of course increase the readiness of all Federated Mission Networking systems immediately, and those will be our main points of contacts for each member state's service chiefs. Your super AI will brief you on your immediate FMN circles. In the event Turkey makes a formal request for military assistance, that will be considered at the top political level—"

"This is crazy!" a new voice shouted. Terry turned to his left to see a junior military attaché from the Israeli government leap to his feet and slam his fist on the desk. As one of only three Major Strategic Allies of NATO, Israel was entitled to a seat at emergency meetings on the unspoken agreement that its attendees would not interrupt proceedings and only speak when invited to do so. The young Israeli man with the shocked face shouted: "Can't you see what's really happening here? Are you all completely blind? We have been warning about this for years. Today it is Turkey, tomorrow it will be Israel, and the next day it will be all of Europe. How could you have been so foolish as to believe the Caliphate's protestations of peace?"

The Secretary General's patience finally snapped and he shouted: "Sit down. You are not permitted to address the NAC unless I allow—"

"We face the end—"

"I said sit down and be quiet."

Terry interceded: "Gentlemen, please. Mr Hasselman, you said a few minutes ago that emotions are running high, so the attaché's… enthusiasm is to a degree understandable." Terry turned to the attaché, "Sir, I'm sure you are quite aware of the—"

But the attaché turned his anger on Terry and spat: "NATO is pathetic. You're a disgrace: to Europe, to democracy, and to the world."

Terry murmured: "That's enough, son."

"How long has it been since NATO did anything, anyway? Twenty years? Thirty? You huff and puff and constantly reduce your budgets and you've lied to your peoples. You lie that they are safe and you can protect them, that the Caliph—"

"I said that's enou—"

"No, it isn't!" the attaché screamed. "Fischel has been warning for years that the Caliphate was not peaceful, that the façade it presented to the world was a charade, that it would not allow the 'unbelievers' to go on in peace. And now, look! He has used all of his forces to invade Turkey, his territory is exposed and you, you *cowards* can only talk of defence—"

"Our computers were wrong," Terry hissed, "and they may be wrong again. We can't trust them. And you need to study history. The Second Caliph didn't react despite the most severe provoca—"

"No, I do not. The Second Caliph may have been a peaceful man, but his successor most certainly is not. And NATO has wilfully ignored the signs, until today, when you finally can't ignore them any longer. And now we have the perfect opportunity to attack the Caliph and you—"

"That's enough," Hasselman cried. "The Israeli attaché will be silent."

A tense pause followed and Terry knew that the Secretary General was too experienced to allow someone else to fill it. Hasselman said: "I'm closing this emergency NAC meeting now, and I conclude it by confirming the invocation of article five and the full activation of all FMNs, on the assumption that our enemy cannot be believed. The Military Committee will meet this afternoon at fourteen hundred hours CEE to discuss the most immediate defence requirements. Another NAC meeting is already scheduled for the same time tomorrow by which time, hopefully, we will have more facts than suppositions. Ladies and gentlemen, I think we should take a moment to send our condolences to those mothers, fathers, husbands, wives and the children who've lost a loved one because of the Third Caliph's unprovoked belligerence today. Thank you for your attendance."

Chapter 14

09.44 Tuesday 7 February 2062

Terry sat back in the chair and let out a sigh as figures left and right of him began to disappear. He pulled the VR glasses off, the auditorium vanished and he was back on the couch in the flat at 10 Downing Street. Napier sat opposite him, her expression as pensive as his own. Next to her, Terry noticed Webb's right eye dart in its socket.

"Ah, prime minister, Sir Terry. More bad news, I'm afraid."

"What's happened now?" Terry asked in a neutral tone.

"United Airlines is reporting the disappearance of its Sydney-Frankfurt flight, BA is saying its lost contact with its Wellington-London flight, and Lufthansa and Emirates are also reporting missing planes, all in the last forty minutes."

"Do they say where contact was lost?"

Webb frowned: "No, but flight monitoring services claim locations in Kazakhstan and over the Caspian Sea."

Terry sipped his tea and tapped a glass panel in the surface of the coffee table. "Simms, John, adjutant to General Sir Terry Tidbury, MOD."

Webb spoke: "If the Caliphate starts shooting down civilian plans, it will cost them a lot in PR."

Napier said: "I'm surprised any are still in the air after the night's events."

Terry replied: "No new flights would've taken off after the attacks on the navies began, but the European Civil Aviation author—"

Terry broke off as the screen in the coffee table came to life with an image of his adjutant. "Yes, Sir Terry?"

"Article five has been invoked and all NATO FMNs are going to full readiness at once. Any news from Turkey?"

Simms's bushy eyebrows came together in consideration. "It's chaos, I'm afraid, Sir Terry. Caliphate ACAs are burning out all equipment with highly directed microwave bursts before their jamming devices block all contact with lost territory. Our SkyWatchers are picking up final comms from Turkish military units on the front line as they're overwhelmed, but there is much confusion."

"Why? The Turkish military knows who the enemy is, yes?"

"Not entirely, Sir. It seems certain units have some sympathy for the Caliphate."

"Any indication of how the invaders are behaving?"

"Not yet, Sir."

Terry queried, "Nothing?"

Simms replied: "The microwave bursts comprehensively burn out all exposed components—"

"But that only affects civilian equipment; their military comms should still work. Haven't we got anything?"

"Any captures would be restricted, so I think that might depend on how much GCHQ feels like sharing."

Terry let out a scoff and said: "Agreed. I'll be on my way back there soon. Organise a meeting with the service chiefs. We have a lot to discuss."

Simms nodded and the connection ended. Terry looked up at Napier and said: "If GCHQ are getting any captures, any captures at all, from the Turkish military, I absolutely need to see them."

Napier replied: "Of course," and then added: "Is there anything else we can start doing now? Anything we should be doing?"

Terry nodded: "Procurement," he said, glancing at Webb. "We need to build up material reserves in case the peace-loving Caliph has broader plans than merely assimilating Turkey."

Webb opened his mouth to speak but Terry put out a hand and said: "No, I don't want to hear there's no money. The money's got to be found, one way or another. It looks like the SkyWatchers and PeaceMakers are already outmatched by the Caliphate's machines, but until we can catch up, we're going to need them. Thousands and thousands of them, I suspect."

"The Treasury is going to love this," Webb said.

Terry said: "How the Treasury feels about it is irrelevant, Mr Webb. We'll also need more funds for our key research facility at Porton Down as soon as possible. If this turns out as I expect, we will have to design, test and build new ACAs in record time. Even if the Third Caliph told the truth this morning—and I don't for a second believe he did—we've got to show him that we're prepared."

"But we are prepared. We were prepared..." the confidence in Webb's voice cracked. He paused and then looked at Terry and Napier in turn. "How could this have happened? How could we not have seen this coming?"

"That," Terry replied, "is a question for the historians. Today, it's one step at a time. The Caliphate is aggressively assimilating Turkey, and nothing's going to save her. But it doesn't necessarily follow that Europe is next. They could advance northeast into Russia and the Caucuses. Certainly there are plenty of Muslims for them in those countries, and that would make Moscow nervous."

Napier said: "We have to bring the hammer down on diplomatic channels. I can't believe no one outside the Caliphate knew this was going to happen." She turned to Webb: "Crispin, research all diplomatic comms for the last year, including intel from the US and our NATO allies, to identify any hint that we should've seen this coming."

Webb replied, "Of course," and his right eye began twitching. Terry watched Napier's aide and decided to hold his tongue. Whether any missed indications could be found mattered little now.

Webb spoke: "Initial research results come up blank. The Caliphate's isolation has been extremely effective."

"What about the Chinese?" Napier asked. "They must have known. They're the Caliphate's key trading partner."

"PM," Terry said with a practised tone of diplomacy, "I'd better be getting back."

"Yes. Yes, of course. Thank you, Terry."

Chapter 15

19.44 Tuesday 7 February 2062

Jane Phillips put her arm around the shoulders of her youngest child and tried to comfort her: "Things like this happen, love. We're all shocked." Jane heard herself speak the words but didn't understand why she sounded so defensive.

Maria said: "But cousin Bernard, dead, and for no reason—"

"We don't know he's gone."

"Two survivors out of how many in that fleet? Five thousand? More?"

Jane felt a pain in her stomach which did little to alleviate the headache that had been grinding behind her forehead for most of the day. The shock defied explanation. These things simply didn't happen any more. When was the last time the Royal Navy had been involved in a proper sea battle? She wracked her memory, all the way back to her schooldays thirty-five years earlier, to briefly studying a long-forgotten skirmish called the Falklands War, nearly a century ago in the 1980s.

"We mustn't give up hope—"

"But so many people, dead, all at once, Mum. It's horrible, it's wrong—"

A new voice spoke: "Nah, happens all the time in games."

Jane spun around to confront her middle child: "Mark, this isn't a game. Real sailors died last night, thousands of them."

Mark gave his mother a nonchalant glance as he walked through the living room, "Yeah, I did hear about it. Was the food I ordered delivered?"

"Yes, it's in your cupboard," Jane answered.

When Mark disappeared into the kitchen, Maria prodded her mother and whispered: "I thought we agreed? You remember what Piccolo said? Much more crap food and Mark will get diabetes."

Jane didn't need her daughter to remind her of what their apartment's super AI had told them about Mark's health. But Mark had always been difficult. Her oldest and youngest, Martin and Maria, were both well-rounded adults: responsible, polite and calm. But Mark had always been surly, insolent and hurtful. His constant immersion in virtual gaming worlds made him an exemplar of one of society's biggest ills, but repeated pleas to moderate his gaming and food consumption only brought stress into the house. At fifty years old, feeling the detrimental health effects of raising three children while working full time as a history teacher, Jane considered that two out of three wasn't bad.

"I know, sweetheart," Jane replied with a faint trace of resignation.

Mark emerged from the kitchen with an armful of cardboard cartons and a one-litre drink in one hand. He said to the two women: "I'm about to enter an S–73 Universe, so I might not come back till tomorrow."

His mother blurted out: "Why don't you stop wasting you life, you stupid little boy?"

Mark replied with a sneer: "You're the ones wasting your lives. What do you gain here, in this world? It's dull and pedantic and tedious and really, really boring. And all of you get upset because I spend so much time in a place that makes me happy, and at the same time, I'm working towards a goal which will make your boring lives a little bit better."

Jane felt Maria squeeze her hand in support, but Jane fought to hold her emotions back.

Mark continued, his strong jaw line jutting forward: "You'll see, all of you. I'll gain one of the Bounties. And when I do, you'll be so grateful to me for allowing you to move to a decent place to live—"

Jane felt her body tremble, but then Maria snapped: "Shut up, Mark. The Bounties are false, they don't even exist—"

"You are so wrong. I've talked to Bounty winners—"

"They are AI, Mark. They're not real people who've won anything."

"Now you're repeating the government's propaganda—"

"No, I'm not. How many reports do you need to see? How many victims of these scams will it take to convince you?"

Mark stepped towards his younger sister, struggling to hold on to his cargo. "There are two sources of those 'reports': one, the government-controlled media who are trying to restrict the gaming companies; two, other gamers, who are putting out false reports to put other gamers off playing for the Bounties. Seriously, sis, you don't know what you're talking about."

Maria hissed: "No, dear brother, it is you who doesn't realise what is going on. While you submerse yourself in the false, pretend worlds where you can die a million times and never feel an ounce of pain, war is coming here, to the real world, where the pain will hurt very much, and where each of us will die only once, and when we do die, there will be few left to mourn us. So go, dear brother, and enjoy your pleasure while it lasts."

Mark scoffed in contempt, turned and left the room. Jane looked at the face of her youngest child, and saw the hard metal of determination in the girl's eyes, and she felt proud of her daughter.

Chapter 16

07.08 Wednesday 8 February 2062

Kivi gripped Paz's hand as the crush of people swept the two young women towards Rabin Square in Tel Aviv.

"Did Seth say where?" Paz asked above the din as the crowd of people flowed like a river along Frishman Street.

Kivi glanced at her best friend and noted the concern in her bright blue eyes. "Close to the edge of the monument. Don't worry, my lens has their location." Kivi wished Paz wouldn't fret. To Kivi, the atmosphere seemed more convivial, like a carnival, the kind of fairs she and Paz used to go to years ago. She glanced down at Paz and raised her voice: "If the rumours are true, I think we're going to hear good news."

With her free hand, Paz brushed stands of black hair from her face and replied: "I can't believe we've attacked the Caliphate, it's so incredible."

"After yesterday and the day before? It was inevit—"

"No, it wasn't," Paz said, and Kivi felt Paz squeeze her hand harder. "The Peace Buffer has kept the peace for years.

What's happened is exactly why it's there: to keep Israel safe from the—"

"Don't be ridiculous." Kivi didn't want to fall out with her friend over such a thing as politics, but sometimes she wondered if Paz realised the seriousness of the situation. "Now the Caliphate has revealed itself to be the warmonger Fischel said it was all along, we had to do something. You've seen the suffering in Turkey—"

"Yes, and it's awful, but it doesn't mean we should've attacked, if we have. How many times have we talked about it, Kivi? I don't understand how you can be happy about this."

"It's not about being happy; it's about being safe."

The pressure of the throng eased as the flow poured into the square. Kivi stood a clear head above most of the people around them, and she noted all of the orthodox black caps that bobbed up and down. High over the thousands of people in the square, the expansive bright blue morning sky shone brightly, flecked with a patchwork of distant cirrocumulus hued a light pink.

"Yeah, but the hate, Kivi, you remember last summer, at Asaf's party? We stayed up the whole night discussing it—"

"I remember, but this is different."

"No, it isn't. This is exactly one of the scenarios we discussed. Do you recall what you said then?"

Kivi felt too much excitement to concentrate on remembering one of the previous summer's many parties. She only wanted to find Seth and the others, as she followed directions from the lens in her eye. She guided and then pulled Paz with her towards the Holocaust Memorial. She heard the splashes as people fell or jumped into the water feature close to the memorial.

Paz reminded her: "You said you believed, finally, there was a real chance to end the century of hatred. You said the

Caliphate was a sensible consolidation of the region and the Peace Buffer Zone would protect us eno—"

"That was when we assumed the Caliphate was peaceful. When we gave them the benefit of the doubt. Before yesterday happened."

"I know it was a shock, but violence can only lead to more violence. You rememb—"

"Seth!" Kivi called and she caught sight of her brother's boyfriend. She dragged Paz through the people and hugged the olive-skinned, muscular Seth, whose smile beamed with pleasure.

"Hey, Sis. You know Deen and Nadin, right?" he said, indicating two smiling young men next to him.

Kivi smiled back and cried, "Hi, guys." She let go of Paz's hand and asked Seth: "What news?"

Seth's smile faded: "Strange."

"How?" she asked.

He spoke into her ear: "We sent our best. We threw everything at them. But our machines just seem to have vanished. So far, no one knows what's happened."

"How could they just vanish?"

Seth shrugged his shoulders.

"So we have attacked them, then?" Paz asked, and Kivi saw the fear in her eyes. "What about America? Did they join in and attack them as well?"

Seth shook his head. "My Dad said he heard that it was unilateral—"

"Fischel trying to look like a hero," Paz said with a frown.

The young man called Nadin said: "Or maybe he understands that we can't rely on our allies like we used to?"

An older, bearded man in a white tallit turned to face the group and wagged a finger at the youngsters: "It was the best time. All of the Caliphate's ACAs are involved attacking

Turkey. Our government realised that they must be defenceless and exposed, and that is why it was better to attack now."

"You seem to be very well informed, Sir," Seth said, but the man just tapped a finger on the side of his nose in reply.

"I don't like it," Paz said. "I thought we were coming here to protest, not celebrate."

Kivi shrugged and said: "What's there to protest if we've already attacked?"

"Then we better pray it succeeds," Paz replied.

Kivi glanced back at Seth and saw his eye twitch. He said nothing so she asked: "News?"

He shook his head, "Still no contact. There's a rumour that the attack must have failed because... Oh, wait. I've got a friend in ACA tech support, and he says for sure our ACAs must have failed."

"At least we're safe enough, yes?" Kivi asked.

"Of course," Seth replied. "I just asked him how he knew, and he said the engineers report no seismic disturbances which they'd expected when the nukes should've—"

"What?" Paz exclaimed. "How many nukes?"

Seth smiled at her, the sunlight reflecting the sheen of sweat on his dark forehead. "All of them, I think."

Paz's mouth hung open for a moment, then she said: "That's madness. The rest of the world will never forgive us... And none of them exploded?"

Kivi shook her head and anger flashed across Seth's face. "What would you prefer, Paz?" Seth asked. "That we wait until it's too late?"

Kivi tutted and said: "I tried explaining that to her on the way here."

Then it was Paz's turn to shake her head. "What's happened to you two? The attack on Turkey has turned you into bloodthirsty degenerates, and I'm appalled—"

"Shut up, Paz," Kivi spat. "You've never learned to recognise when you're being cheated, and you know Fischel did the right thing." Kivi stopped when she heard a low murmur of "Oh, no," from Seth. She spun round to him: "What?"

Seth put his hand out, "Wait," he said, and his right eye twitched. At the time, Kivi's own lens began to malfunction. She noticed other heads in crowd around them dip and shake.

Paz said: "My lens is losing data."

"No, something else is going on." Seth said.

Nadin held out a device in his hand: "My slate's working fine."

Kivi looked at the men in turn and then at Paz's tearstained eyes. Around them, the blare of single-tone sirens rose up in a continuous wailing. Kivi felt a ripple of shock wash over all of the people around her. A man's voice called out: "Must be an earthquake."

Suddenly people began moving, pushing, shoving, but Kivi knew there could be nowhere to go. If an earthquake was about to hit, the middle of Rabin Square was probably one of the safer places to be. The people in the area around her began to thin out.

"We're better off staying here out in the open," Seth shouted.

"What's that?" Paz asked, shielding her eyes with one hand while pointing up at the sky.

"Not sure," Seth answered.

Kivi looked and realised that the black dots in the sky must be ACAs, but such was her confidence she still did not sense any danger.

Seth spoke: "I'm not getting any signal from them. Nadin?"

"Nothing. And that means they're not ours."

"That's not possible," Kivi said, a note of panic in her voice. "They can't be Caliphate machines, they just can't. They're all in Turkey."

"They must be ours," Seth insisted.

The black dots descended out of the hot blue sky in organised waves. In some detached place in her mind, Kivi thought the spectacle beautiful. Hundreds, perhaps thousands of perfectly arranged black spots moving and changing direction and undulating as they approached the city. Abruptly the ground shuddered, and Kivi almost lost her footing.

"What the hell was that?" Nadin asked.

No one answered him as the group glanced at each other with nervous faces. Kivi put a steadying arm on the stonework beneath the inverted metallic pyramid of the Holocaust Memorial. The middle of Rabin Square remained busy but with fewer people than earlier. The densest crowds seemed to be pushing their way out of the square and down the adjoining streets, past the low-rise buildings which lined three sides of the square.

A vast explosion came to Kivi's ears and beyond the square, in the centre of downtown Tel Aviv, the circular Azrieli Center collapsed. The top section appeared to accelerate as it sank into the lower part of the building. When it did, a plume of grey dust billowed out and rose into the air. Another shudder ran through the concrete under Kivi's feet, and indistinctly through the dust she saw another building collapse. She couldn't believe her eyes; she couldn't breathe. Seth and Nadin stood and swore their own incredulity, while Paz had begun weeping in low, pathetic whines.

Then the nearest waves of machines came over the square from the north, proceeded by a surge of agonised screams. Kivi watched the ACAs narrow their focus to where the crowds were thickest, along the roads around the square. Her heart stopped as the thousands of people underneath the ACAs burst into flames. She could see no reason why this should happen: the machines did not appear to do anything, and this confusion compounded her desperate shock.

Seth cried out: "No, no, no, they can't do that. They can't do that."

Kivi turned and looked at him, but Nadin spoke, his voice hoarse with fear and rage: "That's impossible. You can't have a laser on a machine that small," and Kivi understood how the people were being burned.

She gabbed Paz's arm and shouted: "We have to get out of here."

Paz wailed and shook but took a step forward when Kivi yanked her arm.

Seth and Nadin came close and Seth said: "Where the hell do we go?"

Kivi stared at Seth, unable to find an answer. She could not bear to look again. The sounds of chaos and sudden death drummed the air all around her head and she fought to keep the terror at bay. The trembling from the ground told her that buildings in the downtown area continued to collapse; the added heat and smell of burning meat threatened to break her spirit. Beside her, Paz appeared as though her spirit were already broken.

"Let's stay here and hide behind the stonework," she suggested to Seth, certain that Paz was incapable of taking a single step.

He nodded. Kivi turned back to see flames flash and touch more people. The dark, evil machines flew closer to the ground in little groups. They darted and spun and arched and dived and across the length and breadth of the square. People screamed out their agony or lay still in crumpled, crackling heaps. Out towards the edges, the trees burned, the low-rise buildings burned, and the grey and black smoke drifted upwards.

Suddenly, Paz let out a shriek of, "No!" and launched herself out from the memorial, sprinting towards the eastern side.

"Paz!" Kivi shouted, unable to let her friend end her life in such terrified desperation. She had to try to protect her. Kivi ran after her, concentrating on following Paz's long black hair. But burning people were everywhere, many still thrashing and shrieking in agony. Kivi saw Paz stumble and fall among the flaming ruins of her fellow citizens. Above her, a group of the machines made another pass. Paz pushed herself up on one knee, and then her hair and clothes caught fire. She brought her arms up and collapsed into a foetal position.

Kivi took one more step towards her dying friend when another running, screaming, burning victim crashed into her and sent her tumbling to the ground. On her back, she looked up into the bright blue morning sky mottled with flying black shapes. She felt suddenly weak, too weak to move. A hazy irritation began on her skin as four of the black shapes passed overhead. Altogether, she thought, the sky looked like it was filled with locusts. Yes, many locusts, buzzing around looking for food. The heat on her body increased until she couldn't breathe. She tried to pull her arms and legs together against the increasing pain, but her limbs wouldn't move. Kivi closed her eyes, accepted the sudden, overwhelming weakness, and waited for the burning sensation all over her skin to end. When it did, she would help her friend.

Chapter 17

The tall, slim form of Rear Admiral William Rutherford stood up as a waiter showed Sir Terry Tidbury to the expansive table.

"Good of you to agree to lunch, Bill," Terry said as the waiter slid the chair underneath him, and Terry requested freshly squeezed orange juice.

"My pleasure, Sir Terry."

"I think we can dispense with the formalities," Terry said. "Especially in the current circumstances. Are you up to speed with the situation in Israel?"

Rutherford frowned, "Oh, yes. Dreadful business. Apparently the Israelis attacked first, is that right?"

Terry nodded, "And they didn't tell anyone, not even the Americans, until they'd launched—"

"Whyever not?"

"Fischel must have had his reasons."

Rutherford unscrewed the cap of a bottle of water and asked while pouring: "And will he tell us what they were?"

"I don't know. The US sent in a rapid-response team from Naples to get him and any other VIPs out, but that was over two hours ago and there's been no contact with them. In addition, Caliphate Forces deployed another new ACA we haven't seen before."

Rutherford nodded, "Yes, I thought lasers were still too bulky to be mounted on an ACA," he said, and picked up a long menu card.

"So did everyone else, at least until today." Terry said, picking up the menu on his side of the table. Silence settled over the table as the two men considered the dishes. The waiter returned with Terry's drink and took their orders.

"In any case," Terry said when he'd left, "I wanted you to know I'm grateful you chaps in the Senior Service are sharing what you've found out." Terry looked at the Rear Admiral. "I'm sorry your people had to bear the brunt of that, Bill."

"Nonsense, old chap. His Majesty's Royal Navy has always been in the vanguard of England's, shall we say, 'adventures', and none of us expects that to change not only in the foreseeable future, but, in fact, at any time, ever."

Terry smiled and asked: "How's the rest of the service holding up?"

Rutherford's saturnine expression and shadowed eyes gave Terry a hint of the damage the loss of the Mediterranean fleet had done, but the Rear Admiral said: "Oh, I think the Americans got it a lot worse than us. Forty percent of their carrier groups lost in one engagement."

"What's your personal opinion on what the Caliphate hit us with?"

"You've seen the summary report?"

"Of course, but I wanted to hear your appraisal, Bill. I'm hoping the Third Caliph only wants Turkey, and now he's neutralised Israel he'll either strike down into India or go into

110

Russia's underbelly, but if he is thinking about Europe, we're going to need everything we've got."

Rutherford asked: "What do the computers say regarding the likelihood that he is going to attack Europe?"

Terry frowned, "Damn things will tell you anything you want to hear depending on what you ask them, Bill. Their total failure to see this coming has crushed what little trust I had in them. The problem is that the youngsters can't seem to cope without them."

Rutherford smiled and said: "But they grew up with them, and besides, are we really so different? I can remember the first artificial intelligence devices quite well. At Charterhouse, I and my chums developed an AI app as an end-of-sixth-form project. Do you remember those old apps? Things were so much simpler then."

Terry nodded his agreement, happy to allow the rear admiral a moment's nostalgia after the disaster he'd had to cope with. Rutherford continued: "But it's changed so much since then. How did we not see China's inevitable rise to such complete dominance of global affairs? Because whatever they say in public, it's the Chinese and their meddling that's brought us to this disaster."

"I don't know, Bill. I'm not too keen on picking apart the politics behind the how and the why. I want to know if the Caliphate is going to invade Europe, and if it does, how the hell we can defend ourselves."

"Thus far, the only thing we've got is coherence length variation."

Terry nodded. "That's one of the reasons I asked you to lunch. I've read the summary report, but I want to know what you make of it."

"Not sure I can add that much. Wexley on the *Hyperion* had the idea—"

"But it was his idea, not something the ship's super AI suggested?"

"Definitely, yes. He saw what was happening to the American ships and knew they didn't stand a chance, but tried to find a way to delay the inevitable. Once the ship's computer realised that a slight increase in each laser shot's coherence length meant it required fewer shots to knock out one of their machines, it obviously developed that."

"And what were the limits?"

The two men paused to allow the waiter to put the food on the table. Terry looked down at his braised ribs and compared them favourably with Rutherford's rigatoni with ham and cheese in a tomato sauce.

Rutherford extracted his cutlery from the folded linen napkin and said: "Quite restrictive. The tech bods know the fine details, but the trick appears to be randomisation within the available range. The decisive issue during the engagement wasn't so much their swamping of our defences—that's been an understood naval tactic for decades—but the strength in the shielding around their machines. That was quite outrageous."

"If and when an invasion comes, NATO isn't going to have much to hold them back with, and that coherence length variation could play an important role."

The two men shared a glance. Rutherford said: "If the randomisations were sufficiently frequent and sufficiently... random? it would be extremely difficult for any computer to anticipate and react to them, to overcome them."

Terry nodded, "That's interesting: a development which super artificial intelligence would not be able to negate."

"Let's keep that to ourselves for now."

"Indeed."

"Damn."

"What?"

112

Terry reached into his trouser pocket and took out a small, oblong device two centimetres long. He pressed an edge of it and it splayed out into a circle seven centimetres across. The space within the circle appeared empty, and then an image resolved. It had a blue background and the words 'Urgent, return to HQ' appeared in white.

Terry sighed. "It seems I have to go back."

"Before you go," Rutherford said, "there is one thing I wanted to mention to you."

"Certainly."

"I realise that these ACAs will draw much attention, but we're going to have to replace those ships, and that will cost money."

"Bill, I don't have any—"

Rutherford put a hand out and said: "I understand that, old chap. But at the same time, I don't think we can let these damnable machines end four hundred years of Royal Navy history, do you?"

The waiter returned and with deference said: "Excuse me, Sir. Your vehicle is waiting outside."

Terry nodded his thanks, the waiter left, and Terry answered Rutherford: "I'll support any requests you make, but as you might expect, we'll be relying on the Americans for all kinds of support."

"Indeed."

"Sorry I have to go so soon."

Rutherford shook his head and said: "I'll finish this and then I must go as well. I have many widows to visit."

Chapter 18

19.28 Wednesday 8 February 2062

The Englishman looked out at the Beijing skyline and a familiar thrill shivered through him. He stood at the centre of the world. Beijing simply owned all of the superlatives. It was the capital city of the richest and most powerful country; the biggest, the most populous, the place everyone who wasn't here wanted to visit, the city envied and emulated by every other city in the world. It was his natural environment, and every minute he spent here dripped in the vitality of existence itself.

A spark of patriotism flashed and burned inside him, and he wondered if people had felt like this about his home town of London two hundred years earlier. He could imagine a foreign diplomat looking out at St. Paul's or the newly rebuilt Houses of Parliament in the 1860s and marvelling at British supremacy, at how that little island race had conquered three quarters of the world. But so much had changed since then.

He smiled to himself when he recalled the previous night in bed with Marshal Zhou, as his lover had spoken of his family history, and then they'd talked about their countries' histories. In the warm, intimate glow which follows mutual climax, Zhou told the Englishman that, today, five thousand years of Chinese history were at last coalescing in the centre of the 'Middle Kingdom', so that it would finally dominate the world and guide it to a bright, peaceful future. No race on Earth was as patient as the Chinese.

Now, the Englishman scanned the glass and metal towers in the bright morning sunshine, smiling and shaking his head in awe at Sinopec's new headquarters; a vast, spear-like tower which had been designed as an elongated pyramid stretching hundreds of metres into the sky. He saw the canyons between the buildings, and imagined the millions of people down there, from the meanest coolie to the politburo members, from the shady dealers and traders to the thousands of billionaires who maintained a property in the most important capital city in the world, from the thieves and drug addicts to the doctors and charity workers.

The Englishman stood in apartment 4715 of the new Kempinski six-star hotel, opened a mere two weeks previously. He had checked in with his second identity as a seller of English wines to select restaurants, and he'd chosen the Kempinski because his super AI gave this hotel the lowest probability of being discovered. The Chinese government was known to monitor, and attempt to de-encrypt, all quantum comms traffic emanating from the city, but this was a huge undertaking, and when his super AI gave him a low enough probability of detection, the Englishman trusted that he would remain undiscovered. But this risk itself only heightened his pleasure at the life he led.

He strolled the length of the spacious living room and entered the bedroom. He let himself collapse on the wonderfully smooth and soft duvet, puffed up the pillow under his head, and twitched the muscles in his eye so that his lens would encrypt his words. He slowed his breathing and collected his thoughts.

When ready, he spoke aloud: "The Englishman reporting from Beijing. Time of report: nineteen-thirty-two, Wednesday the eighth of February, twenty sixty-two. Report begins. I spent last night with Z. again. We used a notable amount of alcohol and Z. took his usual narcotic, while I feigned taking it, also as usual. I questioned him about the Caliphate and what's happened to Turkey and Israel. To provoke him, I emphasised the sense of shock and fear in Europe, and hinted that few believed China did not know what the Caliphate had been planning, and probably had done for years.

"Z. displayed an element of cynicism allied with more than a trace of indifference. Z. knows his history, and berated Europe for always thinking it was the centre of the universe. He repeated one of his favourite stats, that more Chinese were killed in the Taiping Rebellion in the 1850s than in Europe in the whole of the First World War. Thus feeling that he'd given me a 'better' perspective on global historical events, he went on to concede confusion in his immediate military circle. He wondered if the Chinese intelligence services might have known, but he insisted that no one in the army knew or even expressed an opinion. Up until last Tuesday morning, the Caliphate was a minor subject in Chinese military affairs."

The Englishman paused and admired the ornate cornice above him. He continued: "It is difficult to say with certainty, but I believe Z. was being truthful. The tailored narcotics I gave him should have seen to that. However, irrespective of what the Chinese military did or did not know about the Caliphate's intentions, the future is of most importance now. But when I tried to question Z. on what he expected the Chinese government to do next, including whether they would try to rein the Third Caliph in, he became frivolous and changed the subject. I carried on a little longer, but I could not draw him on what the future might hold. I will try to find out more in the nearest future. Report ends."

Chapter 19

In the emergency meeting room at Ten Downing Street, Terry looked at Crispin Webb as Webb whispered: "Jesus Christ," and wondered what on earth the PM's director of communications had expected. Terry got little pleasure out of civilians suddenly finding themselves out of their depth in a military emergency, but it mattered significantly that they could adapt. So far this week, shock was the dominating force.

In the wall in front of them a large screen showed BBC News. To images of burnt and blasted sheets of twisted metal, the anchor said: "These pictures appear to show the remains of an Israeli Nesher 101–C autonomous combat aircraft. The Office of the Third Caliph claims that Israel attacked the Caliphate with two hundred and fifty-six of these ACAs, each of which was armed with uranium–234 fission warheads. If the Israeli ACAs had got through the Caliphate's defences and reached their targets, it's estimated they would have cost the lives of tens of millions of Caliphate subjects."

Prime Minister Dahra Napier said: "Incredible. Could that evidence have been manufactured somehow? Planted?"

Defence Secretary Phillip Gough stroked his trimmed beard and said: "Not a chance. The world and his wife tracked the Israeli launches and followed them until they disappeared inside Caliphate territory. Frankly, I think we've had the lesser of two horrendous evils. If the Israeli attack had succeeded, serious doses of radiation would've been blowing all around the world for years."

"And what's happening inside Israel now?" Napier asked.

Gough shrugged his shoulders, "We don't know. As with Turkey, when the Caliphate's ACAs gain air superiority in a given battlespace, satellites blanket the area with impenetrable jamming."

"All right," Napier said, "and how do we defeat that?"

Gough hesitated, "Er, we've got experts at Porton Down working on a solution now."

"You mean they can just control any space they like?" Napier asked.

"Not exactly," Gough replied. "It's more about force projection. We agreed to the Caliphate's isolationist stance as it kept the peace, yes? Over twenty years ago, it developed an earlier version of this not to stop us from seeing in, but to stop its subjects from communicating with each other. The First Caliph didn't want any factions and other splinter groups joining together to overthrow him. Now, as long as there was peace, which there was until Tuesday, successive governments accepted the status quo, under pressure from China. But after what's happened the last two days, we're in wholly unchartered territory. The Caliphate has hit our navies, Turkey and now Israel with weapons we didn't know it had and which are, however much we might not like it, actually quite a bit better than ours."

For a moment, the room fell into silence, until Webb muttered: "The press are going to have a field day with this. The bloody Caliph couldn't have managed this any better."

Terry said: "I'm sure he did take global public opinion into account, but the foremost thing to note here is that we have now witnessed two tactically perfect assaults on neighbouring countries. Invading Turkey first and then allowing the Israelis to assume he'd left his own people relatively unprotected was a stroke of genius."

"And," Gough added, "by goading Israel into trying to nuke him, then by defeating that, he's kept the moral high ground by replying with a non-nuclear counterattack."

"I know," Webb sighed. "The global press are horrified at the violence but, if you can believe this, they're broadly supportive of the Cal—"

"That's because of China, Crispin," Napier interrupted. "Most countries in Asia, Africa and South America regard China as the saviour of the world. And the Caliphate is China's creation, so it stands to reason that on other continents, the Caliphate gets the benefit of the doubt." Napier frowned and pinched the bridge of her nose. Terry looked on, wondering how she was really coping.

Napier glanced around the room, at each of the men who surrounded her, and said: "The question is: what happens next? What happens when Turkey is fully assimilated, when those poor Israelis are either destroyed or otherwise released from that dreadful terror? What will the Third Caliph do then?"

"Squonk," Gough called out, addressing the Ministry of Defence's super AI. "Display current probability blocks for future Caliphate action."

The images of the destroyed Israeli Nesher ACA were replaced with a simple block graph.

121

Gough spoke: "Right then, along the bottom we have the most likely options: attack India, attack Russia, attack Europe, or take no further offensive action. Up the side, we have time, from one day to one month from now. Each block contains Squonk's percentage forecasts."

Terry watched the others study the blocks, which gave varying probabilities of the Caliphate's next actions. Terry didn't need to look at the graph because Gough had shown it to him when he was in transit to the meeting, and in any case after this week, he didn't trust Squonk to tell him the sky was blue.

Napier spoke: "The 'take no further offensive action' for the next week is the highest figure, the most probable. Why is that?"

Gough looked at the general and invited him with: "Sir Terry?"

Terry answered: "Normal military doctrine insists the invader needs time to consolidate newly gained territory. In the case of Turkey, Squonk estimates that it will take Caliphate forces at least two weeks to establish full control over the country and begin its assimilation into the Caliphate properly, so they will not take any further military action."

She looked at him pointedly: "Do you agree with it?"

"No, I do not," Terry replied, and waited for one of the others to suggest that the super AI must know better.

None did.

Napier asked: "Why?"

"I'd like to say only because it completely missed this week's staggering events, but it's more than that."

"Go on," Napier said.

"Let me show you what I mean," he said. "Squonk, recalculate this graph to factor in a one-hundred percent certainty that the data contained in the leaked data-pod is in fact true."

The heights of the bars changed, and the 'take no further offensive action' option shrivelled almost to zero. Terry spoke: "This is a little nearer the likelihood of what we can expect."

Napier let out a gasp. She stood and faced Terry with a look of shocked realisation: "Of course, it makes sense now... If he's built such huge military forces, he has to use them. He absolutely must use them."

Terry nodded as he noticed the others' faces drop. "He absolutely cannot, not use that vast an army."

"Three million men under arms, the data-pod claimed," Gough said.

Terry shook his head said to Gough, "Not claimed, but told. It's fact, not planted evidence. It never was." Then he turned to Napier: "That data-pod has been the only reliable thing all along, PM. It has to be accurate. It's the only way the Caliphate could have the volume of arms necessary to attack two large and well-armed countries at the same time, and be the easy victor against both. And with that volume of personnel, guided by their own super AI, I do not believe it will take them two weeks to consolidate their hold on Turkey. The Third Caliph has to move his warriors, soon.

"Now, the one thing only that madman knows is where he's going to deploy those warriors. Is he going to take on India, with the third largest military in the world? Is he going into Russia's underbelly to assimilate the Muslims there, and risk upsetting China in result? Or is he going to turn his attention to the rather weaker Europe and NATO?"

All heads turned to look at the bar chart and saw there was very little difference between the three options.

Napier blinked and said in a tight voice: "I think we should prepare for the worst."

Chapter 20

15.28 Wednesday 8 February 2062

Terry looked around the large, virtual meeting room at the forty or so of his service chiefs of staff and their aides, and asked: "Any questions?"

The vice chief of staff of the RAF, a slight man with a thin nose on a drawn face, said: "Sir Terry, in exercises in the last few years, we had problems with the Greeks and Italians. Are you confident we will be able to rely on them if the Caliphate attacks Europe?"

"I believe nothing concentrates the mind like the prospect of total annihilation. As I mentioned in the presentation, if the Caliphate attacks Europe, we will see a definite increase in performance, but in any case I will be talking with their NATO chiefs in the near future."

"Sir Terry," called the colonel of the Royal Logistics Corps, a severe-looking middle-aged woman with short brown hair. "I think the refugee estimates are a bit on the low side. It's fair to suppose that every last European citizen has seen the pictures from Turkey and Israel, especially Israel, so I think that if the Caliphate does invade Europe, the only people who wouldn't run would be those who couldn't due to physical incapacity. In addition, if they use the ACA with the laser that they've used on the Israelis, we won't be able to fight back. It will be a slaughter."

Terry's adjutant, John Simms, interjected: "The NATO naming committee has ascribed the reporting name 'Lapwing' to that design of Caliphate ACA."

Terry replied: "In the event of an invasion, a great deal will depend on their tactics. Later today, more in-depth scenarios will be available, but right now we're severely hampered by the lack of hard data."

"Can't the spooks help us out more, especially through third countries?" asked a lieutenant-colonel responsible for combat service support.

Terry said: "We're ramping up our intel-gathering in tandem with the Americans and other NATO members, but we have precious little to go on. If war is coming, people, it's going to be completely unlike any other war in our countries' histories. The opportunities for subterfuge simply won't be there."

An aide to the colonel from the Royal Engineers raised a hand and spoke when Terry nodded. "General, one area of concern which you touched on in your presentation concerns comms. If an invasion comes and it moves as quickly as it did in Turkey and Israel, will NATO be able to accelerate reactivation of StratCom?"

"StratCom and the other centres of excellence have been mothballed for the last decade, so it's going to take some time, but NATO is reassessing all of them to determine which will offer the greatest benefit in the event of an invasion."

Terry looked around at his audience, waiting. A moment later, he said: "Okay then, if there are no more questions, we'll close now. Thank you all for attending. I'll conclude by reminding you that some kind of confrontation with the New Persian Caliphate is, in my opinion, inevitable. I sincerely hope I am wrong. But if we look at the events of the last two days, the adventure upon which the Third Caliph has embarked sits easily alongside the most shocking surprise military attacks in history, and to think that his attention lies somewhere other than Europe and NATO is, again in my opinion, a luxury we cannot afford. Please, people, go back to your divisions and regiments and tell them to get ready. As this week has shown, events could move incredibly quickly, and we, the British Armed Forces, who remain the best armed forces the world has ever seen, may soon be forced into a confrontation which we did not seek, but in which we will prevail, as we have prevailed in conflicts for centuries. Good luck."

Terry watched a number of the participants vanish and then removed his own VR glasses to return fully to the kitchen in his home.

"Tea's brewing," he heard his wife Maureen say.

Terry exhaled and got up from the stool to walk around the table and stare at the garden, lost in thought. He knew his wife would never question him about his work, which is what he adored about her. She would wait for him to tell her, and then she would use her formidable intuition to clarify, verify, and ensure he'd missed nothing that could damage him.

"You know, Maureen, I can't quite believe I've just had to talk like that to those chiefs of staff. It seems incredible that a vast machinery has begun functioning, with me at its head."

"If you think about it," she said, stirring his mug of tea and removing the bag when she judged the liquid sufficiently malty, "they probably feel better having you point things out to them clearly."

Terry smiled as he took the mug of tea. "Thank you," he said.

Maureen let out a sigh and also glanced at the garden. "Pity it's not warm enough to sit outside."

The weak February sun washed the green from the lawn, making it appear a sickly, undernourished yellow. The branches on the trees in the corners stuck out, naked, and the borders offered nothing but dirt. The bleakness matched Terry's mood and his fears. He sipped his tea and said: "It's strange. I was due to retire later in the year. A part of me wonders why this has happened now, Maureen. Why this week? Why not any other week? They must have been planning this for years."

"Because it's happened. But it's what you've spent a lifetime being prepared for. I remember when we were courting and you told me that every soldier always hoped for at least one war."

Terry chuckled. "Yes, I remember. But I never believed it would come. It seems so strange that I always thought peace in Europe had achieved some kind of permanency, so much so that until last weekend I didn't give it a second thought."

Their eyes met, and Maureen smiled and said: "No retirement for you yet, Terry."

Chapter 21

15.45 Wednesday 8 February 2062

Berat Kartal cycled past the silent distribution centre on the outskirts of the town of Durasilli. Ahead of him, the sun hued the high clouds a fiery red, and he realised he'd have to stop for the night soon, especially as the temperature had dropped. To take his mind off his aching legs and back and arms, he tried to calculate his averages of speed and distance, and then to extrapolate how long it would take him to reach the port city of Izmir.

However, he couldn't concentrate. The sights he'd seen and the conversations he'd had in the thirty-six hours since fleeing his home in Usak concerned him greatly. Most upsetting had been witnessing the abject shock and panic in what he assumed were otherwise perfectly rational people. But now their devices didn't work anymore, they didn't know what was happening and couldn't find out. Lenses in eyes remained empty and unresponsive; handheld slates spun open to reveal nothingness. And this was only at the individual level. Berat didn't need to imagine the chaos at the levels of communities and local governments and provinces, because he witnessed it as he pedalled on.

The previous night he'd stayed at a distribution centre not dissimilar to the one he now cycled past, where the handful of humans who oversaw the super AI couldn't grasp at all why the centre no longer functioned. Berat had explained patiently how the Caliphate's microwave bursts—very short and very low—burned out unprotected components, and nearly all civilian devices were unprotected. The people to whom he'd given this bad news reacted with anger and frustration, seeming to feel strongly that such a situation shouldn't have been allowed to happen. Berat could only sympathise with them and then be on his way.

Later, he stopped at a vehicle charging station to beg some water. He filled a two-litre plastic bottle and spoke to a policeman, who knew nothing but explained that only military equipment would've survived the microwave bursts. Berat cycled on for a few hours. He noticed people beginning to move. The first refugees of this new war, he thought with mounting bitterness. Families with children carried their most valuable possessions in backpacks or plastic carrier bags. When he stopped for a rest, he greeted and then questioned some of them. Again, anger congealed with frustration to produce a sickly animosity which acted as a cover for the sense of impotence, especially in the men. All headed in the same direction as Berat: the port city of Izmir and the hope of a ship to escape the country.

As the light faded, Berat's attention was caught by a large crowd of people up ahead. He pedalled around pedestrians as the road became busier, and saw a sign that read 'Yelda Restoran'. He decided to chain his bike to the supporting post of a large sign some distance from the throng. Once again, he marvelled at the sense of true exploration. For all of his life, when he arrived at a new destination, his slate or his lens would tell him everything he needed to know. To people of his generation, nothing was a mystery; everything was explained succinctly. Now, Berat found himself approaching people and places with no advance indication of who or what they might be. At some deeper level, he felt thrilled and enriched. To confront a complete stranger with no knowledge of whom they were felt incredibly liberating.

He joined the unthreatening crowd. Families with small children and elderly parents trudged on to the charging station with a little knot of low buildings, likely hoping for some small corner in which to huddle and avoid the chill of the February night. The sound of an argument came from somewhere to his left. He heard the shrill squawk of an elderly grandmother matched against the deep muscular voice of a man. He eased his way nearer.

The elderly woman shouted: "What do you know, eh? This Caliph will kill all of us. I heard from my grandson in Adana they have lasers and are burning all of the young men in each town."

"You don't know what you are talking about, hag," the man chided her. "The Caliphate's warriors are coming to protect us. Did not our great President Demir himself say we would have a vote whether to join—"

"Protect us from what?" another male voice asked.

"Demir is a fat pig," someone else called out.

Berat edged closer and saw through the mass of shoulders and arms an elderly woman standing on a couple of wooden pallets. Her wide face wore a concerned expression and Berat wondered when and how this gathering had begun.

A man in the crowd motioned to the elderly woman: "Your grandson is in Adana; I have a cousin just along from there, on the coast in Mersin, and this morning he told me warriors are processing civilians to get them ready for assimilation. He said the only fighting is from units of the

131

Turkish Army and Police. Remember, everyone, the Third Caliph is the most peaceful leader in the world—"

A few jeering shouts broke out, and then died down as another man, fist shaking next to an angry face of furrowed brow over a thick black beard, insisted: "Rubbish, you're talking rubbish. How can you have been in touch with your 'cousin' if all the electronics were burned out yesterday, eh? And you, old lady, how did you hear from your grandson? Did he send you a carrier pigeon?"

The last question caused a ripple of laughter among the tired and frightened people, but Berat felt the mood change when the first man defended: "I have an older model of slate which kept working longer than most of the devices."

"Or," said the second man with suspicion, "you're something to do with the government and you have protected military equipment on you."

The laughter vanished, but the first man remained passive and calm. He opened his arms in a friendly gesture: "Friend, do we not have enough trouble around us now?"

But the second man spat: "You and I are not friends. And if the Third Caliph is so gentle and merciful, please tell us why he has burned out all of our electronics."

"Because of expected resistance," the man answered without missing a beat. "This is the first part of a very important process which will change all our lives—"

"Yes, by ending most of them," the old woman on the pallets interrupted.

"For the better. But the Third Caliph has to prepare for those who would oppose his teachings."

The second man let out a loud, cynical scoff and stalked away from the gathering. The first man, moving to stand next to the old woman on the pallets, addressed the rest of the crowd: "And that is why I implore you all, that if you are true believers, you should return to your homes, your apartments, and your farms—"

"Rubbish," the old woman said. "Don't listen to these lies. The invaders will kill us all—"

"She does not speak the truth. She speaks of hatred, of poison, and this is not what the benevolent Caliph deals in. The Caliphate believes in building peaceful futures for all of its children…"

Berat could listen no longer, so he backed out of the crowd, wondering what the other people really thought. In the past, he and his friends and his colleagues had kept their opinions to themselves and only spoke openly in trusted company. Everyone realised Demir was dragging the country into dictatorship, but the president's mumbles approving of the Caliphate hadn't been given much weight for the simple fact that if Turkey acceded to the Caliphate, Demir would no longer be the one in charge, except perhaps nominally. He recalled a conversation among his friends a couple of weeks earlier where the prospect of a referendum was dismissed as highly unlikely. Now it hardly mattered.

He backed further away and returned to the tall signpost to which he'd chained his bike. Full darkness had almost arrived, and he considered whether to try to find somewhere to stay warm for the night, or keep pedalling through the darkness and rest in the open in the morning when the sun warmed the air. As the crowd thinned, he sensed someone following him.

He glanced back to see another young man, similar in age and build. When Berat made eye-contact, an accented voice called out: "Hey, is that bike yours?"

Berat increased his slight gait as much as he could, as a sudden burst of adrenalin accelerated his steps on the realisation that he might be obliged to fight to keep his bike.

He realised he hadn't taken anything that he could use as a weapon.

The man repeated: "Hey, is the bike yours?"

Berat spoke over his shoulder, "What if it is?"

"How much do you want for it?"

"It's not for sale."

Berat reached his bike and felt for the key to release the antique padlock and chain he'd used to secure it.

The man stopped some distance away and said: "It's okay. It was just a suggestion. There's a group of us over in the solar hangars. Power and water aren't a problem, but we need money for food, and, you know, there's strength in numbers. I saw you and thought you looked like a smart, reliable guy. Thought maybe you could join us... My name's Panit."

Panit stuck out a hand, but Berat hesitated. He said: "If you need money, why'd you offer to buy my bike?"

Panit smiled and said: "I wanted to know if you were willing to sell it, and if you were I'd help you find a buyer."

"I could probably sell it by myself, you know. And why would I want to share the money with you even if I did?"

"I told you: strength in numbers. Who knows what's going to happen in the coming days and weeks. People need to stick together, and I see you're on your own."

Berat couldn't make a firm decision whether to believe Panit. The expression on his face and his body language seemed genuine, but Berat felt suddenly seized by an irrational fear. Berat said to him: "Let me think about it, okay?"

Panit tilted his head, "Sure," he said. "We're in the solar hangar at the far end. You'll be warm for the night."

"Thanks."

"See you," Panit said, and turned and strolled away.

Berat's logical engineer's mind wondered why he felt so disinclined to join Panit and his friends, but he could find no source for his reluctance. He glanced up at the bright half-moon and star-scattered night sky, as if searching for an answer. He shrugged his shoulders a couple of times to settle the rucksack on his back, sat on the seat, and pedalled to the road. Once on the tarmac, he flicked the little lever to increase the gears and accelerated.

Panit was right: Berat would be warm for the night, cycling ahead of the total chaos which reigned behind them and swept towards them in an unstoppable wave. For tonight, the disaster remained out of sight, out of their knowledge, but Berat knew it was there all the same, ready to overtake them should they dare to rest too long.

Chapter 22

As the autonomous Toyota Rive-All cruised along the M26 towards London, General Sir Terry Tidbury considered military spending options. Distracted by events, he glanced out of the window at the lanes of traffic all crowded with similar vehicles, and admired that so many thousands of them could move in such proximity at high speed and in such safety. For as long as he could remember, there had only ever been one accident and resulting delay, some eight years ago. Otherwise, the traffic around London and the Home Counties ran in a uniform smoothness and precision twenty-four hours a day. Vehicles changed lanes, decelerated and accelerated often with mere centimetres to spare. Perhaps, Terry thought, super artificial intelligence did have some benefits.

"Time to destination?" he asked.

"Seventeen minutes and thirty seconds," the vehicle replied.

Terry forced himself to concentrate on the issues with which the data-feed in his slate presented him. He'd always

137

thought that the Head of the British Army in peacetime was a relatively undemanding job because so much of the work was delegated. Often, Terry's responsibilities consisted of approving deployments, expenditures and training which his colonels knew better than him were required or appropriate. Terry had fewer than forty thousand troops under his command, the lowest number of any head of the British Army in centuries. However, he tended not to dwell on this fact because warfare had changed so much; or, in the case of the British Isles, had ceased altogether. As he looked down at the data on the screen of his slate, he wondered again what the future held.

His adjutant, Simms, flagged options with question marks, but one of the key problems was where to spend the little money the Department of Defence was able to wring out of the Treasury. Terry had already had enough testy debates regarding increasing levels of ACA production before the current crisis erupted, and didn't relish the prospect of more. But now, with this explosion of violence from the previously peaceful Caliphate, money had to be found to fortify strategic defences around the southern coast of England at the very minimum, and preferably all of the British Isles' coastlines.

The vehicle interrupted his thoughts: "Information. An announcement has just been made by the New Persian Caliphate. Would you like to view it on the screen or on your slate?"

The breath stopped in Terry's throat, and for the first time in years he felt a weight in the pit of his stomach. "On the slate, please."

He lifted the device up and looked at the screen, not seeing the other vehicles racing and changing lanes outside. Terry wasn't sure if the figure in the screen was the same handsome, dark-skinned young man who had made the announcement on Tuesday morning, but he also sat at a typical news-reading desk and the official crest of the Third Caliph appeared over his right shoulder.

As he spoke, the English translation scrolled along the bottom of the image: 'The New Persian Caliphate announces its intention to correct an historical wrong. Ever since the Crusades nearly a millennium ago, the Christian infidel has stamped his boot in the Muslim face. Now the day is at hand when this mortal insult will be corrected. The Caliphate gives notice to Europe and the world that the Crusades, as well as the additional injustice that took place in the year of Mohammed 1062, will now be corrected. The Christian infidel in Europe, his power and influence waning for the last fifty years, will find his new role as the subordinate of the superior Muslim. The Caliphate will join with our Turkish brothers to correct this historical mistake, to bring a new balance to a small part of the world which for too long reaped the harvest of slavery and the money-lender's irreligious charging of interest. Now, finally, Europe will be brought to heel and shown the true faith. God is great.'

"Play it again," Terry instructed.

After he'd watched it a second time, he asked the vehicle: "What's the meaning of the second historical reference, the year-of-Mohammed part?"

"Highest probability is the Battle of Vienna, 12 September 1683, during which a multi-national European force led by Polish King Jan Sobieski defeated an invasion of Muslim Ottomans despite being significantly outnumbered. It was the last time Europe was so threatened and, had the multi-national force lost, Europe's future would have been very different. You will arrive at your destination in five minutes."

Terry raised an eyebrow at the vehicle's opining. "Thank you," he said.

He looked at the bleak English countryside outside and felt a strange, calming sensation, as though a threshold had been crossed and now the future took on a dark clarity which had hitherto been obscured by uncertainty. He recalled his basic training as a raw recruit so many years ago, and the one phrase which had stayed with him, yelled out by the training sergeant: "The controlled release of aggression!" This phrase defined more than any other what soldiering meant, and also acted as the pivot from which civilians who had not been in uniform could never comprehend: the military understood the importance of the controlled release of aggression in successfully managing any hostile situation, be it covert confrontation, terrorist attack, skirmish, battle or war.

The data-feed on his slate exploded with comms requests and other inquiries, but he looked at them with disinterest. Soon enough battle would be joined. He exhaled and again looked through the window, noting how the towering buildings of central London crawled into view as the vehicle sped towards them. He asked himself if he were able to face the challenge, if perhaps the PM might not regret her decision to decline his offer of resignation. And then he remembered Maureen's reminder that every soldier hoped for at least one war in their lifetime. He knew, as every soldier knew when a threat materialised, that he would meet the challenge. Once again, Europe would face a mortal threat to its very survival, and the capriciousness of fate had placed him in a key role.

Chapter 23

Crispin Webb watched the Caliphate's broadcast four times, and with each viewing the numbness increased until it threatened to overwhelm him. He deactivated the lens in his eye, walked over to the window and looked out at the bare treetops in St. James's Park, engulfed by a sudden despair that a hitherto certain future had abruptly been thrown into all kinds of doubt.

He paced around the spacious, elegant room. He began to hyperventilate. It wasn't supposed to be like this. He had a first in Political Science from Cambridge. He'd made it to his position as Director of Communications through relentless effort, not through birth or some other dewdrop of good fortune which had come his way by chance. He'd worked hard to support his boss, making her look good as a leader, helping her so the government could cope with the rising seas, the key dividend from the stupidity of generations past who, even when faced with crushing evidence of the damage they were doing to the environment, still continued to allow climate change to proceed apace.

141

Climate change affected the British Isles as it affected many countries around the world, but the blame for it lay with people who for the most part were dead. As long as the boss was seen to deal with flood events in the most professional manner, no one could accuse her of being responsible for the damage and casualties. After that came the usual issues that had beset English prime ministers for decades: unemployment, crime, gaming addiction. And like all prime ministers, the boss had to compromise with the vested interests who didn't want any changes that might eat into their profits.

Crispin spoke his concerns aloud: "Nowhere, absolutely nowhere, does any of this include a bloody war."

He forced himself to control his breathing by counting the seconds between each inhalation and exhalation, which helped only until he replayed the memory of the Third Caliph's announcement. He shook his head and swore, and then told himself to get a grip. In his mind he realised that the announcement had been inevitable, from the moment on Tuesday morning when the first Spider had crashed into the first ship.

His breathing slowed. "Okay, okay," he muttered. He reactivated the lens in his eye and steeled himself. In seconds, all of the data feeds filled up with press releases from around the world along with hundreds of requests for the boss's reaction from every media outlet in the British Isles and Europe.

"Shit, shit, shit," he spat as his eye muscles twitched to refine the data. From all of the media outlets, Crispin knew that only one really mattered: *The Mail*. Its editor, a vicious bulldog of a man called Andy MacSawley, used the outlet as his personal fiefdom to expound his hatreds, which he could do for as long as the Rothermeres kept making money from the outlet. Crispin and the boss knew *The Mail*'s support had contributed to her election victory, although not as much as MacSawley liked to claim.

Crispin twitched his eye and the connection went through to MacSawley. "Cris?" the editor said. "This is a massive fucking disaster. What has the PM got to say about it?"

Crispin gritted his teeth to keep down the anger of his name being shortened in a fashion he loathed, and then replied: "We're still taking it in here, Mac, but you'll know our reaction soon."

"Listen, I can give her some slack, but it won't be long before my readers will start asking exactly how the fuck the government didn't see this coming—"

"Don't give me that bullshit. Who could see anything coming? How many undercover journalists did your predecessor send in years ago, and when was the last time you heard from them, eh?"

"Aye, so you're feeling a touch the smart-arse today, are you? Well, enjoy it while it lasts, Cris. I'm telling you, Napier, her cabinet, and the whole fucking government are going to get ripped to fucking shreds over this disaster; hung, drawn and well-fucking-quartered. Now, get back to me soon. I want a quote and I want it before any of the others. Got that?"

"Wait, Mac," Crispin replied in a warning tone, determined not to be outsmarted. "I think you should remember who gives out the baubles around here. You don't have anything yet, do you, *Mister* MacSawley? So if you want that knighthood, we'll want to see a bit more fucking patriotism from your outlet. If war's coming, we're going to need a lot more than just your usual hate-mongering."

Crispin heard a chuckle followed by, "Aye, lad. Now, piss off." The connection ended.

Crispin attempted to reach his boss, but she had yet to emerge from another appointment. With a further twitch he got through to the boss's PA, Monica. Crispin said: "Have you heard? Where's the boss, for Christ's sake?"

Monica's narrow eyes came together in a frown. "She's having a beauty treatment—"

"What the? Seriously? Europe's about to get invaded and she having a fucking manicure?"

Monica said: "Chill, Crispin. She's having the full service, so it takes a while. She's been in there since before the announcem—"

"I don't care," he almost shouted. "Get her out of there, now—and don't tell me to bloody 'chill'."

"Why?"

"What?"

"Can't we let her have just a few minutes more peace, Crispin? It's out there. The storm's coming, we know that now. This isn't very good news. I think we should let her find out about it when she's looking her best, don't you? It's just a few minutes."

Chapter 24

12.11 Thursday 9 February 2062

Three gruelling hours later, Crispin Webb looked at his boss's red eyes, the only physical sign of what she must have felt. They sat at the vast oak table in the Cabinet Room, the boss in her chair in front of the fireplace, Foreign Secretary Charles Blackwood to her right, Crispin on her left. Opposite them on the wall between the huge windows, hung a large screen which showed the tired-looking face of US President Coll, flanked by members of her Cabinet whom Crispin recognised.

Coll spoke: "We're tabling a motion to condemn the Caliphate's actions and to effect an immediate cessation of exports from and imports to the Caliphate at the emergency session of the UN this evening."

Napier sighed: "Maddie, do you remember last year, when I told you about the League of Nations in the 1930s?"

Coll rubbed her forehead. "Sure, I remember, but you know we can't live in the past, Dahra. The UN carries more weight than you give it credit for."

Napier shook her head. "No, it doesn't. Not any more. China only stays in it out of a dated sense of habit. The Asian Free Trade Area is the most important trade and diplomatic forum to it."

Coll tutted. "Gotta disagree with you there. We're putting a ton of pressure on our allies to find out what the hell is go—"

"As are we, Maddie. But 'pressure' isn't what it used to be, is it?"

"I doan know wh—"

"I've spent the last couple of hours talking to my ambassadors and diplomats in the countries that really matter, Maddie. China, India, Russia, Brazil. You know, the countries with the largest economies and biggest militaries in the world? And I'll tell you what I've found out."

The President looked back at Napier with a testy expression her face.

Napier continued: "First, China will veto your UN motion to condemn the Caliphate's violence and stop imports and exports—"

"No, it wo—"

"Second, it seems we may have underestimated Chinese patronage of the Caliphate and the weight that patronage carries in those countries."

Coll frowned and asked: "What do you mean, they won't support us?"

"We can expect a typical diplomatic fudge. For example, Brazil will send all the condolences we want, but as its trade with China is worth nearly twenty quadrillion Renminbi annually, and the Caliphate was China's creation, Brazil is hardly going to risk antagonising Beijing unduly."

Coll shook her head. "No, diplomacy in peace is one thing, but this is a goddamn war. Whatever our relations were with these countries last week or last year, now everything's changed. We've been in touch with Beijing directly and they're distancing themselves from the Third Caliph's actions, which is a positive sign."

"But how much? So what if the Chinese 'distance themselves' if they won't condemn his outrageous aggression and get him to retract his ludicrous threat to invade Europe? And it's not only Brazil. We've received the official position from India. Ansh Dasgupta is going to make a statement that while the Caliphate's actions were wholly unjustified, the NATO governments must accept some responsibility for stationing naval battle groups so close to Caliphate borders."

"This is crazy," Coll said in irritation. "We can't have the world just accept what's going on here. There has to be outrage. As far as we know, Israel has been entirely wiped out."

"Charles?" Napier said, glancing at her Foreign Secretary.

Blackwood scratched the back of his slender neck with one arm while saying: "Absolutely not, Madam President. But it might pay to look at these developments from their perspective. For example, our super AI has aggregated Chinese media reports since the attack on the navies two days ago, and has found…" his words trailed off as his arm came down to dab at a screen embedded in the oak table top. He took a pair of glasses from the breast pocket of his jacket and put them on. "That approximately seventy-eight percent more coverage was given across all platforms to a bombing carried out by Yunnan separatists at a shopping mall in the city of Lincang, which killed thirty-five and injured a hundred. Indeed, when all Chinese media outlets are aggregated for the last three days, reportage on recent events in Europe is twenty-third in popularity. In short, inside the world's richest and most populous country, what the Caliphate has done this week to NATO, Turkey and Israel is little more than a sideshow."

147

"I didn't realise it was that bad," Crispin heard Napier mutter as he took amusement from Coll's mouth dropping open like a goldfish at feeding time.

Blackwood continued: "The most popular news story concerning recent events in Europe has been in the... *West China City News* outlet, which described what happened and recommended that its readers seriously consider exiting their European investments before the situation worsens." He peered at Coll over the rim of his glasses and added: "I don't think the Chinese government is unduly concerned about any kind of public outcry that they should intercede to rein the Caliph in."

Coll leaned back to consult her Secretary of State, and then said: "Okay, thanks for this. We're in the process of seeing if the USA can't bring a little more pressure to bear on those countries. We still do quite a chunk of business with them, so maybe we can persuade them to support our motion this evening. We'll talk again after the UN vote."

Napier replied: "Very well," and the image of President Coll and the others in the Oval Office vanished.

Crispin reasoned that he didn't need to be diplomatic: "Those bloody Yanks don't have a clue."

Blackwood said: "That's a very opinionated way to put it, Mr Webb, but accurate nevertheless."

Napier said: "They don't seem to understand how little influence we have... Pity Preston Grant isn't around to set them straight."

"The name rings a bell, boss," Crispin said. "Who was he?"

Blackwood answered: "He was arguably the best manager of fires-in-whorehouses the United States of America has ever produced. He would be able to point out to them the flaws in their arguments."

Crispin asked: "So what happened to him?"

Blackwood shrugged and said: "Killed a few years ago in one of those pointless mass murders the Americans do so well."

"If the Third Caliph has the means to carry out his threat, the subsequent mass murder here in Europe could be the biggest and most pointless in history yet," Napier said, looking through the large windows into the weak February sunlight outside.

Crispin gave his boss a moment to think, and then politely coughed and said: "Er, it's time to get the Cabinet meeting underway. Would you like me to show them in?"

Napier tilted her head back and replied: "Yes, please."

Five minutes later, the twenty-three members of Napier's Cabinet had filed in and seated themselves around the huge oak table. The women wore concerned expressions, the men attempted to appear stoic. In addition to the other regular non-ministerial attendees, the Minister of State for Defence and the Minister for the Armed Forces were also shown into the room.

When all were seated, Napier looked at each in turn. She recalled happier times of canvassing and attending post-debate parties at the annual conferences with some of them. She remembered how she'd got to know each of them, their egos, their foibles, their strengths, their limits. She recalled the last election and how she and Crispin had discussed which of the potential cabinet members she could trust, which she couldn't, and those whom it would be better, as Crispin said, to have on the inside of the tent pissing out, rather than on the outside pissing in.

As she gazed at the faces looking at her, the realisation came to her that they expected her to lead them. Since the disaster began on Tuesday, she'd been in a strange kind of quasi-panic combined with a sense of disconnection from reality. Napier could trace her journey to the premiership of

149

England quite easily, because she had it laid out in her journals from the last seventeen years of her political life. For most of them, she'd never really believed she would ever lead the party, and then become prime minister, however much she might have dreamed it when she was merely on the back benches. But with mentoring from the last prime minister but one, and successfully taking on a restructuring of the pension deficit when she was Minister for Work and Pensions, had seen her over the line at the leadership contest ten years previously. The six years of her premiership, at which she'd chaired countless cabinet meetings, had thus far centred on managing the rising sea levels and saving what she could of England's battered and decaying coastline.

However, now she sensed a presence, a weight in the room she could not identify, but which asserted its existence with a certain subtlety. For three hundred and twenty-five years, the most significant decisions concerning these islands had been made in this place, and now, in merely the last forty-eight hours and for reasons she could not fathom, fate had chosen her as the prime minister who would lead England to its next great victory, or who would be the last English prime minister in the country's history.

She saw that the expressions on the faces looking at her showed their owners must have realised the same thing. She attempted to project calm confidence as she scanned and made eye-contact with each person around the table. When she spoke, her words came out clearly and with a sense of purpose: "Hello, everyone. Thanks for coming. It appears we have a spot of bother to sort out, so let's get started, shall we?"

Chapter 25

13.17 Thursday 9 February 2062

"Come on, this is incredible. No one saw this coming, just no one," Mark Phillips said as he stabbed with his fork at a cherry tomato in the salad in the bowl in front of him.

"It's not incredible, it's extremely frightening," Maria replied, eying her older brother with disapproval.

"Pass the dressing, would you?" asked the oldest sibling, Martin.

Their father, Anthony, did so and said: "Listen, kids, this is serious business. It's not like one of your games, Mark."

Mark replied: "You know what, Dad? There's currently around ten-K conspiracy theories which say that we're all just living inside a computer simulation anyway."

Their mother, Jane, tutted and said: "Must we talk politics at the dinner table? This is the first salad we've been able to afford for weeks, can't we just be civil and enjoy a bit of luxury?"

"Yeah," Martin agreed with a smile, "and how often does Mark pull himself away from those games anyway? Nice of you to come and see us for some decent food, brother."

"My pleasure," Mark replied with a sneer. "I do like to see how your boring, ordinary lives are going nowhere, from time to time."

Martin shot back: "At least two of us are boring enough to take on our responsibility to bring in some money."

"I've told you before, brother: Mum and Dad get my U-Bee transferred straight to their account, and that's enough to cover my expenses. For Christ's sake, why does the government pay everyone the U-Bee if we're then supposed to go and work?"

"Because there are still jobs to be had, young man," Anthony replied. "Don't mock your brother and sister for wanting to do something with their lives."

Maria saw Mark's mouth fall open in offence and she knew what was coming: "I am doing something with my life, father. While you all seem to think they're just stupid games, there is method in this madness. After a few years in one of the Universes, I can get a Bounty for us which will help here in the real world—"

Anthony scoffed: "Carrots and donkeys, young Mark."

"Don't say that, fa—"

Anthony put out a calming hand and said: "Listen, son, no one hopes more than me you're right, and the rewards these gaming companies offer will actually materialise, but there're plenty of reports in the media of gamers immersed in the Universes for years on just such promises, and then coming away empty-handed on some technicality buried in the legal—"

"But the disreputable operators were purged last year and since—"

"So that's all well and good then, isn't it?" Anthony broke in. "Now, let's enjoy this delicious dinner your Mum has prepared, shall we?"

During this exchange, Maria noted how her mother's eyes had reddened. During such exchanges among the men, she often thought she saw her mother age, even though from Maria's perspective there seemed little worth worrying about.

Her mother appeared to force a smile and said, "Yes, thank you. Let's enjoy the food. We really don't know how long it'll be before we'll be able to afford this kind of luxury again." She stabbed a cube of white mozzarella with her fork and ate it.

"Don't worry, Mum," Maria said. "Martin and I have got our jobs and we'll keep bringing money in."

Martin added: "I meant to tell you, I've got a chance of promotion to area manager coming up. If I can swing it, it'll mean a few more thousand."

Jane smiled, "You're good kids."

Anthony added: "Yeah, mostly."

"But I don't see the issue of your promotion being decided just yet, dear," Jane said.

"Why's that?" Martin asked, and Maria felt a change come over her mother.

"Because we'll be at war very soon, I expect."

"Don't say that. Just because of what that idiot Caliph said," Anthony replied.

Jane sat back and looked around the table. "As much as I'd rather we didn't discuss these things at dinner, I think you're all missing something. The time is coming for a correction."

Maria watched her two older brothers frown, but Maria knew what her mother was driving at. Thirty years as a history teacher and then a teaching coordinator gave her mother a broader perspective.

Jane continued: "Power among nations is always shifting. Sometimes a nation or block of nations can rise and fall relatively quickly, in just a few years or decades; on other occasions they can last a millennium or more."

Mark said: "Mum, we don't need a lecture right now."

Anthony said: "Be quiet and listen to your mother."

Jane continued: "Europe has had it quite good for the last hundred and twenty years, especially with the USA's protection, but its power has waned. Have you seen the media? No, not the English media which you're used to; I mean, do you know what people in China, Africa and South America think about this?"

"I read a report that there's outrage at the Caliphate's actions, as there should be," Martin said.

Jane shook her head. "Barely. You know you're only getting algo-directed news in your feeds, dear. The super AIs are showing you what they think you want to see, the way it's been for decades." Jane's delicate fingers closed around the stem of her glass of white wine. She took a sip and concluded: "I think Europe and its countries have reached the end of the road, and we should get out before the Caliphate invades."

Anthony held her hand and asked: "But where could we go? We couldn't emigrate, now. We're too old and the kids are—"

"I'm not going anywhere," Mark said. "I reckon the international community will wake up and stop him. For Christ's sake, China and Russia created the bloody Caliphate. Surely they can control it?"

Martin said: "I think Mum's got a point. I agree and think we should maybe find a way to get out of Europe—"

"Look," Anthony began, "even if the Caliphate does invade the mainland, that's over there, we'd be safe enough here. Being an island has always saved us in the past."

"Apart from Julius Caesar and William the Conqueror," Jane noted.

"I'm not sure emigration is the answer, either," Maria said. "According to what I've read, the Caliphate has used all of its armaments to do what it's done to Turkey and Israel. Despite that announcement, I don't think they've got enough machines and soldiers to invade and conquer all of Europe."

Jane gave a slight smile as she looked around the table at her family. "Very well. So Martin and I will take it further and see what options we have. But mark my words, my dears: in terms of the history of nations, it is time for a change. It's time for a major correction."

Chapter 26

Gravel crunched under Professor Duncan Seekings' feet as his long, thin legs strode towards the South Meeting Room at Porton Down military research establishment. He was running slightly late for his appointment to give a presentation on the Caliphate drama to the collected heads of the British Armed Forces, Home Nations' Police forces, and certain people from the USAF. He'd become sidetracked, as was his habit, in his lab a few minutes earlier on reading the latest article by a renowned Chinese scientific research facility, which forecast a material shift in understanding the relationship between matter and energy that had the potential to completely destabilise the global economy in the next decade. If there was one thing guaranteed to set Duncan's blood boiling, it was fellow scientists making over-enthusiastic predictions of how the world was about to change.

He walked on, fuming, oblivious to the cold wind blowing off Salisbury Plain, whipping in between the mix of Victorian red-brick and later white buildings. Duncan had worked at Porton Down, engaged in R&D on ACA propulsion, armaments and defensive shielding, for his entire career and now, well into middle age, he'd seen and heard too much wild speculation over the years to entertain the hope that things would improve or even change with any rapidity. The most egregious example of the last decade had to be the replicator. Duncan shook his head as he recalled the year when 3-D printing evolved into what the Americans decided to call 'replication' in honour of some long-forgotten science fiction programme. Something which had caused virulent enthusiasm for a leap in technology that would change the world forever at the outset, trailed massive disappointment in its wake when the snags appeared.

Duncan muttered aloud: "Bloody fools, never learn. Always snags. They forget there are always snags. Have a good idea, think it's going to change the world, and then—oh look, no, it doesn't. Well, perhaps it can. A bit. But never a lot."

He did concede that from the range of replicators currently available, the construction models were highly effective. His old school friend, Graham English, was involved in their design and often extolled their abilities to Duncan when they met to play snooker. Construction replicators could do all kinds of work very quickly. But the food replicators, those which everyone claimed would end world hunger, remained, after several years, limited to creating only the very unhealthiest food because of numerous problems in replicating fresh food.

His thoughts came back to the present moment with some unwillingness, as he arrived at the entrance to the single-storey building that housed the meeting room. Duncan placed the pad of his left thumb on the scanner and the door beeped and clicked. He pulled it open, and only when he entered and felt the warm air did he appreciate how chilly it was outside.

158

"Such things," he mumbled to himself, "are always relative to the position of the observer." He advanced along the corridor towards the meeting room, still muttering to himself: "And what about super artificial intelligence, eh? How they said that would change the world. And when was that? Twenty years ago? Twenty-five? Just the same: didn't see the snags. Bloody fools."

He pushed the door open and entered the small auditorium. He walked through a break in the tiers of empty benches and stepped up on the small stage. In front of the large screen sat a podium, and Duncan went to it and looked around.

"Hello, Mr English," he called out at the only other person in the room.

"You're late, professor," Mr English replied.

"Yes, yes. Well, I'm here now." He prodded the small screen on the surface of the podium a few times. The light from the ceiling increased as 3-D projectors activated and the benches filled up with the audience. Some of the holographic projections fidgeted as the attendees settled down. Duncan recognised several faces: all of the service chiefs were present, including General Sir Terry Tidbury; the head of the RAF, Air Chief Marshal Raymond Thomas; and Admiral Rutherford of the Royal Navy. In addition, other high-ranking men and women from the regional police forces of all three Home Nations sat in the lower rows, and at the top were a number of civil servants. Around the edges Duncan saw a few US Air Force uniforms sipping at drinks and munching what looked like doughnuts.

"Ah, yes, right. Good. Welcome, everyone," Duncan began in a loud, direct voice, oblivious to the looks of impatience his audience displayed at his few minutes of lateness. "I'm going to bring you up to speed on what the, er, Caliphate has been attacking its, er, enemies with. Do please

159

allow me to describe what we know so far, and then I'll, er, take questions... If you, er, have any, of course. But no interruptions, thank you."

The screen behind him lit up. Duncan took a breath and plunged on: "Right, the first thing to say is that whoever, or rather whatever, is designing the Caliphate's autonomous combat aircraft certainly prefers the ellipsoid. On the screen, you can see the design of the first ACA that attacked the two navy battle groups in the early hours of Tuesday morning, and whose reporting name is, er, 'Blackswan'."

An outline image of a compressed ellipsoid appeared on the screen, in black lines on a turquoise background. Several sharp, angled fins poked out from the body. Numbers resolved detailing its length, height, maximum radii and other dimensions. Duncan continued: "In essence, the Blackswan is a flying bomb transporter, carrying a quite lethal cargo of fifty bomblets that have the reporting name, 'Spider'. I will come to those in a moment. The Blackswan's superstructure is unsurprisingly composed of 3-D ultra-Graphene, which I assume you're all familiar with. Now, what did have us confused was the power source." He looked up at his audience. "However, after intensive research and in combination with its aerial performance statistics, we now believe that an extremely small but powerful fusion unit must be involved."

The professor paused as he wanted the attendees to appreciate the significance of this fact. "This is extremely interesting, because here in Europe and America, fusion-based power sources were thought to be impossible to develop at anything like the volume sufficient to power an ACA of this size. You might have seen them in hospitals where they have several small-scale surgical applications. But it is this power which not only makes the Blackswan so dexterous in the sky, but which also allows the machine's shielding to absorb so much energy. I would like to stress that, currently, NATO forces have nothing that can stand up to this device."

Duncan stopped again to ensure his audience realised the importance of what he was telling them. When satisfied, he went on: "When the Blackswan arrives on target, the Spiders break out of the superstructure and attack."

Behind him, the outline of the Blackswan receded and smaller, ellipsoid-shaped objects emerged from the body. One advanced to the middle of the screen, enlarging as it did so, and similar dimensional data appeared around it. Duncan said: "It is important to note that each Spider has its own super-AI unit, and it is reasonable to assume, although it has not been proven, that Spiders are able to work in unison. When the Spider lands on, or rather crashes into, its target, eight articulated arms break out from the surface. Coupled with its own power unit, these give the Spider a quite remarkable dexterous mobility so it can then travel to the most appropriate location for detonation. You'll appreciate that the chance of a Spider being damaged on colliding with its target is highly unlikely given that it, like its parent, is also constructed from 3-D ultra-Graphene."

On the screen, the eight, triple-jointed arms snapped out from the device, having been folded seamlessly into the surface. Duncan continued: "Initial analysis indicates that a Spider could reach speeds in excess of a hundred kilometres per hour travelling in a straight line on flat terrain. The arrangement and articulation of the arms has, needless to say, been designed to maximise the Spider's dexterity in the most lethal manner. Analysis of blast data picked up by other NATO ACAs involved in the actions in the Mediterranean and Arabian Seas suggests the Spider is also powered by a fusion unit, and utilises a heightened RDX variant explosive with a yield of approximately seven megajoules, or roughly thirty percent more explosive energy than the Equaliser bomblets that the PeaceMaker carries."

The images on the screen withdrew and a new outline emerged; smaller, more elongated, and displaying a clear front and back, but also with sharp fins on the top and bottom and at the sides. The professor spoke: "Now I want to move on to, er, the device which the Caliphate first deployed during the attack against Turkey, and then with rather brutal effectiveness against Israel, and which has been given the reporting name 'Lapwing'. Here, we see quite a remarkable thing: a laser-equipped ACA with a similar power availability as the Blackswan. Thus far, effective lasers have been quite bulky. We use them on ships, tanks and as autonomous, self-propelled weapons. But the received wisdom at NATO has been that a laser powerful enough to be militarily effective, yet light enough to be mounted on an ACA, was at least five years away. In addition, analysis of SkyWatcher data recorded during the battles over Turkey and Israel showed that just three shots from this ACA are sufficient to give an unprotected civilian a fatal level of burns."

Duncan paused and scratched the side of his face. "To summarise: it is safe to assume that both Caliphate ACAs use the same or a very similar power unit, probably fusion based, which affords them performance abilities substantially in excess of the abilities of the SkyWatcher and PeaceMaker ACAs which NATO currently deploys. Here at the English government's key research and development facility, we believe there is an urgent need to develop a new range of ACAs which could respond to the threat that the New Persian Caliphate can now deploy. Thank you for attending. I will—"

Duncan stopped when the American attendees unexpectedly applauded at the conclusion of his presentation, which, given its subject matter, had been the last thing he expected. His brow creased in confusion at what he

162

considered an unnecessary and frivolous display of appreciation, and then he continued: "I will answer any questions you have. Given the urgency of the day's developments, however, I'm sure we all have many other issues to attend to, so does anyone have a question?"

An American Air Force major immediately raised a hand: "Sure, I do. So, seeing as the dumbass raghead has said he's going to invade Europe, if he really does, how many of our ACAs is it gonna take to knock out one of theirs?"

"Difficult to be precise, I'm afraid. So far, our computers have kept on running simulations but initial results are not encouraging. In straightforward air-to-air combat, it could take over thirty PeaceMakers to defeat a single Blackswan, assuming its shielding can be burned through and it releases its Spiders. But unless and until combat occurs, we won't know for sure if a PeaceMaker's Equaliser bomblet has enough punch to burn through a Spider's shielding, let alone actually stop the thing. We still believe that the Pulsar is up to the job, if it can be given the time."

A senior police officer with a craggy face raised his hand: "How long do you think their power sources last?"

"Long enough in a combat situation, I should imagine. If they do employ a fusion power unit, it will depend on a number of variables which we won't know unless and until we obtain and analyse a relatively undamaged device. But it is reasonable to assume the lifetime of the power unit has been designed to be sufficient for most battle situations."

Another hand went up at the back, from among the civil servants. Duncan nodded and a woman with straight brown hair asked: "You said we need to develop a new range of ACAs, but how long will that take?"

"That's really not for me to speculate, madam, but it would certainly take a few years, I should expect."

A gruff male voice shouted out: "But they could invade us at any moment."

Duncan frowned and replied: "And, apart from stating the blindingly obvious, your point is what exactly?"

Some attendees smiled, but Duncan was becoming frustrated. "Any other questions?" he asked the auditorium in a tone which suggested he hoped there would not be. He waited only a few seconds before concluding: "Very well. We will continue our research into these machines and possible countermeasures and such like. Obviously, I don't need to tell you that what you have seen is classified top secret and should not be discussed with anyone with a lower level security clearance than you. Thank you for attending."

The holographic attendees all vanished quickly, and the sole remaining person in the room said in a loud voice: "Very nice, professor."

"Thank you, Mr English," Duncan replied as he deactivated the podium and left the stage. "I was worried I might get a bit of a grilling there."

Mr English left the seat and fell in beside Duncan. "Oh, not a chance, old boy. There's still quite a bit of shock and I got the feeling they just wanted to know what we know about this new enemy."

"Well, the media are being quite unkind to the politicians."

"That's the media's job. Besides, the Caliphate hasn't actually invaded Europe."

"Yet."

"But I believe things might get disagreeable for us if we don't come up with some answers soon."

Duncan stopped at the door to exit the building. He looked down at Mr English and said: "I think we won't have too much trouble finding the answers as to how the Caliphate have got such advanced tech, but coming up with suitable countermeasures is an altogether trickier proposition."

Chapter 27

Crispin Webb watched the screen on the wall in front of them, disliking the feeling of irritated indifference he sensed from the US President.

Napier spoke: "I'm sorry you weren't able to attend the Paris summit, but it wasn't a very good atmosphere."

Coll said: "I was briefed that it went well given the circumstances. The European governments are reacting to the threat."

"Which appears likely to be insurmountable. All of the forecasts are for our annihilation in a matter of weeks." Napier's eyes pleaded with the President and she said: "Please, Maddie, we need everything you can spare."

The corners of Coll's mouth turned down. "Of course the United States will stand by its commitment to NATO, Dahra, but it's going to take time to organise air and ship transportation."

"We don't have time. The Caliph has made his intentions quite clear. He could launch an attack on mainland Europe at any moment. We've begun increasing ACA production but it will take time to build new facilities. We need all the material you can supply. You must begin air transports now."

President Coll said: "Sure, sure. I'll see what I can do," and the screen went blank.

The Foreign Secretary, Charles Blackwood, got up from the couch and paced around the spacious living area. "PM, I don't think you need worry unduly. I'm in almost constant touch with Bill at the State Department, and he's going to make things happen over there however lackadaisical Coll seems to be."

Napier leaned her head back and pinched the bridge of her nose. "Perhaps she's just feeling the pressure a little?"

Crispin got out of his chair and asked: "Glass of white wine, boss?"

"Yes, semi-dry, thank you, Crispin."

"How about you, Charles?" Crispin asked.

"No, thank you, I need to return to my department." Blackwood turned to Napier and said: "Everyone's feeling the pressure, PM. But we've achieved quite a bit in the last couple of days. All of Whitehall and other departments are alive and actively working. John is having outline civil defence plans drawn up to see how we might best protect civilians. On the home front, I think we're getting our act together quite well. We're also working with our European partners to estimate how best we can manage the flood of refugees we expect any invasion to generate. And..." he paused as Crispin delivered the glass of wine into Napier's hand, "I can say with some certainty that your cabinet supports you very much, PM."

Napier sat up, sipped her wine, and said: "They should do when you think about it. After all, the odds aren't looking very good, are they?"

Blackwood nodded in consideration. "On the surface, no. But the Third Caliph may yet be dissuaded from his adventures."

"Yes. Update me in the morning on diplomatic efforts in Beijing, would you?"

"Of course. See you in the morning." Blackwood nodded to Crispin and left the room.

When the door closed behind him, Napier looked at Crispin and said: "Ten years ago, in the leadership race, I came second and he came third in the first round of voting. We went for a walk in the gardens of the conference centre, and he offered his support in return for Chancellor, Home Office or Foreign Office. I declined and told him I wasn't prepared to get into trade-offs which could cause rifts that might damage a future government. He just nodded and walked away, and I thought that was the end of my run. Then, he supported me anyway and I won leadership of the party. When we won the next election, I gave him a junior post in the Foreign Office, and promoted him when that idiot Justin let himself get entrapped at that orgy at the Russian embassy a few years ago."

"Yes, I remember," Crispin said, happy to share memories of simpler times.

Napier looked at him and asked: "He's the only one in the party who has the popularity to replace me. Do you think he'll try?"

Crispin didn't hide his shock at her suggestion: "God, no. Not at all, boss. Your approvals among the party faithful are better than fine. He'd never get the support, not now. The back-benchers have no appetite for anything like that at the moment. Besides, who'd want your job today, in this situation? The position of prime minister of England has got about the same career development prospects as a sanitary worker in Lahore who's just caught bubonic plague."

Napier gave him a weak smile which quickly faded. "But we're getting ripped to pieces in the media, Crispin, with eighty percent of outlets baying for blood, thinking we the government should've known what was happening sooner. They're looking for a political scalp, and I'm not prepared to sacrifice Philip at Defence because I need his advice now. And anyway, no one could have seen this disaster coming."

"I and others are putting a lot of pressure on the media, boss. This won't last. They need to get over the shock and then it'll be the 'we're-all-in-this-together' line. We can't risk a breakdown in civil order, and I'm making sure editors and proprietors know that."

"Thank you… I want to call it a night now. I haven't spent more than five minutes with my family since Tuesday morning, and I'd quite like to read my youngest a bedtime story before she falls asleep. What's the first order of business in the morning?"

"I'll brief you on overnight developments at seven, as usual. Then there's a COBRA meeting at nine. But there's going to be a lot to get through in addition to the international drama. We're due more high tides, all down the east coast. The usual alerts are being sent out, but we can expect some casualties, not least because the army has started pulling units out to consolidate in preparation for potential deployment on the continent."

Webb saw the stress and fatigue in Napier's face. She said: "The way this week is going, those casualties could end up being the lucky ones."

Chapter 28

22.43 Thursday 9 February 2062

Terry Tidbury watched the twinkling London skyline from the modest height of his office at the Ministry of Defence in Whitehall. Behind him the door opened and closed.

"Here you are, Sir Terry," his adjutant John Simms said.

Terry turned and looked at the steam rising from the fresh cup of tea Simms put on his desk. "Thank you. You know, it's been a few years since we've been obliged to stay so late at the office."

"We could let Squonk deal with quite a lot of the logistics," Simms answered.

Terry shook his head. "It makes a good calculator, but I want to crosscheck its results, Simms." He picked up his tea and leaned against his desk. "Squonk, what's the latest intel on Israel?"

The asexual voice answered: "The country's entire surface area is subject to Caliphate interference, but available data gives a ninety-three percent probability that the Caliphate's objective is annihilation rather than assimilation."

"What about survivors? Some must have escaped on boats."

"Caliphate forces are being quite thorough; NATO forces have extracted fewer than one thousand people."

"Christ. And what about Turkey?"

But Squonk said: "Information: incoming communication from General Joseph E. Jones, Supreme Allied Commander, Europe."

Terry stood. "In the screen," he ordered. In an internal wall a large screen came to life with the round, Afro-American face of NATO's most senior soldier in Europe. "Hello, general. Any news on the situation in Israel?" Terry asked.

Jones's grim expression didn't change. "The Caliphate has desisted from killing Israelis fleeing in boats, so at least we're getting some survivors out. But I want to ask you if the British Army can help any more with strengthening our southern border."

"We've got the bulk of our troops out of barracks on flood defence duty, and it's taking time to ramp up our logistics as I'm insisting the super AIs are double-checked. You've deployed the battlefield support lasers we sent over yesterday?"

"Sure, and the two wings of PeaceMakers from the RAF."

"How many troops would you need?"

Jones let out a scoff. "More than we've got in the whole of Europe and probably the US, too. But I'll settle for as many battalions as you can spare. We're concentrating our strategy on the capitals—Athens, Rome, Madrid—as we expect those to be the centre of attention. Those countries are almost fully deployed, but they can't have too much support."

"Are we going to deploy special forces soon?"

Jones gave a humourless smile. "Nope, those guys are going to get the best job when the invasion comes, as they'll go behind enemy lines."

"How much notice do you think we'll get?"

"We'll be lucky to get a few minutes'. I can't imagine it being anymore than that."

Terry grunted his agreement and sipped his tea.

Jones went on: "Our Super AI is providing percentages on hundreds of variations of how they might attack, and all of them look like we're gonna have to roll a hundred double-sixes to hold them off. One thing we have done is re-arm the PeaceMakers with Z-50 Stilettos as they've got the strongest punch."

"And we have the coherence-length variation advantage."

Jones sighed. "I'm not sure that's gonna make a whole lotta difference."

"Because of the numbers?"

"Uh-huh. Athens has got nine BSLs to defend it, Rome the same, Madrid seven."

"Do you think they'll hit us with Blackswans, Lapwings, or a combination?"

"Depends on whether they're aiming for assimilation or annihilation, and that's politics so I can't say, although if they hit us just with Lapwings like they did in Israel, I think it will be worse. If they're aiming for assimilation and attack primarily with Blackswans, we might be able to hold them awhile. Have you seen the right-wingers in the states calling for a nuclear attack?"

Terry chuckled. "Yes, they stick to the line that the Caliphate has exhausted its resources, that the leaked data-pod is still planted evidence."

"You'd almost think they were working for the enemy, wanting Europe to make the same mistake Israel made…"

173

Jones's glance drifted off along with his words. Then he said: "Strange times, general," in a wistful voice.

"Indeed," Terry replied, nonplussed.

Abruptly Jones came back to life: "Okay, that's all for now. I know we're round-the-clock on-call, but try to get some rest before the shooting starts."

"You too, general."

The screen went blank and air whistled through Terry's teeth. He glanced over at his adjutant. "What do you think, Simms?"

"I think SACEUR gave sound advice."

Terry smiled. "How long do you think we have before the Caliphate invades mainland Europe?"

"I would say a great deal depends on how much of a defence Turkey has left."

"Which is where we were when SACEUR called." Terry sipped his tea and said: "Squonk. What is the latest intel from Turkey? How far have Caliphate forces penetrated?"

The voice of the Ministry of Defence's super AI replied: "Organised resistance has collapsed."

Terry looked at Simms. "Then it's going to be our turn soon."

Chapter 29

As Berat Kartal neared the port city of Izmir, his doubts and fears grew stronger. He travelled towards his destination with the scantest knowledge of what lay there. His topographical atlas of Europe told him it was the third most populous city in Turkey. But his lens did not overlay directions to interesting sights to see, places to eat, or cheap hostels for the student travelling on a budget. This lack of real-time data compounded his fear of the disaster which afflicted his country.

His body ached from the constant cycling, lack of food, and the cold weather. Over the last two days, the stream of people on the road had swelled. In the places where he'd stopped, he'd fallen into conversation with some of them, all of which yielded only the same rumours: Caliphate ACAs were flying everywhere bombing and burning people; the Turkish air force and army were destroyed and the remains scattered; and the state had completely broken down.

Twenty kilometres from the city, he'd finally been obliged to dismount from his bike because of the number of people on the road. He thought of them as people, but the word 'refugee' entered his head, and he spent some hours trudging towards his only potential escape considering the precise point at which a 'person' became a 'refugee'. Was there some defining characteristic? Just a few days ago, he'd been a citizen of an acknowledged and secure, if authoritative, nation state. He had a home, he studied at a university, he had friends. So, because these things had changed, had he stopped being a person and become a refugee? Could the moment of change be identified? The only thing he was able to hope he had left were his family, somewhere in the chaos enveloping the country. He felt sure he'd lost his home, and he didn't expect to return to his university. But he decided he would think of the people around him as people, because it didn't seem right to think of them as some lesser persons which the label 'refugee' implied.

The throng passed between the hills which surrounded the city, and the density of people increased. A few hours later, as darkness fell, he found himself in the Bornova district, having obeyed the few policemen at road junctions who appeared to be making valiant efforts to stop the city from being completely overwhelmed.

The river of people eventually spilled into a large area which Berat guessed to be municipal. He followed the flood to one extensive building on the right, and he overheard snippets of conversations which told him it was a hospital. Strings of white light emitters strung along cables hung from makeshift poles, which hued the bobbing heads a weak grey. At various places, the crowd opened out around bonfires which crackled in disused metal containers.

He pushed his bike to queue at a water bowser to refill his plastic bottles. In front of him a family of four also waited. The man turned back, eyed Berat and his bike, and asked:

"Hey, boy, you planning to use that bike to pedal across the sea?"

Berat glanced at the man and saw anger and frustration on his hard face. Next to him huddled a thin, scared-looking woman with two children holding on to her skirt.

"Sorry," was all Berat could utter, unable to imagine the fear those with small children must be feeling.

The man stared at him and asked: "Where are you from?"

"Usak."

"And you pedalled all the way here?"

"Yes."

"I heard Usak has been flattened. The mayor decided to fight rather than surrender, and that was that... You alone?"

"Yes."

"You're lucky, then. You should get down to the docks tonight."

Berat nodded, his eyes drawn to the man's young family. Berat realised that the man must be feeling a certain regret: for his family, for this disaster striking now, when he and his wife had small children to protect, and how this stranger must have wished it were ten years earlier, when he had been like Berat: young and fit and unencumbered.

"Thank you," Berat said.

At length, they refilled their bottles and Berat watched the man and his family join the queue for the soup, which was much longer than the queue for water.

Instead of leaving the camp at once, he made his way through the crowd to a notice board with pieces of A4 paper pinned on it, claiming to be official government advice. He read them with mounting misery, as the sheets tried to represent a semblance of normality; that something more permanent existed when his country was being dismembered and readied for assimilation. The irony struck Berat keenly:

pieces of paper giving advice which merely papered over the cracks of a disintegrating society.

He left the camp and followed his nose to the sea. He took the stranger's advice and abandoned his bicycle among other rubbish under the main highway which lead to the docks. When he passed under the highway and turned back, he saw military vehicles on the road, and briefly entertained the idea of finding out what was going on, before changing his mind lest it cause him more difficulties.

After walking for what felt like kilometres, he realised he'd managed to work his way around some kind of holding area for potential escapees. He warmed to the idea of circumvention, and decided he would likely need some stealth if he were to find a berth on a ship. All the time his imagination questioned how long he and these other people really had. Berat knew that autonomous combat aircraft could travel at many times the speed of sound, and if his country had collapsed and the rumours were more than the result of the stress of the situation, then the machines could arrive at any minute.

Finally, he found some crumpled tarpaulin behind one of many rows of commercial shipping containers. He crouched down beside one and used his sleeping bag as a cushion. He pulled the tarpaulin over him, and despite his hunger and the chill night air, he extracted his paper journal, pen and small torch, and wrote down the day's events.

He awoke the next morning after fitful sleep broken by bad thoughts. He dreamt he had a wife and two small children to protect and felt the burning shame of not being able to do so. His face, toes and fingers were numb from the cold and it took him several minutes of clenching and unclenching for his circulation to return them to feeling. With that, however, came other emotions, and he pushed the tarpaulin to one side, glanced at the massive avenue of metal containers, and set off to find a ship.

Four hours later, Berat ate the first warm food he'd had since leaving his apartment in Usak, a bowl of *iskembe* soup. He felt tears well in the corners of his eyes as he stood by a porthole in the cramped galley of the *Hasköy*, a small and overcrowded ferry. Berat had paid the last of his money to gain passage, and had only been allowed on board the already packed boat because he was alone.

Shuffling elderly people and crying children packed the ferry. His stomach growled as he ate the soup, and the flavours triggered distant memories and feelings of security which had now been lost. Through the porthole he could see the large concrete quay recede as the ferry crawled away from the port. Despite the fetid heat in the galley from the people squeezed inside it, Berat shivered at the prospects for those still ashore. At first, he thought he'd been fortunate to secure passage, but then he questioned if the Caliphate would stop at his country. What if the Third Caliph's appetite had not yet been sated? Had the Caliphate already invaded Russia or India? Berat silently asked himself if he would be safe in Athens, or if he would regret fleeing his home.

Chapter 30

The Englishman lay on his side waiting for the marshal to fall asleep. His thoughts returned to the danger in which Europe now lay. Images of violence and destruction invaded his peace, and his mind's eye overlaid the terrible pictures of suffering he'd seen from Turkey and Israel onto his own country. If the Third Caliph really meant to 'correct an historical wrong', then that would have to include England and the other Home Nations.

His lover suddenly whispered: "You are worried for your home."

The Englishman felt himself flinch at the unexpected sound. Zhou always fell asleep within a few minutes, and suddenly the Englishman sensed the marshal's attentiveness which may, in another life, have qualified as care. "Yes, I am," the Englishman replied.

Zhou said: "There is much pressure from America and the other European countries for the Chinese government to make the Third Caliph stop... But you know that, because you are with the English diplomatic mission."

181

In the darkness, he could not tell if Zhou was making an oblique reference that perhaps the marshal had discovered his secondary role. He said: "Of course I've heard what's happening, although my responsibility is about finding business contacts and representing English companies."

Zhou didn't reply at once, and the Englishman's heart began to canter with the realisation that his lover might not be as enthralled as he thought. Initial infatuation would certainly wear off over time, but had anticipated at least a few months of relative safety before Zhou entered the remorse phase and, possibly, the sudden fear of the Englishman blackmailing him. The Englishman kept the blackmail option in mind only to be used in self-defence, however.

At length, Zhou replied: "I know. But this pressure irritates our diplomats."

"Why?"

"Because, behind closed doors, they realise they share some of the responsibility. But they regard that part of the world as not so important compared to key places like Africa and South America."

"Many people are dying, and many more will if the Third Caliph isn't persuaded to stop."

"I think you might find, my dear, that some peoples are more important than others, and in the eyes of the rest of the world, the countries of Europe are no longer the forces they once were. How many times in the past did a European country sit back and watch as an African or Asian country tore itself apart? This is how the situation now looks to us: just some unimportant part of the world going through an unfortunate but necessary upheaval."

The Englishman wanted to add that the dammed Chinese would also lose too much of their precious 'face' to admit that they'd created the Caliphate and now they'd lost control of it, but instead he said: "But surely there's a very strong humanitarian case for intervention, isn't there?"

"There is always such a case, in every war or disaster or whatever. But there has to be the political will for such intervention, and for the Chinese government, in this case there is no such will."

The Englishman said: "Is there a way it might be created?"

Marshal Zhou sighed and said: "I am tired and want to sleep now. I tell you only this: the Third Caliph agreed to let survivors from Israel escape and has stopped destroying the boats."

"And Turkey?"

"Turkey is to be assimilated, not destroyed like Israel, so his position is more merciful there. Besides, those escaping Turkey will carry the stories of the Caliphate's strengths to the rest of Europe, which will aid the terror that will cause those societies to collapse more quickly, for at length they will be assimilated as well."

The Englishman exhaled as slowly as he could, desperate to seek confirmation as he knew that in London, the key issue was whether Europe would be assimilated or annihilated. He had the answer, but was it true, or did Marshal Zhou intend to send a falsehood through him to NATO? He knew London would aggregate all available data and have the super AI extrapolate the most probable outcome, but he also felt certain that he was London's best and most reliable source here in the most important city in the world.

The marshal turned towards him and rested a thick, heavy forearm on his thigh. As though reading his mind, Zhou whispered in his ear: "My dear, the way the Caliph's armies are behaving, there is little difference between assimilation and annihilation. What you and your shocked and terrified governments have failed to understand, is that the Caliph

183

intends to show the rest of the world that a new military superpower has arrived. He wants India, Russia, Brazil and, yes, even China, to know how much power he has at his disposal. And Europe is to be his sacrificial lamb."

The marshal finished, quite unnecessarily in the Englishman's opinion, with a gentle kiss behind his ear, and whispered: "Goodnight."

Chapter 31

Corporal Rory Moore of 103 Squadron, 21 Engineer Regiment, Royal Engineers, looked at the screen in front of him in mounting dismay. "Shit, shit, shit. Don't buckle, just don't buckle. High tide's in three minutes, so just don't—"

Squonk, the British Army's super AI, interrupted him: "Unit 67–D will buckle in five, four, three, two, one. Unit 67–D has buckled. Estimated volume of flood water—"

"I don't need to know," Rory shrieked at it in frustration. "Compensate, compensate," he demanded, although he knew it wouldn't matter.

"Compensation is not an available option due to the construction replicator's age. Unit 67–D requires a replacement ultra-Graphene ribbon."

"Jesus, can't you rearrange the other units somehow?"

"Jesus isn't here. And no, rearrangement is not an option. Unit 67–D requires a replace—"

"Hardy-fucking-ha, Squonk. Don't try jokes, they don't suit you. Inform HQ squad Delta Four-Two is outbound."

Rory dabbed at panels along the control surface, cursed again, and opened the comms channel to his squad. "Okay, team. You heard what's going on. Standby for take-off." Behind him he heard the clatter of footsteps, and then a new voice said: "Everyone's in, corp."

"Right, Squonk," Rory said. "Power up and set course to Humber Southern Zone."

Squonk answered: "Lift off in twenty, nineteen—"

Rory said testily: "We don't need a fucking countdown," and Squonk stopped.

Another voice in Rory's Squitch said: "This is our last ultra-Graphene ribbon, corp."

"Then let's hope we have no more buckles then, eh?"

"Yup."

"Right, who wants the drop on this? It's Pip's turn, isn't it?"

A young female voice answered: "Sure, can do, corp."

Rory smiled at the sound of the youngest member of his team, Philippa Clarke. He turned around from the monitoring station to look behind him, just as the engines of the autonomous air vehicle reached their familiar take-off pitch. Three of the seats in the rear area were occupied. Pip sat foremost, an impish grin on her round face. Behind her sat Ian Pratt, known as Pratty, and Colin Wimble, referred to as Crimble. The AAV shuddered as it lifted off from their barracks in Ripon, Yorkshire, and began the one-hundred-and-forty kilometre journey to the part of the Humber river defences that had just been breached.

"Don't want to sound like a bore, corp.," Crimble began, scratching at his moustache, "but tell us again what the point of going there now is?"

Rory replied: "Politics, dummy. Brass says we've gotta be seen to be doing something. Keeps the civis happy."

Crimble said: "I reckon they've more important things to worry about now."

Pratty shook his bony head at all of them and said: "But we've got to hover for at least an hour until the water level will've gone down enough for one of us to load the ribbon. And this with the star bore of the squadron," Pratty said with a nod to Crimble.

"Yeah, but then the media calls us 'heroes'," Crimble said, smiling at Pratty's dig.

Rory was about to respond when the communications icon flashed in his eye. "Squad Delta Four-Two," he said in acknowledgement.

"RT, now," said a deep, urgent voice.

"No can do, Captain. We're en-route to a ribbon buckle."

"Shit, where?"

"Humber South."

"So fix it ASAP and get back here, roger?"

Rory wanted to object, but realised that to do so would piss the Captain off more than usual. "Reason for RT urgency, please?"

"You're getting re-tooled for deployment to the continent."

Rory's jaw dropped and he wanted to scream, but he bit down his emotions and replied: "Roger, will RT ASAP."

"Corp.?" Pip enquired.

Rory turned to look at the other three members of his squad. "What do you want first: The great news or the really fan-fucking-tastic news?"

"Are we finally going to do some proper soldiering?" Crimble asked with sarcasm.

Pratty said, "Let me guess: the general's arsehole has collapsed and we've got to build the scaffolding so he can start talking out of it again?"

"Nothing so complicated. All we've got to do is replace that ultra-Graphene ribbon and RT for re-tooling and deployment to the continent."

Pratty's prominent chin jutted further and he snarled, "About fucking time."

Pip said: "We need an hour for the tide to go down enough."

Rory shook his head, "We've got to do a wet replacement."

Crimble said: "Seriously? The Captain can't give us an hour?"

Rory shrugged. "I dunno. Squonk, what's the hurry?"

"Redeployment schedules have been established and they require you to return to barracks by 09.00."

All four members of the squad let out their preferred curses. The AAV flew on and fourteen minutes later it hovered twenty-five metres above the breach in the sea defences over Barrow Haven, a string of over one hundred construction replicators struggling to rebuild sea defences.

Rory said: "Right, Pip, off you go."

Pip moved to the rear of the AAV's cramped interior and unclipped a head unit from the left-hand side panel. She pulled it over her cropped brown hair, unhooked the handheld controllers, and a moment later said: "Squitch linked. Ready."

Rory rolled along the control panels in his chair and activated the external cameras. He said: "Okay, Squonk. Release ultra-Graphene ribbon serial CRP–23."

Squonk replied: "Released."

Screens on the control panel showed a hatch on the underside of the AAV slide open and a tube emerge, suspended on a cable. Pip said: "Okay, let's get this done and get back."

Rory said: "Squonk, tell unit 67–D to open its ribbon hatch."

The super AI replied: "Done."

"You know," Pip began manipulating the handgrips, "if these were modern units, this would all be automatic and we wouldn't even be involved."

"Are you kidding?" Crimble said. "I've got a pal in Germany where they've got the latest models, and he says the ribbons never buckle."

"Okay, Pip," Rory said staring at the monitors. "Just get the ribbon above the hatch." He saw the large cylinder containing the ultra-Graphene ribbon swing back and forth above the waves as it dangled from their aircraft.

Squonk spoke: "Unit 67–D is not responding."

Pip said: "I know… Over the hatch now."

Rory said: "Shit, the unit isn't ejecting the buckled ribbon. Squonk?"

Squonk replied: "Automatic ejection has failed."

All four Royal Engineers swore aloud. Pip asked: "What's the outside temperature?"

Squonk replied: "Plus eleven degrees centigrade."

Pip let go of the handgrips, removed the headgear and looked at Crimble. "Keep control of the replacement, okay?"

"Sure," he replied, scratching his moustache.

Rory said: "No."

Pip looked at him. "What 'no'?"

Rory said: "Pratty's going to do the manual release."

"Why?" Pip demanded.

"Because I said so," Rory replied.

Pip said: "This better not be more of your macho bullshit, corp. Just because I'm a girl, right?"

Pratty put a bony arm out and said: "Relax, Pip. A manual release in these conditions is not an easy—"

"Shut up," Pip spat back. "You guys hate it that girls can do this shit just as well as you."

Sweat prickled the back of Rory's neck. He had to find another reason to keep Pip out of danger without simply pulling rank. He said: "Jesus, Pip. It's got nothing to do with that boys or girls bullshit. There's a serious risk in going out there to do a manu—"

Pip shouted: "Bollocks. I'm going out there, corp., or when we get back I'll file a complaint."

Rory couldn't bear the thought of Pip being in harm's way unnecessarily, and had to reconcile himself with the risk of her filing a complaint with their commanding officer. Perhaps if he told her his true feelings, she might reconsider? But then if he did that and she didn't feel the same way, she'd transfer to another unit and he'd never see her again. He looked at her beautiful face and said: "Pip, I really don't want to pull rank—"

"Good," she broke in, "then don't. I'll get harnessed and perform the manual release."

Squonk said: "HQ is calling, Corporal Moore," at the same moment as the notification icon flashed in his eye.

Still staring at Pip, Rory said: "Put it on the speaker."

The deep, contemptuous voice of the unit's captain boomed in the restricted space: "Squad Delta Four-Two? What the fuck are you monkeys doing out there, over?"

Rory replied: "We need to perform an external manual release to replace the buckled ribbon, Sir."

"No, you do not. Abort the job and return to HQ for re-tooling and deployment, roger?"

"But what about the breach? Tonnes of water are pouring through that—"

"Not your problem, corporal. RT now. And hurry the fuck up. HQ out."

190

Rory said: "Squonk, retract the ultra-Graphene ribbon and take us back to HQ."

"Roger," the super AI responded.

Rory sat back in relief. The other three members of his squad also sat down and buckled in for the return trip. Rory caught the steely look of resentment on Pip's face and thought her pursed lips had never looked more beautiful. For the hundredth time, he asked himself if he should risk telling her how he felt.

Chapter 32

20.46 Friday 10 February 2062

Terry Tidbury's Toyota Rive-All autonomous vehicle sped south along the M26 motorway, heading away from London. He folded his slate up, put it in his pocket, and looked at the distant lights outside, refracted and split and broken by the raindrops streaking along the window.

He felt a pervading sense of melancholy at the day's developments. He'd attended virtual conferences with all of the NATO countries' military chiefs. Despite the strength of the forces ranged against them, generals from each European country discussed the situation in dry, military terms, with barely a shred of emotion, even from the Mediterranean states that had to be the first front-line in the Caliphate's invasion plans. Each country's armed forces were approaching full war-time readiness, with reservists called up and veterans recalled. Many thousands more citizens had made known their availability, which the leaders found reassuring.

In rare moments like these, when Terry was alone and could think clearly about the coming storm, he often caught a strange feeling of unreality. In his mind's eye, he reviewed his years of soldiering, his promotions, the joint exercises, the disciplinary hearings of misbehaving subordinates. Face-offs with the Russian military had been NATO's most strenuous business for many years, while providing support to stretched local civil defence authorities as the sea levels continued their slow but inexorable rise came a close second. He reflected on how much certainty his old life enjoyed. The sea-level rise data was well established, with flood modelling going back decades. All the Home Nations and European governments knew precisely where the flooding would be worst and which areas needed to be evacuated.

He considered the role complacency had played: how willing had European countries been to accept the Caliphate at face value? But he also knew he was no politician. He recalled events from years earlier, and how China and Russia took credit for the Caliphate's creation as a final way to stop decades of bloodshed. He remembered the political leaders of the time had been critical, citing the Caliphate's isolation as a cause for distrust. But as a captain in the British Army with a young family to raise, Terry concentrated on his career and only took notice of political events that might or could have had an effect on that.

As the years passed, the Caliphate remained quiet and isolated. It bothered no one outside its borders, but took no prisoners of those who tried to find out what was happening inside it. Terry shuddered as he recalled the debacle four years earlier when, without his knowledge, a squad of four special forces troops had been sent into Caliphate territory, and had been caught and executed, their bodies displayed to the international media. While those troops lost their lives, in result several colonels and lieutenant generals had merely lost their careers.

The vehicle sensed Terry's shudder and asked: "Are you cold, sir?"

"No. How much longer?"

"Six minutes."

But now, in less than a week, the accepted global order had been turned on its head. Terry recalled the day's other discussions and debates. He worried that the defences were ridiculously thin outside the cities, although he accepted that the defenders were obliged to concentrate on their capitals. Thus, the Greek Army deployed the bulk of its forces around Athens; the Italians around Rome, and the Spanish around Madrid. The French, Germans and Poles were deploying as fast as possible, although tactically the Caliphate was not expected to attack the more northerly countries until it had overrun the southern ones.

Terry sensed strongly that the result of the coming invasion was a foregone conclusion. The bald truth remained: NATO forces were outnumbered and outgunned. In such situation, it would take an incredibly incompetent commander to lose any military action. And Terry felt sure everyone else in NATO realised that it could not happen because of super artificial intelligence. In addition, the Caliphate did not require especially talented individuals at corps and divisional levels because super AI could oversee the entire operation: the Caliphate's ACAs and warriors would only have to go where and do what they were told, and then do battle. This level of involvement of artificial intelligence left little room for either side to make strategic or tactical errors of which the opposing side could take advantage.

Heavier rain lashed the windows outside the vehicle; hard, insistent, battering the impregnable glass. To Terry, the sound made him think of the thousands of Caliphate ACAs which threatened at any moment to begin their attack on Europe. In truth, he was surprised that he travelled home on this Friday evening. In the morning, he'd expected the day to see the invasion begin. But it had not.

Terry recognised the buildings the vehicle passed through the rain and realised he would arrive home soon, something of a surprise for his wife Maureen, because he'd told her in the morning that he could be very late. As his journey reached its end, he recalled his wife's words: that every soldier hoped for one war in his or her lifetime. Terry said aloud: "Indeed, but it would've been nicer if we had even the slightest chance of winning it."

Chapter 33

07.19 Saturday 11 February 2062

Captain Raptis of the 12th Mechanised Infantry Division, IV Corps of the Hellenic Army, looked out at the red-flecked cirrocumulus above Athens and waited. The breeze tasted cool and fresh, as though it also awaited the day's events with a keen curiosity. He'd readied his troops as much as possible: weapons checked, Squitches functioning. At the briefing the previous evening, there'd been enough strange looks among them as the tactics bordered on the suicidal. Doctrine insisted that only one's own ACAs could defeat an attack by an enemy's ACAs.

The troops were not impressed. After the briefing, he'd had private talks with some squad leaders. While complaints were vociferous and to a degree justified, on the other hand the majority of the men and women understood the imperative of throwing everything into the battle. They knew NATO would bring as many PeaceMakers to the fight as it could, but they also knew the Blackswans and Lapwings were far superior machines. That's why the hills to the northeast and southeast of Athens now bristled with an array of the most powerful weapons NATO possessed. battlefield support lasers protected key political and architectural sites, backed up by autonomous, unmanned Leopard tanks and over a hundred batteries of RIM–214 Standard surface-to-air missiles. The troops were each equipped with Z-50 Stilettos, shoulder-fired smart missiles.

Raptis scanned the sky as the red hues on the cloud brightened to sheer gold and the dawn advanced. He questioned how long they would have to wait for the promised invasion. He reflected that the problem with adrenalin was that it seldom stayed in one's blood for very long. While it was easy to become aggressive, the feeling soon waned, often leaving tiredness in its wake. Thus, it was impossible for anyone to stay at the highest level of alertness for a substantial length of time. Raptis asked himself if they would come today, tomorrow, or—

His thoughts were broken by a single word spoken in his Squitch: "Incoming."

He felt relief: Corporal Drakos, who'd announced the contact, had maintained a professional indifference, as though he'd been informing the regiment of the arrival of an order of pizza.

Raptis strode the few steps back to the mobile command centre and entered the long, trailer-sized vehicle. Inside was a bustle of activity as monitors displayed lines of light denoting the approaching ACAs.

One of the signals troops manning the centre called out: "Tracking two hundred and fifty-six incoming signals. Signature is hostile."

"Are they Blackswans or Lapwings?" Raptis asked.

The trooper glanced at him and said: "They are Blackswans, sir. All of them."

"Where are ours?"

"Locked-on, one minute out."

198

With a twitch of an eye muscle, Raptis opened comms to his company of troops. "Attention, we have incoming, people. Free the BSL and Leopards. Our PeaceMakers will launch their missiles, but they might not be very effective. The less-worse news is that these are Blackswans, not Lapwings, so keep your eyes sharp when they release their Spiders. Remember: we do not know how strong the Spiders' shielding is, so engage with caution. So far, we have no movements of any types of vehicles which could carry an invasion force, but they may be on the way, or more likely ready to go. Good luck."

He twitched his eye muscle again to close the transmission channel, told the troopers to evacuate if targeted, and went outside the command centre to witness the confrontation. He recalled the briefing and how the super AI at headquarters had hurriedly updated potential invasion scenarios based on an attack by Turkey. From his position on hill thirty-five, he looked south at the Acropolis and could see the Aegean Sea in the far distance. Below and all around him lay the thousands of homes, fifty-five hospitals, over a hundred schools, and dozens of government offices, small businesses, numerous kilometres of roads, and all of the other pieces which fitted together to make up a society. And it was now his job to help protect it.

He swallowed when he looked at the sky and saw rows of tiny black dots streak across it and then descend in undulating, geometric waves. In his ear, the Hellenic Army's super AI announced: "Hostiles engaged; friendly missiles inbound."

From behind him, he heard the repeated 'click-clack' of the Battlefield Support Laser. This sound was important because the laser pulses were invisible, and Raptis had learned to concentrate on that telltale click-clack to know that the device was in fact engaging the enemy.

He glanced behind him, and in the sky above the command centre hundreds of streaks of white lines rushed into the battlespace above Athens. As he watched the NATO missiles and speeding ACAs converge, he recalled the image of the poor woman and her child in Istanbul, pictured in the instant a Spider embraced them in its claws a fraction of a second before detonating.

The click-clack of the Battlefield Support Laser stopped as the NATO missiles ducked and dived to follow the evasive manoeuvres of the Blackswans. The missiles found targets and distant pops and bursts of black smoke hung in the sky. Raptis watched keenly, but the Spiders appeared to have been reduced to wreckage, spiralling down to the streets below. He did the maths: two hundred and fifty-six Blackswans carried twelve thousand, eight hundred Spiders. When fitted with the air-to-air model of the RIM–214 smart missile, each PeaceMaker carried thirty-six missiles, which an even fight when the surface batteries of RIM–214s were considered.

Further waves of missiles arrived in the battlespace as more wings of Blackswans descended in sweeping geometrical patterns that fascinated Raptis. Amid the explosions and the shrieking noise from chunks of metal falling to earth, the cirrocumulus high above the battle moved off and the day came on, the sky bright and blue and fresh. The puffs of smoke from the first engagements began to soften and merge. Raptis looked at the debris created by the explosions and followed some pieces down into the city, wondering how much damage they were doing.

After two minutes of ferocious combat, the battle appeared to be winding down. He didn't believe this first attack could be all they would send. In any event, the PeaceMakers which had provided the missiles to defeat the enemy force were now obliged to retire to bases further north to re-arm. This would take at least thirty minutes. Raptis recalled the briefing they'd had on the naval engagement the previous Tuesday and how the defences had been swamped, and he questioned how much more awaited Athens.

As if in answer, Corporal Drakos in the mobile command centre reported: "SkyWatchers detecting one thousand and sixty-four new hostile contacts approaching, ETA two minutes. We have ten squadrons of armed PeaceMakers in theatre, now locking on."

Raptis shook his head in resignation. The next part of the engagement would see eight thousand, six hundred and forty NATO missiles take on fifty-three thousand, two hundred Spiders. He twitched his eye to open comms to his troops hidden in defensive dugouts further down the hill, feeling the responsibility of his rank. "All teams, standby. Things may start to get busier soon. Make sure your Stilettos and Pickups are ready to go; we might not get much time to use them."

He heard his Commanding Officer's voice in his ear: "Sector three, report."

"Sector three, standing by," Raptis answered. It occurred to Raptis that an invasion force might not choose to begin with Athens, and could prefer to get a foothold where the defensive line was weaker, which, despite full mobilisation, included many places around Greece's rugged coastal areas. In his ear, the other sectors reported their readiness.

He withdrew closer to the mobile command centre just as the first wings of the next wave of Blackswans spun down out of the bright blue sky. The Battlefield Support Laser began its click-clack and Raptis imagined the heat of the pulses as they hit the shielding around the Blackswans. A moment later, the laser stopped and numerous streaks of white raced in from further inland. Pops and blotches of black cloud began to fill the battlespace above the city. He stared in fascination as the confrontation played out above him. After a moment, the white streaks thinned out.

Raptis watched Blackswans approach the ground unobstructed. A wave of around ten descended in a curved line towards the Acropolis, and Raptis caught his breath when he realised that the Parthenon and other ancient buildings must be their target. He twitched his eye so that his Squitch zoomed in on the area. The first two Caliphate ACAs disintegrated in fiery explosions; the next two received a cloud of Stiletto missiles and blew up. But despite two missile hits, the next Blackswan deployed its Spiders, which left the body of the ACA in a cone formation, spinning to the ground. Raptis swore aloud when he saw for himself how quickly these monstrous mobile bombs moved after they hit the ground. Their appendages snapped open and twenty or more of them swarmed over the Battlefield Support Laser and detonated in unison. The shock of the explosion made Raptis take an involuntary step backwards, even though he was over three kilometres away.

He deactivated the zoom and stared aghast at the scene. Dozens more Blackswans swooped down to disgorge hundreds of Spiders. In the heat-haze they appeared to move almost in slow motion, disappearing among the columns of Greece's most well-known landmark. A second later, silent clouds of yellow and grey dust billowed up. The columns of the Parthenon buckled and toppled over into the dust.

Raptis gasped, unable to comprehend the scale of the disaster. Many more Spiders fell into the vast cloud of dust which now hung where the Parthenon had been. The sounds of the explosions came to his ears, and these jarred him back to his professional presence and responsibilities. A new-found hatred for these machines and those who'd sent them ignited inside him.

A voice spoke urgently in his ear: "Captain? Captain Raptis? We've got hundreds of incoming. Super AI is telling us we will be overwhelmed in less than thirty seconds."

Raptis put a finger to his ear and yelled: "Get out! Arm yourselves and evacuate the command post." He began to withdraw from the mobile command centre, moving down the hill to join his troops. He became aware of the crowded sky above him. Now that the Blackswans had achieved air superiority, they cruised to specific positions before releasing their cargoes. Raptis saw the Battlefield Support Laser next to the command centre suffer the same fate as the one which had been defending the Acropolis: its weapons burned through and destroyed the first pair of Blackswans, but soon it was overwhelmed. Rapis had to leap and run to avoid the debris of a falling Blackswan. When he looked back, the earth shook under the impact of ten or more Spiders detonating on and around the Battlefield Support Laser and command centre, far more than was required to destroy it.

Raptis watched as thousands of Spiders fell like a deadly black rain over the whole city. Blooms of smoke followed bright orange flashes in numerous locations on the patchwork quilt of buildings below him. In some areas, larger conflagrations grew. He twitched his eye and shouted: "Hill thirty-five, calling for reinforcements. Command centre and BSL destroyed, many casualties, over."

He waited for a response but when none came, he switched channels and heard a cacophony of similar distress calls, demands for reinforcements, and pleas for medical support. Other units in the city were being similarly decimated, and he decided he had to do something. With a bitterness and anger he'd never believed he would feel, he looked out over his city as thousands of Spiders rained down on it, bringing unimaginable destruction and death.

He opened a comms channel to his units on the hillside. "Okay, troops. Command and the BSL are knocked out. All companies report in."

"Kilo three-two. Holding position. Almost out of ammo."

"Lima four-three. Leopards knocked out. We are withdrawing with wounded. If anyone knows where we can get some GenoFluid packs, we would be happy to get our hands on them."

Then the voice of Corporal Metaxas spoke in his ear: "Mike five-four here, sir. Our Leopards are holding out. We are in a good defensive overhang. A Spider needs five shots all-in to defeat its shielding. The best we have worked out is three shots from the Leopard and then a couple of Stilettos. After that, a few shots from a Pickup will take it out."

Raptis waited for his other companies to report in, but he heard no more and had to assume they were unable to respond. He realised that if he still had the mobile command centre, he'd have access to their life signs and would know their condition. But now he felt the imperative to move off the hill. The battle had become a rout. He looked out over the city and his heart broke: palls of dirty black smoke hung over vast areas, and he saw tongues of orange flame flash within them. Blackswans cruised down, released their cargo of Spiders, and departed the battlespace. The Spiders decided autonomously how they could cause the maximum damage, disruption and death, and proceeded to the most effective location for detonation.

Surveying the appalling damage being inflicted on his country's capital city, Raptis asked himself what defence there could be against it. He recalled again the image of the young Turkish woman and her son being enveloped by the Spider in Istanbul, and questioned how long he and his men had before the battlespace became so swamped with Spiders that they would be able, here also in Athens, to target actual individuals for such brutal eradication.

"All troops, fall back. Let us get down to where we might defend a hospital. Set your Squitches to follow me."

Captain Raptis didn't wait for any acknowledgements but proceeded into the relatively dense forest on the hillside, where he hoped he and his troops could reach the city and provide some aid. The one fact that staggered him, which made him despair for the future, was the observation that in each moment of this bright Saturday morning, hundreds if not thousands of Athenians were being killed, and he expected to join them shortly. But their enemy, NATO's enemy, didn't have to put a single flesh-and-blood warrior into the battle. While the Greeks in Athens burned and died with troops of the Hellenic Army, the Third Caliph merely expended material. NATO lost valuable, competent soldiers while in return the Caliphate lost easily replaceable chunks of metal. As Raptis led his troops off hill thirty-five to try to save even a handful of civilian lives, he wondered what on earth could save Europe from this pestilence.

Chapter 34

08.03 Saturday 11 February 2062

On the opposite side of Athens, Turkish engineering student Berat Kartal stared in shock as the Parthenon dissolved in clouds of yellow and grey dust. Like all the other refugees from Turkey, he'd had no reliable news since the Caliphate invaded his country the previous Monday. When the ferry on which he'd escaped from the port city of Izmir docked at Athens, the authorities had made only rudimentary identification checks, despite the risk of Caliphate sympathisers slipping in among the thousands of people genuinely fleeing for their lives.

He'd immediately sought out an expatriate Turkish business, a restaurant close to the port, and at first refused to believe the news about Israel and the Third Caliph's announcement that the whole of Europe was to be either assimilated or annihilated. The restaurant owner, a large, well-fed man who looked to be around Berat's father's age, had offered Berat more help in addition to the *Lahmacun* and side order of *Kuru Fasulye* which had restored Berat so much.

Berat knew that a fellow Turk would never expect anything in return for the help, but he wished he could offer something. However, as before, the young engineering student reacted to the owner's hospitality with an inexplicable urge to move on. The guilt he felt at accepting the food without giving anything in return, even though it was not expected, shrivelled next to his fear of the forthcoming storm. He thanked the restaurant owner for his charity, wished him luck, and left.

He spent the night in a school that had been converted into a refugee centre. He slept fitfully after recording the day's events in his paper journal. A few of the other refugees tried to engage him in conversation, and he remained polite but short with them. In the morning, he filled his water bottles and resolved to escape Athens as soon as possible.

Now, he stood in a nondescript backstreet, having surmised early on in the attack that key transport infrastructure could be the primary target for the Caliphate's ACAs, after the military defenders had been dealt with. With no enthusiasm, he congratulated himself on his foresight: he could have easily been caught up in this battle. What Berat had not expected was that the Caliphate's machines would target Greece's most significant historical monuments for destruction.

Giving a final glance at the pall of smoke and dust which had begun to sink down the rocky outcrop on which the Parthenon and other ancient buildings of the Acropolis were built, Berat hurried on, heading away from the city centre. The sense of impending destruction made him quicken his step as he hastened along streets lined with shops and businesses whose frontages consisted of sun-bleached concrete blocks, bare windows, and chipped and fading signs. Others jogged with him, trying to find a way to escape the violence. From the occasional window or doorway, people would put their heads out and bark questions in Greek, which Berat didn't understand. At one junction lay the burning wreck of one of the Caliphate's machines which had smashed into a workshop of some kind.

At every break in the buildings, he looked to his right to see the smoke and dust spread down from where the Parthenon used to be. As he ran, he noticed the number of black dots in the sky increase. He stopped, chest heaving, at a residential junction from which he saw a large portion of Athens. Caliphate ACAs filled the sky. The engineer in Berat admired their geometrical flight patterns.

On the ground, however, all was chaos: fires raged; sirens wailed distantly; and deep, booming explosions seemed to echo off the sky itself. As he gulped in lungfuls of warm morning air, he could taste the smoke and explosives and burnt plastic. To his left, he watched a wave of smaller machines disgorged from a larger one swoop down and crash into a major elevated road junction. Berat stared, fascinated, as they appeared to grow two groups of four legs and crawl swiftly away. They dispersed and he realised what the movements meant just as twenty or more puffs of smoke blew out from the most vulnerable points on the structure. At once, the entire junction collapsed.

Berat's mouth hung open as he scanned the rest of the city, and he reeled at the brilliance of the tactic. He'd heard of the fate that Israel had met when it tried to neutralise the Caliphate with a massive, pre-emptive nuclear strike. In comparison, this was a stroke of genius: rather than huge bombs that flattened everything and expelled lethal radioactivity for the winds to blow everywhere, here he witnessed an overwhelming piecemeal operation, with thousands of highly mobile and autonomous bombs which each knew the very best place to detonate to maximise death and destruction.

Berat retreated towards the relative anonymity of the backstreets as his mind pointed out a new and more worrying conclusion. When the key targets had been blown up, the remaining autonomous bombs would then turn their attention the less important targets. And so on. He turned into a back street of low-rise residential villas, some well-kept, others dilapidated, and jogged on as his conclusion refined itself further: the sky over Athens must have contained thousands of these flying bombs, and he didn't think for a moment that when all the soldiers and NATO armaments had been destroyed, and then all the key infrastructure on which the city depended had gone, the machines left over would simply fly off. There could be enough to begin targeting individual residences, or even individual people.

Panic gripped Berat and he started to run along the anonymous, deserted street. His imagination placed one of these flying death machines right behind him, watching him, following him, amused at his pathetic attempt to escape with his life.

He reached the end of the street, arriving at another non-descript junction of low-rise buildings with empty plots here and there that were covered in low, dry scrub. He spun around checking the sky. Distant black shapes zoomed across the bright blue morning. Sounds of thumps came to his ears which had to be explosions. Suddenly, he heard a shriek: a black dot travelling very quickly disappeared behind a residential property back along the street which Berat had just run down. The windows blew out and the flat roof seemed to jump in the air, before it collapsed into the house. The boom of the explosion ended with the tinkle of shattered glass. Berat thought he heard screaming.

"Hsst! Hey, you!"

Berat looked to his left to see a figure poking out from under a half-open overhead garage door. The garage was part of the nearest house and a short driveway from the road went down to it at an angle of forty-five degrees.

The young man made an urgent wave with his hand, urging Berat to join him in safety. Berat took a hesitant step towards him but then stopped. The man's face had bad symmetry and abruptly, inexplicably, Berat sensed danger. His breath regained, he turned and ran, deciding to go left.

Above him, black dots zipped and raced around the fringes of his vision. One grew larger as it sped almost overhead. Berat fought his panic and struggled to think rationally regarding how the super AI guiding these flying bombs would choose their targets now that probably little of anything important remained to be destroyed in the city. The thought entered his head that the Caliphate's super AI might have hacked data records and, after the minute or so it would need to process the information, it now knew every resident of Athens and everything about them. Thus, it could target those individuals whom it identified as being most likely to resist assimilation.

As his chest began hurting again, he saw on his right an old building. He ran to it, its shabby appearance encouraging the belief in Berat that it would be uninhabited. Another explosion shook the ground under his feet, and he swore in frustration as, when he reached the building, the old wooden door refused to open. In frustration he took a step back and kicked at the rusted handle. It fell off and landed in the sand. The door swung back and Berat entered to see shrouds which could only be covering antique vehicles.

In relief, Berat realised that the shed hadn't been visited in some time. There was a workbench along one wall, so he pulled a dirty dust sheet off one of the cars and crumpled it up. He kicked away some plastic bottles of engine oil and old tyres, crawled under the work bench, and crouched down, using the dust sheet as a cushion and a blanket. The motes went in his mouth and tasted of rusted, corroded metal; they went into his nose and smelled of the decay that nothing other than time can inflict on man and his lofty ambitions.

Tears welled in the corners of Berat's eyes. At some deep level in his soul, he could feel the thousands of Athenian lives being brutally snuffed out this morning. His thoughts returned to his beloved Turkey and his family and friends there. He thought of all the ancient, historical places in his own country and how the Caliphate must also have destroyed those. He hoped the people he cared for the most had found some way to survive, but suspected they may not have. He recalled the jokes and smiles of his father and uncles and knew they would never submit to a false version of their faith, to a foul corruption of what Allah and Islam really represented.

The bright morning sun shone in through a high window, and underneath Berat the ground shuddered from a new explosion nearby, in time with the shuddering of his shoulders as the tears flowed.

Chapter 35

Trainee nurse Serena Rizzi pulled another trolley full of GenoFluid packs out of the storeroom on the second floor of the Santa Maria hospital in the centre of Rome. An automaton would normally do this work, but with the Third Caliph's announcement of violence against Europe, the Board had decided to 'manualise' as much as possible in the event of a software control breach.

"Where are the packs, Serena?" a voice barked in her ear.

"On the way, Doctor Benini," she replied.

"Hurry up, please."

She reached the lift at the end of the brightly lit corridor and pressed the call panel. Her body began to shake again. She couldn't cope with any delay. Outside, a few minutes ago, the promised invasion had started. At least, she thought it was an invasion. So far, it seemed to be a battle among machines in the sky, with death and destruction raining down on the hapless city and its panic-stricken residents. And this is what made Serena shake: panic. As long as she had something to do, she could cope. But having to wait, even for a moment, made her aware of the pops and metallic shrieks and thumps and crashes outside the hospital in the city, where bombs detonated and missiles exploded. She glared at the reflection of her oval face and shoulder-length, brown hair in the shiny steel doors, whose unevenness distorted her image, and told herself she must keep herself together for the sake of the injured.

The lift chimed and the doors opened. She stood to the side to allow a paramedic to push a bed out of the lift on which rested a young and very pregnant woman, gasping for air.

Serena entered the lift, the doors closed, and she slapped the '0' icon. She inhaled gradually to control her nerves as the lift descended with painful slowness, but the sounds from outside had frayed them. She recalled the previous day's shift, and the staff meeting held by Doctor Francesco Costa, one of the hospital's most renowned surgeons. He wanted as many of the staff to be as prepared as possible for the promised invasion. He knew most of them had never had to deal with serious burns and blunt-force trauma injuries. Serena shivered again when she remembered his descriptions of the injuries he'd treated in Chile during the Super-AI war there a few years ago. Nevertheless, Dr Costa reassured them that the military had positioned defensive weapons around all of Rome's main hospitals, and these would therefore be some of the safest places in the whole city.

The lift chimed, the doors opened, and with relief Serena came back to the present. She pushed the trolley into the broad space on the ground floor of the east wing and gasped at how many more injured casualties had arrived in the few moments it had taken her to fetch the GenoFluid packs. The area had nearly filled with people of all ages. Everyone was distressed; only the very badly injured or dead remained still.

"Over here, quickly," called Doctor Benini, a handsome young man who had flirted with her just a couple of weeks earlier. Now there was neither the time nor the inclination.

She pushed the trolley over the little free space that remained, and frightened and anguished, pain-filled faces looked at her as she passed. She arrived at a woman lying on a bed and lifted a GenoFluid pack out of the trolley.

"Thank you," Doctor Benini said as he took the pack from her, which was the size and weight of a pillow. A translucent whiteness undulated inside the pack. On one side there was a small black command panel. Doctor Benini touched the panel and spoke: "Massive blunt-force trauma to right hand. Severe subcutaneous contusions across most of the body, suggesting intramuscular and periosteal contusions as well. Several lesions of varying severity, mainly on the right side of the body."

Serena looked down at the injured woman with sympathy. Due to the dust and debris on her face and in her hair, it was impossible to tell her age; she could've been twenty or forty years old. Her smashed right hand rested across her blood-stained blouse on her stomach. Doctor Benini laid the GenoFluid pack slowly on the woman's stomach, directly over the hand.

"Okay, right, that's good," he said, his eye twitching. "Are you getting this?" he asked Serena.

"Yes," she replied.

"Good."

The data running across Serena's vision gave the patient's name, address, age and options to view her medical history. It also told Serena that the patient was three weeks pregnant, but that the internal bruising suggested a ninety-eight percent probability that the foetus would abort.

Serena smiled into the woman's terrified eyes, and held her undamaged left hand, noting the pretty flower pattern on the fourth fingernail. The woman mumbled her thanks and Serena knew the GenoFluid pack had begun its work. The nano-bots moved into the patient's bloodstream through the pack's surface, which was solid to the touch, but allowed free passage back and forth to the nano-bots it contained. The hospital had the most modern packs which contained the broadest range of bots yet developed: anaesthetic bots to block pain; disinfecting bots to neutralise infections; bots to repair all three main types of contusion; programmable bots which assembled at a location to effect a specific repair such as closing a torn vessel or artery; 'clone' bots which combined to adopt the characteristics of key elements in the body, such as haemoglobin in cases of severe blood loss; 'dumb' bots which the super AI could program to bind together in specific ways to promote and accelerate tissue repair, so broken bones could heal in hours instead of weeks. Given the extent of the damage to her hand, Serena realised this patient would likely require some reconstructive surgery that was beyond the GenoFluid pack's abilities.

New lettering scrolled up in Serena's vision as the super AI managing the GenoFluid pack told her that severe contusions around the patient's uterus ensured the foetus could not be saved.

The woman spoke to Serena: "The pain is easing now. Thank you so much."

Serena held her hand more tightly. "Try to rest, and don't move. The GenoFluid pack works best if you keep as still as possible, okay?"

The woman nodded and smiled.

"I'll come back soon," Serena said, and returned to her trolley. Doctor Benini had moved on to the next patient and Serena noticed more injured people had arrived. She went to Doctor Benini, nodding soberly at the other doctors and nurses working among the wounded.

Doctor Benini looked at her: "I know you care, but we really don't have the time to give them the personal touch. Could you stop with the chit-chat, please?"

As if to support him, a commotion broke out at the north entrance as the doors flew open and a bald man, covered from head to toe in blood and looking like he cradled something in front of his stomach, staggered in and bellowed out a loud, incomprehensible shout. Then, he fell to his knees. His arms came away from his stomach and off-white intestines spilled out from him. Two nurses and a doctor rushed to help.

Doctor Benini muttered, "Christ, this is bad," and he looked at Serena.

She opened her mouth but a sudden explosion close to the hospital made her gasp.

"They're getting closer," Benini said. "Come on. Pass me another pack."

The next bed contained an unconscious young man with crushed legs. Benini placed the GenoFluid pack over the patient's upper thighs and both he and Serena read the data the super AI controlling the pack relayed to them about the patient. Remarkably, it detected a congenital heart defect in this man which hadn't been noted before, but which carried a very high probability of killing him within the next ten years. The super AI confirmed that, in addition to the patient's injuries, it would send heart-specific bots to repair the defect.

There came another explosion outside and a wave of gasps went up from the far side of the area when two of the windows shattered. Serena's concern grew and she wondered where this would end. Her thoughts ran to her extended

217

family, her friends, to all of the people who meant something to her. But as she looked around this crowded, bloody space in her hospital, as she heard the whimpers and cries and pleas for help, she understood that every single person meant something to her.

For the next hour, she and Doctor Benini and all of the other staff at the Santa Maria hospital worked tirelessly to give aid to the civilian victims of the Third Caliph's aggression. Serena had to return to the GenoFluid storeroom on the second floor a number of times, and with each visit she looked out of the windows on the south side, down at the city, and saw the increasing smoke and fires and destruction. She forced herself to look away; she told herself she had to help the injured.

The first wounded soldiers began to arrive shortly after one o'clock. The head doctor ordered Serena and Doctor Benini to the reception area in the west building. As they hurried across the courtyard full of wounded and dying, most of whom rested in relative peace with GenoFluid packs to comfort them, Benini said: "The Army have their own medical facilities. What are they doing sending their casualties here?"

"I don't know. Perhaps they have too many wounded?"

Benini shook his head and gave a grim smile. "My girlfriend warned me not to come to work today."

"Really?"

"Said she'd had a premonition. Told me to register sick or take an unplanned vacation day. Pleaded for us to go up to her parents' place in the hills near Genoa. Never thought she'd be—"

He broke off when shouts went up further ahead.

"Oh, God. What now?" Serena said, while looking for the nurse or doctor in charge in this part of the hospital. She realised the medical staff were more difficult to identify because their white uniforms had turned crimson with blood, until she looked at her own and realised she looked like a butcher.

Someone grabbed her arm. "Did Gallo send you?"

She looked into the sweaty and urgent face of a doctor she didn't recognise. "Er, yes."

"Good," the doctor replied. "Then both of you start with the serious cases which aren't terminal. Leave the walking wounded, no matter how much they complain. The packs are over there," he pointed to double doors on the far side of the large and packed reception area.

Serena nodded and she and Benini hurried around beds, stretchers on the floor and injured people.

"I'll grab a few packs and you get started. Look, here come more of them," Benini said, motioning to sets of doors at the entrance as vehicles arrived outside.

Serena looked at him. "But that's my job," she said.

He smiled. "Yes, but the guy-soldiers will be cheered up if the first thing they see when they get here is a pretty trainee nurse."

Serena hurried over to join another doctor and nurse at the entrance. One military orderly at the side of an ambulance looked at Serena and called: "Have you still got GenoFluid packs?"

She nodded.

"Good." The side of the ambulance retracted to reveal a line of four stretchers with injured soldiers head to toe. Inside lay a further three such rows. "These on the outside are the worst cases, just about blown to pieces."

She went to the head of the first wounded soldier and they lifted the stretcher off. She asked the orderly: "You have so many wounded you've run out of packs?"

The orderly glanced behind him as he walked backwards towards the doors, and looked at her and said: "Ran out in the first hour."

They went through the doors and Serena said: "It's a slaughter out there, isn't it?"

The orderly gave her an ironic smile: "Not yet, but it won't be long."

They lowered the stretcher down by a wall. Serena looked at the young male face of the patient and wondered how handsome he had been before shrapnel had taken off his lower jaw.

Benini arrived, glanced at the unconscious soldier on the stretcher and said: "If he survives, he's going to need a lot more than a GenoFluid pack." He knelt down, placed a pack over the soldier's chest, and described the patient's condition, prioritising repairs to the man's destroyed face.

"Come on," the orderly said to Serena. "Let's get the next."

They returned to the ambulance and the orderly abruptly said: "Shit, that's great."

"What?" Serena asked

He looked at her: "You're not getting the emergency military feed?"

"No, why would I? I work for the hosp—"

The orderly scoffed. "Our airborne defences are nearly finished. And we knew this would happen all week, ever since that mad bastard smashed Turkey and Israel."

Serena tried to compose herself; she wanted to appear confident and capable in front of this stranger, despite her own inner turmoil. She felt herself beginning to shake again. She and the orderly lifted off the next stretcher, which held another unconscious soldier covered in blood. She said: "But it can't be so bad. I read that although we don't have so many ACAs, they can still hold off—"

Then the orderly laughed at her and sneered: "You shouldn't waste your time here, lovely girl. When they run out of missiles and the tanks are finally finished, and that's not going to be long, we're going to get the order to evacuate and that will be the end of this lot."

"What?"

"You think we'll have time to get all these injured out ahead of the invaders? Forget it, lovely girl."

"Don't patronise me, orderly," she said. "The army is supposed to defend us. You do your job and I'll do mine."

The orderly laughed again as they lowered the stretcher to the floor. Serena gave him a withering look and left to get another GenoFluid pack. She hurried to the supply area under an ornate stone arch, nearly tripping over other patients. She grabbed one and went to Benini. "Doctor," she said, "Next one's over there. I can't tell what the major injuries are—"

Benini looked up at her. "You'll have to deal with it, Serena." He lowered his voice. "I think I'm going to lose this one. I have to monitor the pack."

Serena nodded and returned to the patient, catching a sideways glance from the medical orderly, who was being helped by Pisano, a fellow junior nurse.

She turned back to the wounded soldier and tried to identify the most serious injuries. The man looked quite peaceful and she wondered if he'd already died. She placed the GenoFluid pack on his chest and activated it, muttering to it about multiple, life-threatening injuries. The pack began working and details scrolled in the front of Serena's vision. She read his name, rank and number in the Italian Army, and accessed his medical records, which showed he had been a healthy young man.

A moment later, the pack detailed all of the pieces of shrapnel which had been blown into his body, mainly from in front and to the right of him. Hundreds of lesions ran through his legs and torso. The super AI told her the bots would not be able to remove all of the shrapnel because many pieces were too large to dissolve, and the patient would need more traditional surgery to be performed by a supervised android.

Serena sighed and wondered how long this young man would be able to hold on. Before going to the next patient, she waited for the pack's super AI to confirm the patient was stable when his eyes suddenly snapped open.

She leaned towards his face, unnerved by the terror in his eyes. "It's okay," she said, "you're in hospital now and you're safe. You have a GenoFluid pack attached to you so please try to keep still."

The terror left his grey eyes slowly and Serena thought she saw a wave of relief cross his face. His lips moved. Serena considered he might be praying. His eyebrows came together, and she realised he wanted to tell her something.

She leaned close to his pockmarked, bloodied face. "Run," he whispered.

She pulled back and looked at him with curiosity. She put her ear to his mouth again. "Run," he repeated. Then he whispered: "The Squitch… Defences outside overwhelmed."

"I won't leave my patients," she replied, her spirit sinking.

"Run," he mouthed, and then passed out. The pack's super AI told her it had anesthetised the patient for his own safety.

Serena looked around at everyone else. She saw Benini on the other side of the reception area, across a sea of injured people. She stood up and the hospital's general alarm went off. She flinched, recalling the annual drill they had and the huge inconvenience it caused everyone. Now, it wasn't a drill. The pulsing single tone increased in pitch, dropped and increased repeatedly. Serena didn't know what to do, which struck her as ironic because they drilled what to do every year.

222

Benini was suddenly in front of her, grabbing her upper arms and shouting above the alarm and above the screams: "Come on, we have to get out, now!"

She stared at him. "No."

"What?" he cried. "We must evacuate."

She pulled his arms off her and repeated: "No. I'm not leaving them."

"But you can't save—"

An explosion erupted outside above the building, shaking it. Benini grabbed Serena as they both fell to the floor. The screaming around them grew louder. Seconds passed, and she heard Benini cry: "Oh, God, the pack's split. The pack's split."

She struggled to lift her head and then coughed on all the dust which had suddenly appeared. Benini faced her, a look of horror on his face and opaque liquid on his hands. Serena knew that the piercing of a GenoFluid pack with patients in these conditions would be fatal. She pushed herself up, knowing only that she had to get another pack. She looked down at the floor, at the dirty grey dust and bits of wood and glass, and then at her hands, which had fresh blood on them running over and dripping off her dust-covered skin.

A clacking sound came to her ears and black shapes moved down past the windows. Her spirit rose up in protest at the sight of the Spiders. She would not give in. She took long strides to the supply area under the stone arch. She glanced back at all of the wounded patients, her patients, and looked on in disgust as Benini struggled over the injured and the debris to escape the building. When he reached the furthest doorway, eighteen Spiders at key points outside the building detonated simultaneously, and Serena looked up to see the ceiling of the Santa Maria hospital collapse on all of them.

Chapter 36

"We're getting reports of tens of thousands of casualties, Sir Terry. Just what the hell are their armies doing?"

"Try to keep calm, Mr Gough. It's a rout for NATO forces, but we had a good idea what was coming. Our enemy appears to have inexhaustible supplies of munitions at his disposal."

The two men strode along a gothic corridor inside the rebuilt Houses of Parliament. Napier's defence minister, Phillip Gough, only enjoyed his ministerial position due to political favours he'd done in the past. Since his appointment, he admitted to Terry that he had little knowledge of military affairs. Terry hadn't minded this because it gave Terry a chance to ensure the defence minister was correctly informed. However, Gough had this last week developed a penchant for becoming irritatingly emotional at worrying news. The two men turned a corner and continued walking. Terry admired the architecture and could sense the atmosphere of angry concern inside the vast building. He wondered if and when the concern would turn to fear.

"But it's a disaster," Gough shrieked, throwing his thick forearms in the air. "It's a complete shit festival, it's the wor—"

"Shut up, Mr Gough," Terry snapped, struggling to keep his voice even. "I'll remind you that thousands of men and women are, at this moment, getting maimed and killed trying to save as many civilians as they can, and now is hardly the time for hysterics."

"Perhaps, but the threatened invasion hasn't even begun and we're already almost defenceless."

"That won't last for long. Our ACA plants are ramping production up and the Americans will soon begin sending reinforcements."

"Have you seen the media? Have you read what they're saying?"

"That's not my concern."

"It's a complete disaster for the government."

Terry glanced at Gough with mild amusement in his eyes. He pointed out: "Do you realise the Caliphate could launch a massive aerial assault probably anywhere in Europe? That what's happening today in Athens and Rome could be Paris and London tomorrow? And until we get substantial reinforcements, we are just as exposed as those cities?"

Gough gulped hard before saying: "Yes, of course. But, with respect, Sir Terry, I would've thought the fact that war is highly likely one way or another, and it probably won't be restricted to ACAs, would make you see the urgent need for a positive media spin on this. Do you think the British and NATO forces currently have sufficient personnel to defeat a Caliphate invasion?"

Terry smiled at Gough's rhetorical tone. They arrived at the ornate, Gothic doors to the prime minister's emergency room, and Terry turned to Gough: "My political masters give me tasks, and I carry them out to the best of my and the British Army's ability. But if in the future we should need to drastically increase recruitment, then the most powerful woman in England, or perhaps one of her ministers, really should bring some pressure to bear on this country's media to gather support for the forthcoming struggle, wouldn't you agree, Mr Gough?"

Gough opened his mouth but the doors swung open before he could speak.

Terry strode into the room first. Low winter sunlight poured in through the windows that overlooked the river. Murmuring people stood in front of the large east wall, which displayed eight different image feeds from various locations. These included SkyWatcher ACAs above Athens and Rome, and digital social sharing platforms that disseminated chilling sequences of people suffering and dying in real time.

Terry approached the prime minister, who stood watching the screens with the head of MI5, David Perkins. Terry recalled the friction of their earlier meetings and questioned if Perkins had the wit to realise that the current disaster enveloping the continent was slightly more important than mere personality clashes.

Napier said: "Terry, thank you for coming. This is a little different from what we usually do in this room. Rising sea levels are no longer our first concern."

Terry saw Perkins's eyebrows rise at the tone of familiarity in Napier's voice, but he offered his hand and said: "Hello again, Sir Terry, we're not sure if this is the invasion or not."

Terry shook it and replied: "From what I've seen, these are terror raids, designed to scare us, nothing more."

Perkins's forehead creased: "What for?"

"To drive refugees north from southern Europe to encourage the rest of the continent to surrender. They will flee, taking with them stories of death and destruction, which you can already see on these screens. These will cause a massive wave of panic among civilian populations and put insurmountable pressure on civilian infrastructure. Any new intel from GCHQ?"

Perkins shook his head, "Nothing substantial."

Terry said: "It would help if we knew what Beijing knows."

Napier glanced at the two men and said: "Most of the rest of the world seems to think it's Europe's own fault."

Perkins brushed the front of his jacket with his hand and said: "That's only their official position because they don't want to antagonise China."

"Perhaps," Napier replied, "and that a number of countries wonder where the Third Caliph will turn his attention once he has put Europe to the sword." She glared at the two men. "You've seen the latest projections?"

Terry said: "A great deal depends on how many flesh-and-blood troops they can deploy, PM. There is still an awful lot of guesswork going into these—"

Anger flashed across her face: "If they decide they need to use any flesh-and-blood soldiers at all. Analyses of what they did in Israel have convinced me they don't need to invade with anything more than enough of those flying lasers, and we have precious little defence against them. And how can you be sure this isn't the beginning of the invasion?"

Terry answered: "Because it would have begun by now. They must be using their own version of super artificial intelligence, and that has undoubtedly given a selection of the most effective invasion scenarios, and I'm sure our own computers will confirm none of those scenarios includes waiting so long after the initial assaults. Besides, any continent-wide invasion absolutely must begin on a minimum of two fronts, probably more. Their tactics today are clear to anyone with an understanding of these things."

Napier's eyebrows rose at the implied criticism, so Terry added: "This is how I can be reasonably certain that today's events are a terror raid, not the prelude to an invasion. This is tactical, PM, not strategic. The enemy wants to sow as much panic and confusion as he can, to drive as many civilians as possible to flee northwards, to place Europe's infrastructure under intolerable stress, and hinder or prevent NATO forces from deploying units to defend the likely invasion when it does come."

"So when will it come?" Perkins asked, a note of shocked diffidence in his voice.

Terry replied while scanning the images of palls of black smoke drifting over the ruins of Athens and Rome: "In my opinion, which our computers may or may not contradict, anything from two days to two weeks, certainly no longer than that, but the enemy will still want to allow some time for the panic to spread."

Napier's aide, Crispin Webb, arrived from the other side of the room. "Excuse me. Boss, I've just spoken to Linda at COBRA. She reports that we've got more very high tides due next week and has asked if the army can redeploy troops to assist civil defence with maintaining the construction replicators."

Napier looked at Terry, who said: "We have to meet our NATO commitments first, PM. But I'll see if we can't spare some reserves."

"Pass that back to Linda, would you, Crispin?"

Crispin nodded and turned to go, but Terry grabbed his arm. "Mr Webb, when you have a moment, the defence minister would like to have a word with you concerning getting the media on board."

Crispin looked from Terry to Gough, who nodded his confirmation. Crispin left.

Terry spoke to the others: "However, while these terror raids might be good tactics, they are also a strategic mistake."

"How is that?" Perkins asked.

Terry answered: "Look at the raw data up there," and nodded at the large screen. To the left of the images of destruction and chaos, a slim column gave continually updated statistics of estimated numbers of deaths and injuries in each city, buildings destroyed, and enemy ACAs attacking and NATO machines defending.

Terry continued: "Near the bottom of the list there's a figure for the number of enemy ACAs brought down. Today, unlike during the attacks on the navies on Tuesday morning, those Blackswans aren't sinking to the bottom of the ocean. For the first time, when those attacks are over, we're going to get our hands on the Caliphate's actual hardware, and that will tell us all kinds of things."

"Indeed," Perkins agreed.

"I'm not sure I would have made that strategic concession for the tactical gain," Terry added.

"My god," Napier said in a heavy voice, "look at the casualty figures. Can you even imagine what those poor people must be going through?"

"The worst destruction Europe's seen in a hundred and twenty years," Perkins said flatly.

"We're going to have even bigger problems when the invasion does come," Terry said.

"Meaning?" Napier asked.

"You see, in addition to the thirty thousand-odd estimated civilian casualties, we've also had several thousand dead and injured from the militaries. The Hellenic and Italian Armies are getting beaten up today. The Italian Army alone has lost five percent of its entire strength since this morning.

Meanwhile, our enemy is expending only machines, and his armies remain safe inside Caliphate territory, waiting. Those machines are killing professional soldiers for whom the army was a way of life. Who are we going to replace them with?"

The shocked realisation on the faces of the head of MI5 and the prime minister confirmed to Terry that they now understood an important reality in this war.

Perkins shook his head. "I need to get back to HQ. I'll keep both of you appraised if we get any hard-and-fast intel on a potential invasion date."

"Thank you," Terry said. When Perkins left, he looked at Napier and lowered his voice: "What's happening today in Athens and Rome is certain to happen here, sooner or later, and I confidently expect to lose many of my best troops in the next few weeks. We're going to have to replace them, and we can only do that from the general population. Your aide over there, Webb, keeps whining on about the media."

"Yes, I know," Napier said.

Terry moved in closer: "Personally, I don't really have a great deal of time for all the frivolity and vapidity in which today's media generally deal, but I would like to point out to you, PM, that someone needs to pull them on board. I mentioned this earlier to the defence minister. Things are going to get very violent very soon; we're going to see that kind of destruction," he indicated the screens, "all over Europe and the Home Nations. If we're going to stand even the slimmest chance of lasting more than mere days, then we're going to have to get everything right. There is absolutely no room for any errors, small or large. And one of the key things is having a general public which understands that the enemy is out there, not here in your government."

"I can hardly tell the media outlets what to tell people."

"Why not?"

"Because, if I want to get re-elected..." her words trailed off under Terry's stare of mild amusement.

"Yes, I see. But you might want to have a word with the health department."

"Why?"

"Have you seen the latest obesity stats?"

Terry smiled, "Now, I see," he said.

Crispin Webb arrived and said: "Boss, it's time now. The chamber is filling up."

Napier said: "Very well. I have to go and make a statement to the house."

"On a Saturday?" Terry queried.

Napier smiled with good-natured envy that England's top soldier had only a loose grasp of politics. "Emergency sitting. Even members of parliament can put in a little overtime when international events demand rapid reactions."

Chapter 37

19.23 Saturday 11 February 2062

Having been dealt the first jack yet again, Maria Phillips shuffled the pack of cards.

Her father fidgeted next to her at the dining table, scratching at his thinning brown hair. He said: "I still think we should leave. We should get out of Europe."

Her older brother, Martin, smiled opposite her and shook his head. "We spoke about this, Dad. Just where would we go, exactly?" he asked in a rhetorical tone.

Maria dealt the cards.

"I dunno yet, but I've been thinking we should get out before it's too late."

Martin said: "You and Mum are too old now, at any rate."

Maria said: "And don't you think that's what half of Europe is trying to do at the moment, Dad?"

She sensed her father's resolve wilt under the common sense of his children. "All right, so me and your mother, perhaps we are too old to get out, but you kids aren't. You're just the right ages to emigrate somewhere safer, like New Zealand or Australia."

Having dealt seven cards in front of each of them, Maria put down the rest of the pack, picked up a pen, and said: "Okay then, forecast whist, second round, clubs are trumps. Your first call and lead, Dad. How many tricks do you want?"

Anthony looked at his cards. "Oh, you're a good daughter and no mistake," he said with sarcasm. "Go on, put me down for three."

Maria glanced at Mark, who said at once: "Yeah, I'll have three as well."

Maria looked at her own cards and grimaced. "So I can't have one... I'm having two, so we're one over-called. Your lead, Dad."

Anthony said: "I'll start as I mean to go on this evening, kiddie-winkies," and threw down the ace of trumps.

Maria groaned along with Martin. The latter put down the four of clubs, while Maria reluctantly gave up her queen of clubs and said: "Dad, that was so one of my two."

Anthony let out a chuckle. Martin looked at Maria and asked: "Shall I tell him now?"

"Go on," Maria replied.

"What?" Anthony said, as he collected the first trick and laid the jack of clubs.

"Dad," Martin began, looking at Anthony's jack and shaking his head, "I've got quite a few feeds running in my lens, and I can tell you that we have zero chance of getting out of England, unless you own and can captain an ocean-going vessel which you've kept secret from the rest of us for all of our lives."

"Yeah," Anthony grumbled, "I've got one right here, in my back pocket."

Martin threw down the ten of clubs while Maria laid the four of diamonds.

"Thank you very much," Anthony said, collecting the second trick. "Just one more trick for me," and he laid the ace of hearts.

Martin spoke while laying the seven of clubs: "Nope, you're not having that trick. What I mean, Dad, is that the only real chance any of us would have is to try to get transport west, to Wales, and then maybe get a boat to Ireland. Civilian air transport has been suspended since the attacks on the navies when those planes went missing, and you can bet that's not going to start again any time soon."

"But there must be other ways, surely?" Anthony asked.

Martin shook his head. "There aren't, Dad. The government controls everything. Super AI controls all transport. And they've put in place emergency powers which let the police take control over all that Super—"

"Bloody old bill," Maria's father spat.

"Bloody or not," Martin went on, "they've got the law on their side. They decide what gets priority for transport, and it doesn't matter whatever ordinary people want, if the police say 'no', that's that."

"So we're trapped, here in happy East Grinstead, is that it?"

Martin shrugged as he collected the third trick of the hand, the first of the three he wanted. He then laid the king of diamonds.

Maria smiled as she put the ace of diamonds down and said: "We're happy and safe in East Grinstead, Dad." Her smile faded. "You might want to spare a thought for those poor people in Athens and Rome."

Anthony looked at his eldest child and asked: "What's the latest news, Martin?"

Martin's eye twitched and he said: "Hmm, mainly speculation. Officially the death toll in Athens is three hundred and twenty, while in Rome it's over five hundred, but all reports are suggesting that thousands must have been killed."

Anthony tossed out the ten of diamonds and Maria collected the trick. He said, "My god, I can't remember the last time something like that happened in Europe."

Maria laid the king of spades.

"Well," Martin said. "I've made a decision. If the invasion does start, I'm going to join up."

Maria saw her father react. For a moment, she worried they would begin a row, but her father's weathered face softened and he said: "Are you sure, son?"

"Oh, yeah," Martin replied, and Maria felt a small flash of emotion which part of her brain recognised as pride.

Anthony threw down the seven of spades on Maria's king. "You know you have some family in the forces, not least poor cousin Bernie in the navy, but—"

"Yeah, I know, Dad," Martin interrupted. "But if the bleaker assessments turn out to be true, then we're all in the deepest shit imaginable, and I've decide I'd rather go down fighting. That's your second trick, Maz," he said, laying the five of spades.

Maria collected the cards. "Right, that's all I want. So, Dad, you want one of these, while Martin needs both of them. And I need to lose the lead." She put down the five of diamonds and saw her brother wink at her.

"Damn, wrong suit," her father said, putting down the six of hearts.

Martin said: "Thanks, Maz," laid the nine of diamonds, and collected the trick. "Okay, Dad. As you would say: have you kept the right suit?" Martin's grin warmed Maria as her brother put down the seven of diamonds.

"Nice one, dearest brother," Maria said with warmth as she laid her final card, the nine of hearts.

"You cheeky little bugger," Anthony said. "You know I haven't got any diamonds left."

"You not got a trump, Dad?" Martin said with a smile.

"Bugger," Anthony said, throwing down his final card, the queen of spades. "I suppose you kiddie-winkies are bound to get lucky from time to time."

Picking up the pen and recording the scores, Maria announced: "So that's thirteen for Martin, twelve for me, and oh, er, only two for you, Dad."

Anthony flashed two of his three children a warm smile and said: "It's a good thing you've got a father who knows that a game of forecast whist has seven hands. Seriously, do either of you think you're going to get another bonus?"

Maria looked at Martin and rolled her eyes. Martin winked and said: "Dad's deal for six, Maz."

Anthony sighed and said: "Such a pity your brother spends all his time inside those bloody games."

Maria said: "I think his intentions are good, Dad. He's got this idea of winning a Bounty to make all our lives easier."

Her father scoffed as he shuffled the pack. "Doesn't he read the media? Doesn't he see the interviews with all the gamers who've spent years in the Universes and got nothing?"

Martin said: "Try and tell him and he comes straight back with all the other gamers he's spoken to who say that those stories are false, planted by the government to try and get people to stop total immersive gaming."

Anthony dealt each of them six cards.

Maria said: "It depends on who you want to believe. For every person who says they've been cheated, Mark will show you someone who's gained a Bounty and is living the life." She picked up the pen. "Your first call and lead, Martin."

"A week ago I would've said it didn't matter that much, but now it does. That boy needs to think about what he's

237

going to do if things do get really bad," Anthony said, looking at his cards.

Martin also looked at his cards and said: "And I heard the government is also going to stop paying the U-Bee… I'll have a silly two, Maz."

Maria made a note and said: "I'll have two as well. You can't have two, Dad."

Anthony said: "No way they'll stop the U-Bee, there'd be riots on the streets if the government tried that… I'll have one, then."

"Right, there's one spare. Your lead, Martin."

Martin looked at the others. "Does it matter? Does anything matter anymore? So what if there're riots on the streets? That's nothing compare to what's coming. Look at the state of Athens and Rome. That's going to be all of Europe in a few weeks."

"Maybe it won't be?" Maria offered, not wishing the atmosphere to become morose.

Martin scoffed at her.

Their father said: "Come on, let's not worry about things we can't change." He looked at Martin: "Play the game, lad."

Martin scoffed again and threw down the ace of trumps.

Chapter 38

Dahra Napier sat back on the cream couch and let her aching neck and shoulders sink into the smooth, welcoming upholstery. Five minutes; she only needed five minutes. She regulated her breathing, an exercise she'd used since she first entered the English parliament in the 2046 election. While she closed her eyes and counted the time between inhalation, pause, and exhalation, pause, she reflected how much had happened in her sixteen years as a parliamentarian, and how suddenly everything had changed.

Not for a moment had she thought anything like this abrupt and brutal war would or could mark the end of her premiership. Her major political goals of this parliament, which had guided all of her decisions until the previous Monday night, faded out of sight as she thought of them: to manage the protection of England's coastline, to bring unemployment down, and to rein in the exploitative power of the immersive gaming industry. The thought occurred to her just how much those gaming companies might welcome this explosion of violence, for she suspected many more ordinary citizens would run to the total immersive gaming worlds to hide from this, the real world. On reflection, could she really blame them?

The statement she'd given to the house of commons that afternoon had made the chamber echo with cries of concerns and a barrage of obtuse observations. The leader of the opposition, the stiff and hesitant David Bentley, had laced his reciprocal statement with lashings of the childish sarcasm he and his MPs thought passed for wit, and the supportive questions and observations from her own party felt more laboured and sycophantic than usual. At length, she took comfort from the fact that in the five days since the world had gone mad, she hadn't lost a single minister to public pressure, despite the media's best efforts. And regarding the media, Sir Terry Tidbury had undoubtedly been correct.

She let out one final long exhalation and said: "Okay. Crispin, Monica, you can come in now."

Her two aides hurried into the room. Napier stood up, stretched, and asked the new arrivals, "Wine?"

Webb and Monica smiled, nodded and thanked their boss in unison. Napier went over to an ornate occasional table on which a bottle of white wine chilled in an ice bucket. After seven years, the housekeepers at Ten Downing Street had learned the occupant's preferences.

"Any interesting feedback on this afternoon?" she asked as she filled three glasses.

"Initial reactions are positive," Webb began. "Focus groups rate you strongly on determination and reliability, in any case. On Monday, we'll begin our monthly polling research to establish the—"

"No, you won't," Napier smiled as she handed a glass to each of them. She returned to the table and collected her own, before striding to the windows and looking out into the darkness. She gazed at the yellow and green hue from the glass of wine, followed the minute bubbles as they rose to the surface, and wondered how much longer she had to enjoy such luxury.

She spoke to her aides without turning around: "Did you make the enquiries I asked you to?"

Monica said: "I've sounded out a couple of the senior content editors and they seemed to be expecting something a bit more than a memo."

"Which outlets?" Napier asked.

"*The Telegraph* and *Buzzfeed*."

Webb spoke: "I had a chat with that psychopathic vulture MacSawley at *The Mail* and only just managed to keep him in check on the implied threat that he wouldn't get a gong at the end of your premiership."

Napier turned to face them. "As long as it was only implied, although the end of my premiership may come a lot sooner than they think. Don't any of those fools realise the gravity of the situation?"

Monica answered, bright and animated: "I think they realise how serious it is, ma'am, but they want the person responsible for not seeing it coming. They want blood."

"Oh," Napier replied, her thin eyebrows rising, "very soon they're going to get all the blood they want, and lots more besides." The sudden blinking of Monica's eyes conveyed the aide's sense of shock to Napier.

Webb said: "*The Times* is, as usual, more sober, but that's been behind a paywall for half a century, so its reach among the general public is negligible."

Napier looked at Monica. "You said they expected more than a memo. How much more?"

Monica blew air out through her teeth and replied: "What you'd normally do when you need an important favour: invite them all round here for a slap-up meal and drinks."

Napier grimaced, "I thought so. Awful people, journalists. The worst part of my job is having to sup with them… Well, it used to be the worst part."

Webb said: "It wouldn't be a bad move, boss. We can get everything organised and have all, or most, at least, of the important editors here towards the end of next week."

Napier gave him a withering look. "Do you have any idea what the situation could be by the end of next week?" she asked rhetorically.

"Well, obviously—" Webb began.

"No, I want this communicated tonight. We simply don't have a moment to lose."

"Of course, boss," Webb said.

Napier said: "Memo begins: Top secret, highly classified. For distribution to all media editors and owners with outlets with an English, Home Nations and/or international impact exceeding one-point-one on the Gosforth Social Penetration Scale. Important communication from the office of the prime minister of England.

"Dear Sirs and Madams, the frightening and appalling events of the last few days have completely upended our way of life, and now we stand on the threshold of a future which looks black indeed. As the government works tirelessly with our friends and allies in Europe and NATO to find responses to the indefensible actions of the New Persian Caliphate, the danger which has become so apparently sudden… No, wait. Change the second clause to: the danger which has so abruptly overtaken all our lives threatens to engulf us in a level of violence not seen in Europe for well over a century.

"There are a number of objectives the English and other European governments need to achieve if we are to have even the slimmest hope of surviving this storm. One of those regards our populations and how the majority of our citizens respond to this terrible threat to our societies and way of life.

"In this respect, the media has a vital role to play." Napier stopped talking and sipped her wine, composing her thoughts. She continued: "I believe… No, change that: The government believes the time has arrived when the whole country needs to pull together to face this most powerful of foes. While it is understandable that the shock of the suddenness of this week's events would lead to a strong desire to find and punish those responsible for some imagined oversight or intelligence failure, the truth is that the only individual responsible for the situation resides in Tehran.

"Therefore, the government believes that you, the media, now need to step up to your responsibilities not only to maintain factual, accurate reporting of events, but also to ensure that citizens understand the full danger that threatens us: a war which will probably entail the worst destruction Europe has seen since the Second World War. Citizens need to be informed, assisted and educated, rather than scared out of their wits. They require guidance on how to prepare, how they can contribute to Europe's defence. At no time in the last one hundred and twenty years has it been more important that our communities and our societies come together and work together, and, ultimately, fight together.

"I cannot underestimate the importance of your role in this significant task. The time for recrimination amongst us is over. We must face the coming storm with all our energy focused on this new and powerful enemy. Let us draw now on the best qualities of our humanity, our strength, our resilience, our determination… Very sincerest regards, prime minister, first lord of the treasury, etc, etc."

Napier watched her two aides as she finished the memo, and their reactions satisfied her that it was sufficient.

Monica asked: "Shall we put an R-Notice on it?"

Napier replied: "Certainly not. We're still an open society, for now."

Webb said: "Boss, I suggest replacing 'surviving' as you might be questioned on that word. In this sentence: 'There are a number of objectives the English and other European governments need to achieve if we are to have even the slimmest hope of surviving this storm,' I recommend saying 'if we are to battle this storm,' as that would not imply you might have some secret plan to defeat the Caliphate."

Napier said: "I only wish I had. How about 'successfully battle the storm'? I'd like to include the very occasional positive word if I can."

Webb nodded. "Of course," he said.

"Good," Napier replied, and sipped her wine. "Send paper copies out with my seal and signature by courier as soon as you can, please."

Both of the aides nodded.

"Will that be all for now, boss?" Webb asked.

Napier let out a sigh and looked at them. She briefly wondered what they really felt about the violence that would shortly engulf Europe, but stamped on the thought at once because of her growing fatigue. "Yes, thank you," she replied.

"Okay, boss," Webb said. "I'll brief you first thing tomorrow, assuming nothing vastly dramatic happens overnight."

"I'll trust your judgement on whether something's important enough to have me woken, Crispin."

Crispin nodded. "And then you've got the party leaders' meeting at the house, over breakfast at nine. There's two hours for that, and then—"

Webb stopped when Napier held out a hand. "Certainly, we'll get through everything, but now I need to see my fam—"

Monica said: "Wow, that's interesting."

"What is it?" Napier asked.

244

"Protests are being planned for tomorrow in a number of cities."

Napier controlled her feelings. "Against my government?"

She watched the heads of her two aides twitch from side to side as they followed whatever their lenses were showing them.

Webb said: "Not really, no. Peace protests… Yes, London, Cambridge, Manchester, Birmingham, Lincoln."

Monica added: "The live feeds are showing the number of people planning to go. The total has reached a quarter of a million in the last three minutes."

"Filtering now," Webb announced. "The usual suspects: Greens, Marxists. They're talking about showing the Third Caliph that, and I quote: 'The English people are a peace-loving race who do not deserve to pay for the mistakes of past generations yet again,' although I don't know what that's supposed to mean."

Monica suggested, "Climate change?" and Webb grunted his agreement.

"Crispin," Napier said, "send a subsidiary alert to all police forces to be extra vigilant for racist attacks. They need to make sure nothing gains traction on that front."

"Will do, but it's highly improbab—"

"How many English Muslims did the home office record as leaving the country and potentially entering the Caliphate last year?" Napier asked.

Crispin's eye muscles twitched for a moment. He said: "Fewer than five hundred. The downward trend hasn't changed in years, boss."

"Yes, I know, but I wanted to be sure. I don't want the last remnants of the hard right dredging their tired propaganda up again."

"Boss, super-AI filtering is showing very little cause for concern on that front. What we're looking at is a rapidly growing wannabe peace movement. Yup, the fringe parties are already trying to negotiate linkage for the media to report, but I anticipate no serious violence, either racist or other."

Napier sighed and said: "Okay, then. Thank you, both of you."

"Okay," Webb said, "we'll call it a night now, boss. It looks like the protests are going to be quite widespread and vocal tomorrow."

Napier replied with cynicism: "They can bleat like sheep all they want, and I promise it will have absolutely no influence whatsoever on the future."

Chapter 39

08.00 Sunday 12 February 2062

Terry Tidbury sipped his fourth cup of tea of the morning and stared at the familiar NATO crest on the wall screen, its blue background lightened by the bright winter sunlight streaming in through the office windows.

"Still no sign of troop movements, Sir Terry," Simms, his adjutant, reported.

"I was concerned they might have begun something overnight; there was an outside chance."

Simms sat down in a chair on Terry's right and said: "Indeed. I certainly expected yesterday's attacks to be the beginning of the invasion."

"So did I," Terry replied. "But it seems the enemy wanted to give us all a nice bloody nose first." He sipped his tea and then asked: "How long have you been my adjutant now, Simms?"

"Two years this June, Sir Terry."

"It is two. Time has been passing so quickly lately, I wondered if—" Terry stopped when the screen chimed and came to life with an empty desk that belonged to General

Joseph E. Jones, Supreme Allied Commander, Europe. The well-built African-American heaved into view, looking lethal in his combat fatigues. Rather than sit behind the desk, he sat on the front of it, and took up a larger part of the screen. Along the bottom, thumbnail images appeared as others joined the meeting. No one spoke until all of the generals and chiefs of staff who were slated to join had logged in.

When Terry counted fifteen thumbnails along the bottom of the screen, General Jones took a swig from a Coke bottle and began: "Welcome, chiefs. First, let me start by expressing my country's condolences to the Italian and Hellenic Armies for the unprovoked attacks they had to endure yesterday. I think I can speak for all of us here, and indeed many thousands of others in Europe, when I say that, in honesty, we expected those attacks on Athens and Rome to be the beginning of the main invasion. Now, on the one hand that turned out not to be the case, which gave some a little bit of comfort, that for whatever reason the enemy has paused; but on the other, this doesn't detract from the truly terrible loss of life those two cities have suffered.

"This meeting is to establish how we can deploy the best defence to stop the invasion when it comes. Our computers are suggesting that we don't have a whole lotta options here, but we need to work with what we got. This graphic here gives us Ample Annie's most highly recommended deployments, after refining feedback from each member's super AI."

A map of Spain enlarged from a thumbnail that contained differently coloured shapes denoting the locations of NATO deployments. Jones spoke: "We have elements of the Spanish Army, French units and elements of the British Army, and as of today, we have three hundred PeaceMakers assigned to this anticipated front. As you can see, we're covering an 'arc of approach' as those are the most likely points the Caliphate will land."

Spain moved off to the left and Italy came into view, similarly decorated with coloured shapes to denote the locations of deployments. Jones went on: "In Italy, we are still reassessing after yesterday's apparent terror attack, but in addition to the Italian Army, we have three brigades of the German 13th Mechanized. Ample Annie and the others were not able to agree on likely invasion points, so if the enemy's gonna give us a little extra time, we'll push the units southwards from Rome so we don't risk turning the south of the country into one huge battlefield. Currently, we can field two hundred and fifty PeaceMakers in this theatre."

The image moved again to the left and down, so that the landmass of Greece, surrounded by hundreds of islands, moved to the centre. Jones continued: "The Hellenic Army also suffered quite badly yesterday, but General Kokinos assures me the action merely whetted appetites among his troops. Another two-hundred-and-fifty PeaceMakers have been deployed on this front. In addition, over the last few days the Greeks have been reinforced with elements of the Polish First Army under the command of General Pakla, and I think we all know how General Pakla and his troops will respond to any attempted invasion."

Terry smiled at the good-natured joke with the Polish general's reputation for his uncompromising approach to his profession.

The image withdrew to bring Bulgaria and northern Turkey into the frame. Jones said: "As a subsidiary front, we need also to take into account that the enemy will use the land border for the initial transportation of Caliphate troops. Our super AIs all forecast that for a swift and successful invasion, the enemy must use some kind of air transportation, a one-route land entry from Turkey will not be enough, and anyways we'd likely be able to contain that. On this fourth front, we're gonna have a mix of Bulgarian, Romanian, Polish, Hungarian and Serbian forces, and they'll be supported with another two hundred PeaceMakers."

The map shrank back into a thumbnail in the top-left of the screen to reveal Jones still sitting casually on the front of his desk. He went on: "In addition to the forces deployed, I think we can say we're now fully alive to the threat that's presented itself on our southern borders. I would like to thank all of you for the efforts you've been making in your own countries. The good news is that ACA production is forecast to increase over one thousand percent. German industry in particular says it can retool civilian plants in forty-eight to seventy-two hours, so let's hope the enemy gives us a few more days at least.

"Also, the UK and France have upped manufacture of battlefield support lasers. As most of you probably know, the key issue is the manufacture of parts which can't be replicated, then the logistics of deployment when we know that a massive invasion could start at any minute. Finally, I'm happy to let you know that the *USS George Washington* put to sea out of Naval Station Norfolk in the early hours. She'll steam up to Philadelphia and NY to protect the first convoy of material for Europe, which will leave this afternoon." A polite ripple of applause greeted this announcement. "So that's about where we are right now. Any questions?"

Terry recognised General Keller of the German Army, who spoke accented English from his thumbnail at the bottom of the screen: "We have to rely on civilian infrastructure to cope with the people fleeing north. Could not this be a greater hindrance than currently anticipated?"

Jones shrugged his shoulders: "We gotta work with these figures and hope the transport networks can stand the strain. We have to rely on the computers to manage the expected volumes and adjust according to how many civilians try to head north."

The Hungarian chief of staff then asked: "What's the naval situation? Does the enemy even have any ships?"

Jones shook his head: "Not so far as we've seen, but I wouldn't discount the Caliphate using ships for attack or for troop transport. One plus is that the US and Royal Navy still have five submarines in the Med. They were en-route to join the battle group last Tuesday so missed the action, which I think we should regard as a touch of good fortune. We are planning to use them for covert comms when the invasion begins. In addition, we've got another twelve subs en-route to the Med. Not sure yet what role they'll play, but personally I'm hoping the enemy will invade using surface ships and we'll have a say about how many troops he can land. Any more questions?"

Silence greeted his enquiry, so Jones said: "Okay. So thank you for attending, ladies and gentlemen. This afternoon there's a chiefs of staff meeting with virtual attendance mandatory for all chiefs and generals. We have an update briefing from US Strategic Command, who've been taking a closer look at the enemy's kit, and we'll be trying to establish ways of neutralising some of his advantages... while we've still got time."

Chapter 40

Trainee nurse Serena Rizzi returned to consciousness with her memories intact, so therefore with some surprise. She opened her eyes to see a magnolia ceiling above her. She recalled the last thing she had seen: the yellow stone arch at the Santa Maria hospital. She remembered the fleeting glance of Spiders as they clattered past the overrun reception area, down into earth outside the building. She sighed at the recollection of the ceiling coming down on all of them.

"Hello, how do you feel?" asked a nurse who had suddenly appeared next to the bed.

"I'm not sure yet," Serena replied with a weak smile. She could feel the smooth surface of a GenoFluid pack over her legs, and for the first time in her life, she understood what patients meant when they described a 'soft tingling' sensation as the pack worked. She looked up at the nurse and saw a face not much older than her own. The woman's dark eyes smiled with concern, and Serena noticed a large, brown birthmark in the middle of her right cheek.

"You're going to be all right in a few days, so try not to worry."

"I don't understand. How did I survive? I remember the building was coming down, the Spiders had destroyed—"

"You were saved by the arch you were standing under. It kept the debris off your body and head... but your legs will need some time to get better."

"Thank you," Serena said. "How many others were saved?"

The nurse looked downwards, and Serena knew the answer at once. The nurse said: "No one. I'm sorry."

Serena's mind ran to the injured citizens she and Doctor Benini and all the other staff had been trying to save, all the work wasted. She looked at the nurse now treating her: "What day is it?"

"Sunday."

"Good, only a day. Has the invasion started?"

"No, not yet."

"And how is Rome?"

Tears welled in the nurse's eyes, and she stammered: "Bad. The Vatican is destroyed. All of the culture, so much... Thousands are dead. It is the worst in the history of Rome, worse even than the Visigoths... I must go now, I have many more injured to attend to. You are very lucky to have a bed." The nurse dabbed the tears from her cheek and left Serena.

She laid her head back on the pillow and considered the last thing the nurse had said. Yes, she had been lucky, but why? Why was she alive when the entire building collapsed and everyone else perished? The seed of a resolution began to germinate inside Serena. In a moment of revelation, she realised she'd been spared for a reason, a higher purpose. She glanced along the bed and looked at the GenoFluid pack, staring and picturing its miniscule nano-bots going back and forth repairing and regenerating her smashed legs.

She whispered to herself: "A few days. Dear God, just grant me a few days."

Chapter 41

20.42 Sunday 12 February 2062

In Beijing, the Englishman's difficult day worsened in the evening, when he arrived at Marshal Zhou's private quarters in the compound. The Englishman didn't need to worry about the marshal's subordinates knowing of their liaisons, because the marshal enjoyed a great deal of power in his own fiefdom, but at the same time the Englishman suspected that other elements of the Chinese military also knew, and would use the knowledge for their own gain at the marshal's expense. On a normal day, the Englishman could manage and even gain a sense of pleasure from the danger.

But today had been problematic. The aide to the ambassador from whom he normally got his drugs had prevaricated. The Englishman needed the little white pills to ensure the marshal enjoyed himself sufficiently. The ambassador's aide said she didn't have any, then changed her mind and said she did. The exchange unnerved him, because although the taking of recreational drugs was officially frowned on, everyone accepted that it happened. The aide's reluctance might have been in response to a potential crackdown by the ambassador. And the Englishman did not want to have to find another supplier.

Then, while travelling across the city to the compound, he'd watched news feeds from England and other European countries which carried pictures of protests and demonstrations calling for peace at any cost. An overwhelming sense of futility enveloped him: if people were stupid enough to believe that such actions could or would have any bearing on the course of events, then they were likely to get exactly what they deserved.

The door to the marshal's apartment opened and the Englishman smiled.

"Come," said the marshal, his narrow eyes piercing into the Englishman's, and his fleshy jowls wobbling into a smile.

The Englishman entered; the door closed.

The marshal put his arms around the Englishman's waist and said: "I still miss you, every day."

"And I miss you," the Englishman replied, a touch automatically.

The marshal's eyes narrowed further. "You do not sound very sincere," he said. The suspicious look intensified. "You look like you do not miss me so much."

Inside, the Englishman cursed himself for his lapse of concentration. He stared back at Zhou's hostile suspicion. "I do, I do," he said. "It's just—"

"Just what, eh?"

The Englishman took a long breath and composed himself. A lie popped into his head and he told it easily: "I have family in Rome, and I can't reach them. My younger sister. She has an Italian boyfriend. They were visiting his family on vacation in the city, seeing all those sights that have now been destroyed."

The marshal paused, and the Englishman wondered if he would buy it. His features softened and he embraced the

Englishman. "My poor boy," he said. "You must be so worried."

The Englishman pulled back and gave out a sniffle. He nodded: "Thank you. Yes, the violence was truly terrible... I'm thinking of returning to the UK, I think I must—"

"No, you must not," Zhou broke in, appearing to take the conversation more seriously. "We talked. You will be safer here in Beijing. If you go back to Eur—"

"But the invasion could begin at any time. It could've started since I arrived here a few minutes ago. I'm very scared for my—"

Zhou's face flickered and he said: "Wait."

The Englishman stopped and sensed Zhou's demeanour change.

Zhou said: "Let us drink first. Did you bring our pleasure tablets?"

The Englishman forced a reluctant smile. "Yes," he said.

Zhou walked further into the apartment and entered the living area. The Englishman followed in silence. The far wall hummed as the cover to hidden shelves rolled upwards. Zhou selected two glasses and said: "I have some of the *Mei Kuei Lu Chiew* you like."

"Thank you."

Zhou took the bottle of the rose-flavoured *Baijiu* and poured generous measures. He offered one to the Englishman, who took it. "To another evening of wonderful escape," Zhou said.

Two hours later, groggy from the little white pills and the *Baijiu*, the Englishman realised that he hadn't felt this bad for a long time. He concluded that he was looking at two sides of the same coin: the thrill of the subterfuge also caused the occasional sick feeling. Perhaps, he reasoned, the cause did stem from the worsening situation in Europe. He glanced

259

back at the marshal. The darkness hid the details of his body, but he had been as energetic as usual and the Englishman could feel Zhou's semen escape him in a slick dribble.

"Thank you," the Englishman's lover whispered in the dark.

The Englishman laid back down and snuggled closer to the marshal. "I thank you," he whispered back.

"My dear," the marshal began, "I know you worry still, but there is little you or I can do to change what will happen."

"It's the uncertainty, that's the—"

"Then let me give you a small piece of certainty. The invasion will not start tomorrow or the next day."

"What? How can you—"

"Don't ask too many questions, my dear. I care about you, so I care also for those whom you care about. So tell them that they have until next Sunday morning, and then perhaps we can sleep a little better tonight, yes?"

Every nerve inside the Englishman tingled. Again, he wished he could question the marshal openly but he dare not. He chided himself silently: beggars can't be choosers, and he wasn't likely to get better intelligence from anywhere else. The temptation to tell London at once, to twitch his eye muscles and contact Control and tell them he knew when the invasion would start, drove his heart to beat ever faster. He felt certain the marshal must sense his excitement, but in a moment of abandon he decided he didn't care. All that mattered now was that he got the information to London.

The marshal surprised him when he suddenly chuckled and whispered: "We had a briefing today, and our intelligence said that the Third Caliph only wishes to make Europe wait on his pleasure. You can imagine the logistics involved in such an invasion, so he chose Sunday as the ideal compromise between keeping supremacy on the battlefield and allowing the greatest possible spread of terror."

The Englishman's throat had dried and his heart thumped, but in an effort to keep to the game he whispered back: "Thank you for giving my family a chance."

Zhou grunted: "I doubt it will make any difference, my dear. You should consider that Europe will soon have a new ruler."

Chapter 42

Professor Duncan Seekings trudged along the gravel drive towards the office attached to his lab. He'd spent the morning wracking his brains trying to establish how the fusion units in the Caliphate's ACAs worked. Now he had an important conference, but for the evening he'd promised his friend Graham a few frames of snooker. Part of his mind set to work thinking up excuses not to go.

He opened the door to his untidy office and muttered aloud: "On the other hand, it might be useful to bounce some ideas off him. Now, where's the bloody..." He searched around the room and spotted the glasses folded on a shelf among piles of papers and books. "Ah, good. Perhaps something to drink? No, it won't last that long. But what if it does? Oh well, let's hope it won't. Now then..." He settled down on the couch in the middle of the room which faced the only window.

He put the glasses on and looked around him. To his left and right, and in front of and behind him, several rows of other attendees extended out in a large semi-circle. Other heads did the same as his and twisted this way and that, despite the fact that a small attendance list resolved in the bottom-right corner of the view. The professor thought he recognised some faces, and then muttered to himself: "I'm sure everyone who should be here, is."

In the centre stood a podium on which leaned the imposing, broad-shouldered form of Bjarne Hasselman, the Secretary General of the North Atlantic Council, NATO's governing body. Next to him stood two younger men with a screen behind them that displayed the NATO crest.

"Ladies and gentlemen," Hasselman began, "good morning, at least to those of you from America, and good afternoon or evening or night to the rest of you. I would like to introduce to you two space warfare experts from the US Strategic Command, Mr John Parsons and Mr Dan Griffin."

The two Americans gave the audience confident, bright smiles, but Duncan scoffed inside as they appeared to him to be little older than teenagers, and he was amazed they could be considered experts at anything, apart from, possibly, how to tie their shoelaces.

Hasselman continued: "The NAC has identified the priority issues to which we need answers if we we're going to make any progress against the Persian Caliphate. Top of this list is their ability to prevent any electronic penetration of their airspace. Gentlemen?"

The Secretary of the NAC stepped away from the podium and took a seat in the audience. The taller of the two Americans, whose names the professor had already forgotten, stepped forward and spoke: "Hi everyone. Thanks for attending this North Atlantic Council meeting. And I just wanna remind you all that everything you see and hear is top secret."

Duncan scoffed aloud at that. A couple of heads nearby glanced at him, so he changed the settings to mute his own voice, that he might speak aloud in his office, but what he said would not be audible to any of the other attendees.

The American, either John or Dan, continued: "The Caliphate has been a closed political entity since its formation over twenty years ago."

The professor muttered: "Oh goody, let's start with the bleeding obvious, shall we?"

"Until a few days ago, that was much more a political issue than a military one, and I'm sure I don't need to give you folks a history lesson."

"Might be history to you, young fella, but some of us lived through that and it seems like only yesterday," Duncan said.

"If you look at this image behind me, you'll see what we call the 'Caliphate's Nest', a layered system of several tens of satellites which hold geostationary orbits over Caliphate territory."

Duncan became intrigued and analysed the image. It showed the locations of more than seventy satellites in orbits ranging from one hundred and fifty kilometres to over ninety thousand kilometres.

"Now, this nest is constructed to do two things: to prevent anyone outside Caliphate territory seeing in, and to stop any Caliphate subject seeing out. However, that hasn't stopped the USAF trying to breach this barrier. The problem is that our satellites can glean very little hard data before they go dark. For the last ten years or so, the information we've been getting has all pointed to a political entity which is stable and broadly peaceful, as its leaders claim.

"Over the last forty-eight hours, the USAF has mounted attacks on selected parts of the nest but to little avail. Our satellites are probably being taken out by more powerful lasers. It's likely the Caliphate might have developed different tech to us. Nevertheless, the key issue here is that, to break through their cloak of electromagnetic darkness, we need to destroy those satellites."

"Why are the attacks failing?" asked the German chief of staff.

"Er, excuse me?" the American stuttered.

"Why are the attacks failing?" the German repeated.

"As I said, we suspect our satellites are probably—"

"Why do you always say 'probably' and 'likely'? Do you not *know* anything?"

The professor could see the American's hold on his temper begin to slip. "I told you: we cannot be one hundred percent sure exactly how they are taking our satellites out."

"Pah," said the German dismissively, "it must be because they have more powerful lasers, which means they have much stronger power units."

The American replied with anger: "Sure, that's the easy route: just to assume you know what's going on. But you need to look at the variables. Light, especially when it's concentrated into a beam designed to burn something to destruction, behaves differently at different altitudes. Once you get to a certain height, you're transitioning from an air environment to an airless environment. We're attacking Caliphate satellites in broad elliptical orbits, which means the wavelengths—"

"Rubbish," the German shouted. "Super AI should easily compensate for such variables and millions more besides—"

"Wait," a new voice said. All heads spun to look at the speaker as he stood. Duncan recognised the young, slender man as one of the authors of a recent paper he'd read on the application of fusion tech in deep undersea exploration. "Oh what's his name? Louis something, from France... Ripper? Rayer? Reyer?" He looked at the attendance list to see the young man's name highlighted because he now spoke.

Reyer glanced at the attendees with a placid face. The English he spoke carried a heavy French accent: "This is really very clear to anyone who has even a basic understanding of nuclear fusion."

The German questioner said: "Would you care to enlighten us?"

Reyer replied: "It is the propulsion systems of their satellites which are the source of all our difficulties. And that is because they are built around a muon-based fusion reactor."

The professor scoffed and noted similar reactions from other attendees with a scientific background. He muttered: "And how do you think they've suffice—" but stopped when Reyer continued speaking.

"Their artificial intelligence must have truly found a needle in a haystack."

"And what's that supposed to mean?" asked one of the Americans, looking irked that his presentation had become an open debate.

The American received a Gallic shrug, and the professor found himself obliged to admit a grudging admiration for the young French nuclear physicist. Reyer continued laconically: "There are a very great many atomic and subatomic particles which have numerous uses. In a fusion reaction, a muon particle, in general, has only a one percent chance of sticking to an alpha particle. What has happened here, as anyone with even a modest knowledge of physics will realise, is that the Caliphate's computers have found a way to overcome this limitation on muon performance—"

"Oh yeah? How?" the American asked with a sneer.

Reyer's left eyebrow rose in a look of mild indifference. "Is it not obvious? Oh, I suppose not to—"

"Yeah, yeah, just get on with it, Frenchy," the American spat back.

Reyer's expression didn't change. He said: "My initial research suggests that in a certain type of high-pressured hydrogen-based containment field, it might be possible to generate substantially increased power. However, the parameters of this containment field are highly specific. What the Caliphate has achieved is several years ahead of where NATO is."

"That absolutely cannot be the goddamn answer to why their kit outmatches ours in just about every goddamn depart—"

"And that is just where you are wrong, Mr Parsons. It answers everything. It answers how their satellite nest can be so impregnable; it answers why their ACA shielding is so much stronger than ours; it answers how they can mount a laser on an ACA and give it the lethality and dexterity of their Lapwing. And it leaves NATO, and in consequence our countries, very, very exposed."

Even though he attended only virtually, Duncan sensed the shock as it rippled around the conference room. Then the American gathered himself and spoke with hesitation: "And can you share that 'initial research'?"

"It already is shared, automatically. Each NATO country's and armed service's artificial intelligence has access to it."

Parsons looked at his colleague and shrugged his shoulders. The colleague stepped forward and said: "Well, folks, it looks like Mr... Excuse me, what's your name, sir?"

"Louis Reyer."

"Thank you. It looks like Mr Reyer's contribution today has changed the fundamental dynamics and has, er, kinda—"

The man stopped talking as Duncan ripped the glasses from his head and thus left the conference. He got off the couch and paced around the room. "Well, well, well, a proper little genius… And French, too. Will wonders never cease?" He went through to a small kitchenette at the rear and put the kettle on. "Tea," he muttered. "Nothing can get solved without a decent cup of tea." He grabbed a mug from the sink and threw a teabag in it. "Squonk," he barked, addressing the Ministry of Defence's super AI, "Louis Reyer, French scientist. Access his research, please."

The kettle boiled and the professor made his tea. He spent the next two hours reviewing Reyer's research, his respect for the young French scientist increasing throughout. At the end, he stared into the cold, empty tea mug and muttered: "The fellow's right, of course. But it will take us years to catch up. And we're due to be put to the sword any day now. Hmm, tricky."

Chapter 43

07.42 Monday 13 February 2062

Corporal Rory Moore of 103 Squadron, 21 Engineer Regiment, Royal Engineers, fidgeted in his seat and wondered when they would finally get going. To either side of him sat the other members of Squad Delta Four-Two: Crimble, Pratty, and his adored Pip. Around them, the rest of 103 Squadron itched, bantered, and blathered their way through the minutes until their Commanding Officer deigned to speak to them. Rory looked up at the ceiling of the hangar and then around him at the rows of hundreds of his fellow Engineers, and felt the intense heat from the small ball of regimental pride inside him, which burned as fiercely as any sun.

An elbow in his ribs from Crimble brought him back to the moment. "Where d'you reckon they're sending us then, eh?"

"What?" Rory said in exasperation. "The Falkland Islands, I expect."

Crimble's eyes narrowed. "Really? You reckon?"

Rory despaired and replied: "No, not really."

From beyond Crimble, Pip pushed her slim body forward and said to the men: "I've heard the real name of the mission is Operation Certain Death."

"And that's why they'll get us to make a will before we embark," announced Pratty, reclining on the other side of Rory with his legs sticking out, ready to trip an inattentive squaddie.

Pip began: "Have you guys got anything worth making a will for, apart from—" but stopped when the sergeants around the hangar barked out an order.

At once, eight hundred royal engineers stood to attention as their commanding officer, Colonel Doyle, entered the hangar. He and his aide strode to a raised podium in front of the soldiers. Rory couldn't stop a wry smile forming on his face as he saw the colonel's moustache, an exact copy of which Crimble had grown.

The colonel stared at his troops for a moment, nodding in apparent satisfaction with an encouraging half-smile on his face, and then he said: "As you were." The soldiers sat back down and Doyle went on: "I won't keep you long. As you all know now, we expect an invasion of the European mainland by the New Persian Caliphate to begin at any moment. It is our job to make a major contribution to upsetting the Third Caliph and his outrageous plans.

"You are a vitally important part of the British Expeditionary Force. You are one of the first regiments to have the privilege of deploying to southern Spain, and it is highly probable that you will play a key defensive role when the invasion begins. You will have all support with which the armed forces of NATO, working in unison, can provide you.

"I shan't try to deceive you, troops. I have too much respect for you to do that. Operation Defensive Arc will see us outmatched and outgunned. However, I remain convinced that if NATO is to successfully defend the European mainland from this foe, which has so abruptly exploded upon us, you will find the resourcefulness to do so. Each of you, remember that you represent one thousand years of history of providing service to the British, now the English, crown. Take a moment to reflect on all that the royal engineers have achieved down the centuries, and understand that what you embark upon today is the next step in our on-going and illustrious history. Thank you."

The colonel took a step back. The sergeants barked and the soldiers stood to attention. The colonel saluted them, and the eight hundred returned the salute. Doyle and his aide strode off to Rory's left. A sergeant walked up to the podium, scooped it up and wandered off in the opposite direction. Rory heard a deep thump and the vast hangar doors in front of them slid open. The bright morning sunlight revealed a runway beyond, on which sat the three Autonomous Air Transports which would take them and their equipment to Spain.

Crimble stroked his moustache with a thumb and forefinger, and said: "Oh, look. Boeing 818s. I wonder how old they are."

"Any idea, Pratty?" Rory asked.

Pratty tutted and said: "Been in service twenty-one years, long-since superseded by the 828. Top speed Mach 6.5; maximum cargo weight—"

Pip broke in with a cheerful: "Maximum number of coffins that will fit inside it, Pratty?"

Crimble said: "You think Brass is going to have the time to put us in a coffin and bring us back?"

Rory said: "If they bring the Lapwings in, it'll be a cremation with our ashes scattered over Spain."

"And so Operation Certain Death gets underway," Pip said with her impish grin that made Rory's affection for her burn a little more fiercely.

Abruptly his Squitch indicated in his eyesight which AAT he and his squad should board. "Okay, guys, you got that?"

The other three mumbled their confirmations, and all four joined the other two-hundred-and-fifty royal engineers who trudged towards the foremost aircraft, as the rest split to board the other aircraft. Rory swallowed his affection for Pip back down yet again as he had so many times. They were heading into what would soon become a warzone, and the gallows' humour became as good a protection as their weapons would likely be when the invasion began.

Chapter 44

09.13 Tuesday 14 February 2062

Terry glanced at the attendees at the COBRA meeting and noted how the composition changed depending on what was on the agenda. Several people attended each meeting: the PM and her aide, the Head of MI5, David Perkins, and either other cabinet ministers or top civil servants. Junior ministers sometimes appeared, and today the conference table was crowded with three chief constables and two fire brigade chiefs.

Perkins prodded the screen in the desk in front of him and announced. "The new intel is clear: the invasion will not begin until this Sunday, 19 February. Our forces have five days to prepare."

"What about the source?" Terry asked.

"The same source as the data-pod which we all thought was planted evidence."

"Speak for yourself," Terry said. "How sure can you be that the source is still reliable?"

"We have in place a protocol if the source is compromised. The source claims they have good leverage over the contact that provides the intel."

"Can you tell us anything about the contact?" Terry asked.

"Only that it's very good."

"I should hope so," Terry said.

Perkins shot Terry a reproachful glance, and then said: "I've shared this intel with our allies, but I think this is a major breakthrough, frankly speaking."

Terry saw Napier smile ruefully. She said: "It is very useful, Mr Perkins, and I thank you for sharing it with our allies, but for us to regard new intelligence as a 'major breakthrough', it would have to involve a revelation which might offer us a slight chance of avoiding the bleak fate our computers tell us is a certainty."

Terry glanced at the civilians around the table and recalled the first COBRA meeting which the head of MI5 had attended just over two weeks before. Terry remembered how they'd dismissed his request to make extra funding available for increasing ACA production, and then Perkins had questioned his judgement. The assumed threat of an attack by the Caliphate then had been eight percent. Now it was ninety-eight-point-seven percent. With melancholy he thought of all the lives that had been lost in the intervening time, and all those yet to die. A voice inside reminded him of his duty and his job.

He spoke to Perkins: "Is there any way at all we could get corroboration from other sources?"

Perkins replied: "We're working hard, especially with the Americans. The CIA has some strong contacts in the Chinese conglomerates in Africa. If we do get corroboration, I will disseminate it at once."

"If we accept this intel as accurate, it should allow logistics to improve," Terry said. "But I don't think we should let the ground troops know."

Napier looked at him. "Can that be stopped? If we've already shared this with our allies, I'd imagine it will become common knowledge among the lower ranks quite soon."

"I have another North Atlantic Council meeting at eleven, and in any case I'll raise it with SACEUR before then."

"Very well. Now I'd like to bring in Chief Constable Holloway of the Surrey Constabulary. One of the strongest concerns, not only according to media outlets but also among the general population, is the threat of terror attacks on England and the Home Nations similar to those endured by Athens and Rome at the weekend. Chief Constable Holloway has been nominated to head a committee to establish the likelihood of such attacks and draw up recommendations regarding what can be done to ensure citizens' safety."

The chief constable, a dark-skinned middle-aged man whose flat nose and rounded jaw spoke of Slavic roots, cleared his throat and said: "The Civil Defence Committee has established some basic tenets. Firstly, according to the latest research, there is no question regarding whether the Caliphate's ACAs can reach the British Isles. According to our scientists, depending on how their power availability is utilised, they could have a range of up to one thousand kilometres."

Terry groaned inside. Holloway seemed to be one of those speakers for whom addressing any kind of audience or making an announcement led to a reliance on filler words. In addition, Holloway had a low monotone delivery which Terry was certain would put half the room to sleep in moments, and the rest not long afterwards.

The chief constable went on: "Second, should an attack on the Home Nations be launched, the security services would have no more than a few moments of warning. Unfortunately, it would be difficult to keep knowledge of an approaching attack from the general population—"

"But why ever should we want to?" Napier broke in.

Holloway looked surprised: "Panic, prime minister. We wouldn't want to cause unnecessary panic in the civilian population."

"So what do you propose?" she asked, incredulous.

"It would be helpful if we could put in place a system to limit citizens' ability to communicate. Built around key 'trigger' words, we would be able to—"

Napier erupted: "Absolutely out of the question. England is a free country. No matter the threat, I will not drag us back to the days of monitoring citizens to a level which all but obliterates their privacy. I can remember as a girl how those governments used to monitor everyone's mobile phones and their emails and completely destroyed any pretence that the general population had any privacy. And I swore then that, if I were ever in my life in a position to influence the issue, I would give ordinary citizens back their privacy."

Holloway stammered: "Yes, of course. You're quite correct. But these are not ordinary times. We face a mortal enemy—"

Napier's hand slapped down on the table and her voice dripped with sarcasm: "Really? Well, what can I say? How will we ever be able to thank you for pointing this out to us?"

Terry's senses came alive at the abrupt realisation that Napier may have been pushed too far. But at once flickers of a deeper thought process resolved on the prime minister's face. She exhaled, inhaled deeply and said: "Chief Constable Holloway, and the rest of you for that matter, we face something unprecedented in our lifetimes. For almost one hundred and twenty years, we have had peace in Europe. We have had problems, too, but for the most part, Europeans have been able to live the lives they wished to. Today, all that has gone. But as we choose how we best defend ourselves, we must not lose sight of what we are and what our country stands for.

"The people of England cannot be micromanaged in such a way as to deny them information to which they have a right. Besides which, any similar attack would likely cause thousands of casualties, so we need communities to help each other as much as possible. Certainly the police and fire brigades will be overwhelmed."

Holloway said with incredulity: "Have you seen the protests? How often do you get briefed—"

"Thank you, chief," Crispin Webb broke in with a sneer. "The PM is briefed regularly on current events—"

"That's good to hear," Holloway shot back. "Because ordinary people are frightened. They're feeling threatened, exposed, and can't believe that the authorities might not be able to protect them. In addition to the peace protests which we have sparking off every evening in numerous towns and cities, we're also seeing alarming increases in crime, and I have anecdotal evidence that hospitals are noting more suicides than usual."

Napier turned to Webb. "Crispin," she asked, "how many people died in sea defence breaches around the coast of England last year?"

Webb's eye twitched and he replied: "Three hundred and twenty-two confirmed drownings and disappearances; a further forty-three aggravated fatalities."

"How many people died in domestic accidents?"

"Eighty-one."

"And how many in road traffic accidents?"

"Nine."

Napier turned and her look took in everyone in the room. "We don't know how many perished in Athens and Rome, but we can be sure it runs to the tens of thousands.

That's a different kind of disaster, and it is ridiculous to pretend to the citizens of this country that their government and armed forces can somehow protect them from such an onslaught."

"If and when it happens," Holloway interjected.

"It already has," Napier replied in exasperation. "We've all seen the pictures from those cities, from Turkey, and worst of all the wholesale slaughter in Israel. This is what the people of England will shortly have to endure."

Holloway said: "One of the better suggestions I've received is to recreate the civil defence corps."

"What's that?" Perkins asked.

"A volunteer force, mainly of civilians. It existed from 1949 to 1968, and although run under the direction of the home office, each county's authority was pretty autonomous. Then, the corps' main duty was to be ready to respond to a nuclear attack. Given today's technology, something like this would be very useful in the event of a massed Caliphate ACA attack like those on Athens and Rome. In fact, we're already seeing local communities form unofficial virtual networks, detailing where the deepest cellars are located. Many are suggesting that in the event of an attack, local government super AIs should empty vehicle termini by sending all vehicles onto the roads so people can shelter in their underground parking areas."

Napier said: "That's an excellent idea, Holloway. Liaise with the Home Secretary and get the ball rolling on this. It's important these local communities see central government stepping up to support where possible."

Terry added: "These civil defence authorities could also coordinate the surveys for building shelters."

Napier sat back, apparently satisfied, and said: "Good. Now I only need to get the treasury on board."

Chapter 45

22.15 Tuesday 14 February 2062

"Maureen is still such a magnificent cook, Earl. I ain't never had a Beef Wellington as good as that," Studs Stevens said.

Terry smiled. "I think she appreciated your kind words, Suds. Shall we?" He opened the humidor and offered it to Stevens.

The American smiled at the sight of the four Montecristo number twos laying in an orderly row inside the box. He took one and ran it under his nose. Terry also took one and both men picked up their snifters. They strolled back to the chairs arranged in front of the panoramic windows that looked out over the English Channel a couple of hundred metres below.

They lit their cigars and Terry took in the familiar surroundings of the one indulgence in his home: the smoking room. The distant crash of waves washed off the windows and walls. Terry sipped his brandy and said: "I think the view is somehow better when it's dark."

"I agree," Studs replied. "We can picture our future more easily."

Terry grunted: "Easy for you to say. Tomorrow you get on an AAT and return to the US. And I've got a feeling you're going to be as safe as you Americans always are over there when there's a war in Europe."

Studs smiled and then asked: "What do you think about the intel?"

"The way things have been going so far, I'll take almost any intel at face value, Suds. I don't understand why the enemy waits like this. If he does have so many warriors and ACAs all ready to go, why the terror attacks on Athens and Rome? Why not simply come right at us, before we're even properly ready with the precious few defences we've got?"

"Looks like downright sadism to me."

"What's the mood across the pond, really, Suds? Napier and Coll aren't getting on, and we're going to need US help, like always."

Stevens sipped his brandy and said: "Coll may be the commander in chief, but the US doesn't go to war on the whim of any president. NATO has a pretty good image in Congress, Earl, and if she doesn't authorise the support for our NATO obligations, she'll have all kinds of problems. Anyways, she's been giving the authorisations just fine up to now, so don't worry."

"I witnessed the last call she had with the PM. It was real stilettos-at-dawn stuff."

Stevens chuckled. "I think Coll has the same problem as every leader of the European countries: twitchy populations who don't know if they want peace, or if they want security, or revenge."

"And hardly understanding that they won't get any of those; that the choice has already been taken away from them."

Stevens murmured his agreement and more spicy, woody cigar smoke wafted up to the ceiling. He asked: "How about your relationship with SACEUR?"

"Very good. I like General Jones."

"Yeah, he's one tough bastard."

"Just what I thought."

"How did today's NAC meeting go?"

Terry paused before replying: "There's a sense of unreality developing about them, Suds. Day after day we discuss deployments, strategies, and countermeasures. The computers run thousands of simulations based on hundreds of variables. But the numbers are hopeless. England, France, Germany and Poland will demand that their wings of PeaceMakers are needed for home defence, instead of pooling all our resources to make Defensive Arc as strong as possible. And you know the worst part?"

Stevens didn't answer.

"The reason they allude to but don't say out loud is because they think Defensive Arc is doomed from the outset."

"Jesus," Stevens breathed.

"Of course, when you look at what we've got and what we're likely to be hit with, that is actually a reasonable deduction. The damn computers are forecasting Europe's complete collapse in a matter of weeks... I really hate those bloody things."

Stevens let out another chuckle and said: "We sure rely on them far too much, Earl."

"But the youngsters have never known a time without them. A quarter of a century ago, these things were aides, and suddenly they just seemed to take over without anyone actually wondering if it really was the right thing to do."

"Ah, come on, that's true with so many things. But super-artificial intelligence was bound to be a game changer, and anyone would argue for the benefits—"

"I don't have a problem with the benefits, Suds, but I've got to think of morale, for Christ's sake. You remember the world war two bomber pilots over Germany, yes? On each mission they had a one-in-twenty chance of being shot down, but a tour of duty was set at thirty missions, so on the balance of probabilities they realised they were not going to make it through one tour of duty. Now, we've got to convince troops to fight and these troops have access to data which tells them that—"

"Whoa, hold on a minute. Back in the second world war, those airmen still flew, even though they knew the odds."

"Yes, because they would've been thrown in prison otherwise. What are my captains, colonels and brigadiers supposed to do if troops refuse to fight?"

"Earl, I understand you, I really do, but you need to look back a little further in history, at some of the truly heroic things our armies have done."

Terry blew cigar smoke out in front of him and took a large sip of brandy which, he thought, might have looked to Stevens like a gulp. He would never reveal the depth of his fears to anyone other than Suds, but now, late in the evening after a salubrious meal among the laughter and warmth of trusted friends, Terry revealed his anxiety for what the future held.

Terry glanced into Suds' weathered face, noting the progress of the scar above the airman's right eye, incurred during an exercise twenty years previously. This scar had deepened into his flesh as the years rolled by. Terry said: "We're heading for certain defeat, Suds. My boss, Dahra Napier, prime minister of England and first lord of the treasury, fears that she will be the last prime minister of England. What she does not seem to consider is that many of her subordinates share her despondency in their respective roles."

Stevens' faced hardened as he waved his half-spent Montecristo number two in Terry's face and spat: "Don't give me that goddamn mawkish bullshit, Earl. The reason you're the most senior soldier in the British armed forces is because you're the best they've got, you asshole. Yup, it sure looks like all of us are just about bent over the goddamn sty and the pig farmer is gonna stuff his dick up our asses, but that don't give you the right to get all goddamn mawkish for yourself. You got that, dumbass?"

The smoke from Stevens' cigar stung Terry's eye, but he did not react, absorbing the trifling pain as a real soldier should. At length, Terry replied: "I know, but please, my friend, allow me the luxury of a moment's despair for the lives I will cast into the furnace for no benefit. Grant me a measure of melancholy for the poor souls who will shortly be obliged to leave this Earth in the most excruciating physical pain imaginable—"

"Earl, you are really beginning to piss me off. You want me to start quoting Shakespeare at you? Which one of those plays was it where the king claimed that he was not responsible for his soldiers' deaths, huh? Something about all the arms and legs rising up from the Thames or some goddamn bullshit?"

"That was Hen—"

"I don't give a shit. That was then and this is now. Whatever you think, however you feel, Sir Terrance goddamn Tidbury, knight of the realm, His Majesty's loyal servant, you gotta drop all that history. Just let it go, man. Do your job. We have been soldiers all our lives. Sure, we never expected this—"

"And that was our biggest mistake."

"Horseshit. You know the history, Earl. Sure, much of what the Caliphate put out over the years was propaganda, but as long as it kept itself to itself, who really gave a shit? Just

285

tell me: how could we have known? Name one single way we could've found out what was really going on, huh? Contact with the outside world has always been restricted to trade at its ports. No diplomats, no missions, no NGOs, no transport, no nothing. Just a flurry of drowned wannabe defectors washing up on European shores with hearts shredded by nano-bots."

Terry's forehead creased: "There must have been something we could've done."

"They've had over twenty years to get their shit together. I'm willing to bet the Second Caliph was actually the least mad, but number three has really excelled himself."

"Pity our clever computers didn't see this coming, isn't it?"

Stevens puffed out another cloud of blue smoke. "They did. They—and we—just didn't give it any priority. They said the chances of something like this were so small," he shrugged, "so we didn't give it the attention it actually deserved. We took the average probabilities and defended ourselves according to those forecasts."

"Suds, I've never had a problem risking troops for a fair tactical or strategic gain, but this invasion, when it comes, is going to be—"

"The defining moment of your career as a soldier, Earl. That's what it's gonna be because that's what it's gotta be. You know you're not the first general to face what, on the surface, appears to be certain defeat. What NATO troops have to do is slow the invaders down. Once they're outside Caliphate territory, we'll only have to find and exploit their weaknesses, and there ain't no invading army in history that ain't had some weaknesses. Remember, we'll have home advantage."

Terry gave Stevens a rueful smile. "I hadn't looked at it like that. Must be old age."

"There's one other thing,"

"What's that?"

286

"We've got millions of refugees on the move, and one of our jobs is gonna be making sure as many of them can escape as possible."

Terry lifted his snifter up and toasted: "To the invasion, then."

Stevens eyed his comrade and repeated the toast.

Chapter 46

Berat Kartal's feet hurt. He felt as though he'd been walking all night, but he'd woken only an hour or so earlier. Since the attack on Athens the previous Saturday, he'd pushed on. He understood now he was truly a refugee: he had no money and he relied on the charity of others. A part of his brain told him he should seek some casual labour to get money to eat properly and perhaps buy a bike, but he chastised himself for old thinking. The rationality of his life up until a week earlier made no more sense than behaving as though the moon really were made of cheese. Now, rationality served only a single purpose: survival.

On his right, the early sun of the new day rose higher and its light flashed off the surrounding hills and low mountains as he kept trudging on the endless road. His feet hurt because of the blisters on his soles. Since Saturday, he calculated he'd walked over one hundred kilometres. He kept records of time and distances in his paper journal, so appreciated his figures could be inaccurate, but the absence of modern tech forced him to utilise his academic abilities to the maximum.

On the road that headed north-eastwards, the occasional autonomous vehicle crept past him and the other refugees, packed full of people. Often, they were obliged to travel at less speed than even a bike due to the refugees moving on foot. Those lucky enough to have secured a place aboard a vehicle cast disapproving glares down at the more unfortunate people who had to walk. Without those walkers getting in the way, the autonomous vehicles would be able to increase their speed, but he sensed that few of the refugees on foot felt any sympathy for those in the vehicles. Berat reflected that none of them knew if or when an invasion would begin; the one thing they had in common was the desire to remove themselves from the potential battlefields.

Berat looked at the hills and low scrub mountains which surrounded him and thought how pleasant it would be to climb them. He sighed in resignation at yet another clash of the rationality of yesterday with the brutal reality of today. The stinging pain from his soles made him want to rest again, but he knew he must push on for another two hours at least before the sun rose high and the heat increased.

He'd wanted very much to try to gain a seat on an official government autonomous transport leaving the area, but he could not justify any entitlement to such convenience. He was a fit young man of twenty-three years—how could he plead for charity and take a place from which a child or a disabled or elderly person could benefit? Given his youth and physical fitness, no matter how much rationality screamed at him to claw any advantage he could to escape the coming storm as quickly as possible, an overwhelming sense of justice forced him to take the harder path, on the chance that someone less fortunate than him may find a place and have an opportunity to escape.

He trudged on, experimenting with each footfall how he might minimise the pain, landing his foot on the left edge, then the right, then the heel. The most painful blisters were on the ball and around the edges. For a few steps he gave up and accepted the agony, and then tried again to find a less painful way to land his feet on the ground.

He overtook other refugees frequently, for they were often families struggling with small children or elderly relatives. From time to time he heard the Turkish language, but his reticence kept his own mouth closed. In any case, he suspected no one fleeing Athens would have any knowledge of his home country. He sensed most of the other people fought against their own fears; more than a few men had over the last three days opinionated loudly in their groups, but Berat could not understand them. The sounds of the wailing children and quietly sobbing grandmothers required no translation.

Berat heard a commotion begin in the distance behind him and grow louder as it neared. He stopped and turned around. Other people further back waved and some gave little cheers at something travelling in the field next to the road, throwing up a cloud of dust behind it. For the first time in days, he smiled in joyful shock as an old tractor went trundling past the line of refugees. Its driver, a middle-aged man with dark, leathered skin, stared ahead with a look of grim determination. Around him clung a woman and five children of various ages. Berat's smile broadened as the tractor continued, and marvelled at the farmer's ingenuity: the machine was decades old and probably hadn't been used in years, and the farmer must have stockpiled the special fuel for it because it was almost impossible to purchase.

He followed the little cloud of dust as the tractor continued on its way, grateful for a brief, unexpected respite from the relentless need to flee. He put his head down, gritted his teeth in anticipation of the pain from the soles of his feet, and continued walking.

Chapter 47

Crispin Webb stared at the boss's lined face and wondered if she really was starting to age or if it was just his imagination.

She lifted her head, looked at him, and said: "Do I look so bad, Crispin?"

Wrong footed, Crispin stammered: "No, er, of course not, boss. You know, these are tough days for all of us."

Napier shrugged and got up from the couch. "In some ways, very tough; in others, less so." She walked over to the window and looked out at the grey-slate rooftops of Whitehall which matched the slate-grey clouds. "I should thank you, the media are behaving much better now."

"No need to thank me, boss. You wrote the memo. You know, not all of them are ever going to be on board—"

"Like all things in politics, I only need a majority," she said, turning back to face him, and they shared a smile. She went on: "And the majority are on board now. Did you see that feature in *The Mail* today?"

Crispin nodded, "That will make people reconsider, and world war two is the last really serious war we were involved in, even though it was so long ago. If media outlets can keep going back to that great victory, it'll help us. And it was funny: you know how we use the idiom 'Dunkirk spirit'? I never knew the etymology behind it until I read that feature article today."

Napier shook her head: "Don't they teach you kids anything at school these days?"

Crispin felt relief to see a spark of the old boss, as she smiled so rarely now. He said: "I went to St. Paul's, and some of their AI teaching assistants were very good. But that's not what matters at the moment. The media is organised, next we need to—"

"When's the next cabinet meeting?"

"Midday."

"Euro leaders' conference?"

"One-thirty. I managed to get you half an hour for lunch after cabinet."

"Thank you. Will President Coll attend the ELC?"

"Er, hang on," Crispin's eye muscles twitched and his glance drifted. Then he said: "Looks like it. It's in her calendar, even though it'll be six-thirty over there."

"Good. What's the latest on the civil defence groups?"

Crispin's eye muscles manipulated the data feeds in his lens again and he answered: "Hmm, the chief supers have got the working groups up and running. They're using the police forces' super AI to coordinate the details."

"How soon will they be operational?"

"Recruitment is under way and many local community groups are responding positively to it. Training will begin next week, once suitable candidates have been selected and interviewed. This is good, boss. You're successfully reaching out to the grass roots and that's pushing up your approval ratings."

"Oh, jolly good," Napier replied, and Crispin caught her familiar sarcasm. "That will be extremely helpful when I seek re-election… Oh, no, it won't, because I've just remembered that Europe is about to be invaded and destroyed, and I am the last prime minister of England."

"Boss, you can't know—"

"It's all right, Crispin," Napier replied. "In some strange way I feel freer than I ever have. Freed from all that politicking and sniping to score points from the opposition; freed from having to waste energy worrying about so many little things that used to take on so much relative importance in peacetime. But now? Can you imagine, Crispin, that all of us here might only have a few weeks left to live, that all of this history which we inhabit and continue, the hundreds of years of tradition, all of it could be gone in the flash of Spiders' detonations?"

Crispin swallowed and realised he didn't want to talk about it. It seemed too severe, too unreal. The look in his boss's eyes unnerved him in the extreme, so he decided to do what a good employee should do, and deflect her. "Yes, well, boss, until that actually happens, we have to keep the ship of state on an even keel—"

"Oh, quiet," Napier interrupted him, tucking a strand of auburn hair behind her ear. "So how are we going to raise the required funds for rearmament? Have you heard from Pamela at the treasury? What's the state of our gold reserves?"

Crispin said: "We do still have over two hundred tonnes… Perhaps you would like to read her memo?"

She shook her head. "Summarise its conclusions for me, would you?"

Crispin knew his boss's deep dislike for figures. She was a strong humanist and a brilliant strategist, but little irritated her more than numbers and the world of financing. He said: "We can increase the money supply in the country to accelerate national production of ACAs; we can sell gold reserves to expand our ability to build defences—"

"I was in touch with Tom," Napier began, recalling her verbose and evasive Chancellor of the Exchequer, "and he said something about a bond issue, or was it promissory notes? Can we do that?"

"We can certainly try, boss," Crispin replied, keeping the groan of frustration inside him.

"But?"

"Let's put it like this: asking international investors to buy bits of paper from the government of a country over whose very existence hangs a dark cloud of uncertainty means that the return we'd have to offer to get them to bite would have to be so high that even if England survived until maturity, the pay out obligations would bankrupt the treasury."

"So you'd say that's a 'no' then, would you?"

Crispin nodded. "Pam has said one idea gaining traction at the treasury is to suspend Universal Basic Income payments to free up more—"

Napier shook her head: "Can't stop paying the U-Bee, that's one of the untouchables."

"As I said, that's just hearsay. Pam doesn't expect Tom to put it forward at cabinet."

"Wouldn't matter if he did, no one else would support the idea in any case so it would be a waste of time."

"I'll communicate that back through Pam, just to be on the safe side."

Napier sighed and said: "And tell Pamela to encourage Tom to find some other working solution, even if it's just to print more money."

"Very well," Crispin replied, and then noted new data running up the feeds in his lens. "Ah, boss. Getting new data."

"What is it now?" Napier asked with the faintest trace of resignation.

"More bad news, I'm afraid. The met office is forecasting progressively increasing high tides, up to a maximum swell of an extra two metres on Sunday morning."

"A metaphor for the tide of violence about to engulf Europe?"

A small flare of panic flashed inside Crispin when he glanced into his boss's eyes. He'd never seen her look so vulnerable yet distant; so wounded yet serene. He groped inside to find some words, any words. "Boss... We didn't choose this. We didn't ask for this and no one, absolutely no one, could've seen this coming. It's not our fault—"

"Of course it isn't. We are but the custodians of the end." She crossed the room and approached him. "I was talking to my husband in bed last night, and he suggested that I should try to be as careful and prudent as possible, lest history judge my premiership too harshly. Do you know what I said to him?"

Crispin shook his head, barely able to draw breath.

Napier whispered: "I said: 'What history?' You see, we are but custodians of the end, my dear Crispin. We have mere weeks, possibly months, and all of our history ends. And before it gets to us, before the Spiders and Lapwings level the houses of parliament and all London, I am obliged to send thousands of innocent people to their deaths."

Crispin didn't blink, but did manage to breathe in.

Napier took a step back. "Time's getting on. Let's get to cabinet. As you said, we still need to keep the ship of state on an even keel, especially as we sail towards the iceberg." She turned and made for the door, and then added over her shoulder: "They did teach you about the *Titanic* at school, didn't they?"

Chapter 48

L ieutenant General Studs Stevens stood at the rear of the underground command control room at the vast March Air Force Base in southern California and observed the young techs monitoring the progress of the attack which had just begun in the high atmosphere above the territory of the New Persian Caliphate.

He fought to overcome the jetlag, having arrived back from England only a few hours earlier. He'd slept fitfully on the flight, unnerved by Earl's near-implosion after dinner on the Tuesday evening, and now felt his concentration drifting as the USAF's PeaceMaker ACAs converged on the western rim of the Caliphate's satellite nest. He put this down to old age: all of his physical senses seemed to desert him for a second, and he felt as though he might collapse, until they suddenly returned and he could focus once again.

Stevens felt another stab of regret that he'd been born too late. The USAF, like England's RAF and the air forces of every other country, employed no pilots. All air forces were entirely made up of tech specialists and maintenance teams, and their superiors. But even these were seldom needed: the tech teams monitored the super artificial intelligence units as they self-diagnosed and self-corrected any problems, and the maintenance teams merely supervised the robots which repaired and maintained the ACAs.

Stevens had joined the USAF just as human pilots became redundant. More than two decades had passed since a human had flown a combat mission. There was still great enthusiasm for amateur flying of upgraded old aircraft at public air displays, but these remained firmly in the realms of pastime. Humans flying the last piloted planes into war against modern ACAs and expecting to win made as much sense as a caveman taking his cudgel and expecting to best a machine gun post.

One of the tech sergeants sitting around the command control desk announced: "Attack wings approaching targets. Are we gonna be discreet, sir?"

Stevens pushed himself off the wall and strolled up to the desk, stopping behind the tech sergeant's seat. "Hell no, sarge," he said. "We're at war now, and there ain't no need to pretend we're just going for a stroll in low-Earth orbit, minding our own business. Now we can hit them head on. You send both wings in and give 'em hell."

"Yes, sir," came the satisfied reply.

Above the large desk, a holographic representation of the battlespace above Caliphate territory shimmered. At its centre sat an image of the Caliphate 'nest', seventy satellites in orbits ranging from one hundred and fifty kilometres to over ninety thousand kilometres, represented by gold pyramids with information panels next to them. From outside this space, several silver lines approached them from over the Atlantic Ocean, climbing rapidly.

"Okay," the tech sergeant said, "Ample Annie has decided the best target is a group of four Caliphate machines at an altitude of eight-five thousand metres, and it projects a near-certainty that their destruction will open electronic signals traffic."

"Monitoring stations?" Stevens asked.

"All report active and following events as they unfold. If we breakthrough, we'll scoop up whatever leaks out."

Stevens breathed easily as the confrontation unfolded. Not for the first time, his regret at missing the era of manned warplanes was tempered by the realisation that the approaching confrontation would see zero casualties. In a few moments, tonnes of intelligent metal and explosives would clash but no people would be killed.

"Ample Annie is launching Ramparts in ten, nine, eight..."

As the tech sergeant counted down, Stevens watched the holographic display, hoping for the best but fearing the worst. The US military's super AI, Ample Annie, forecast a probability of this mission's success—defined as any signals' breach of the Caliphate's airspace—at between seven and sixteen percent. But everyone from the President down wanted to do something, anything, to attack the enemy, and to be seen doing so. The instinctive reaction had been to throw hundreds of missiles, everything the USAF had, at the Caliphate's nest, but Stevens convinced the Chief of Staff and the Secretary of Defense that making a more moderate first attack was the better tactical option.

"Ramparts away," called the tech sergeant.

In the display, more lines of silver light left the PeaceMakers and accelerated ahead of them towards a group of four gold pyramids in the middle of the image. Stevens sensed more expectation than the attack deserved.

"Okay," the tech sergeant began again, "Ramparts at Mach seven and increasing... Enemy satellites discharging now… Ramparts taking evasive action… Exterior temperatures rising…"

Stevens shook his head as, one after the other, the silver lines denoting the Rampart missiles disappeared. A ripple of tuts and groans went around the room as the Caliphate's satellites vaporised the last missile.

The tech sergeant reported: "All missiles destroyed; no digital breach of Caliphate airspace made."

Stevens hid his disappointment. "Okay, people. Thanks for all your effort. Ample Annie will have some useful data from this attack anyway, so that's one good thing to take away."

The tech sergeant who'd narrated the brief encounter sat back in his chair and muttered: "Goddamn ragheads. We should be using our nukes. They'd piss right through their satellites' shielding, no problem."

Stevens caught the comment. He went back to the man, leaned down and said to him: "You know something? Nothing would make the chief raghead happier than if we went at him with our nukes. And you know why?"

The tech sergeant gulped and said: "Er—"

"'Cos then he'd take 'em out and come at us with his own nukes. Israel tried that, and you remember what happened to Israel, don't you?"

Chapter 49

14.44 Thursday 16 February 2062

Maria Phillips walked past the shops along East Grinstead high street. She pulled her jacket tighter against the strong breeze that carried spats of rain. She marvelled at how her life, and the lives of everyone she knew, had changed so completely in the last few days. One week earlier, her biggest fears had centred on her older brother Mark and his near constant immersion in gaming worlds. She also recalled some minor health scare concerning her father, but only that it involved him having to make a few dietary adjustments.

Now, as she walked towards her home, she saw two police officers and a municipal manager supervising a small device about the size of a dog as it trundled slowly along the road. She took out her slate, spun it open, and the screen told her the device checked the status of super-AI node connections under the road. Maria shook her head when she realised that the super AI could do that itself with almost one hundred percent reliability.

"That's how sure they want to be," she murmured to herself.

A few minutes later, she arrived at her home, one dwelling in a uniform row of semi-detached houses, anonymous like so many others in the streets around hers. The door opened at her approach as she looked up to make sure Billy still sat on the ridge tiles on the roof. She smiled and recalled the day she'd first seen the large wooden rabbit her father had carved for her as a birthday gift. But that was so many years ago. Billy was weathered now, the brown wood having faded to a dirty grey, but she loved him still.

She went through the door, glancing at her slate to see that only her mother and brother Mark were at home. "Hi, Mum," she called out.

Jane emerged from the living room and hugged her as the front door slid closed again.

Maria saw the redness in her mother's eyes. "What's happened?"

Jane sighed, "It's your brother."

"Mark?"

"Of course. It would hardly be Martin."

Maria followed her mother through the hall and into the kitchen. "Do you really think he will join the Armed Forces?"

Jane put the kettle on. "I expect so. As the oldest, Martin's always been the most responsible of you lot."

"So what's the matter with Mark?"

"A package arrived for him."

"What was it?"

Jane put two mugs on the surface and sighed. "He's gone and got himself a total immersion suit."

"But he agreed he wouldn't do that," Maria exclaimed, horrified. "Depending on the model, he could spend days in a Universe at a time."

Her mother shuddered. "And do you know how they do that? The suit has got... 'sacks' where he'll... go to the toilet, which he'll have to empty when he does come back. Really, it's disgusting."

Maria felt a flash of sympathy and decided not to tell her mother what happened at the World Gaming Championships held every year in Australia, where such issues had been known to decide winners and losers in a number of categories. "But how did he get the money for that? I never thought he'd—"

"He was here, not twenty minutes ago. He was angry. I asked him the same thing."

"And?"

Maria's mother poured the boiling water into the mugs, put the kettle back on its UG point, and sniffed. "He said he'd finally achieved sponsorship. And his new sponsor paid for the suit."

"Oh no," Maria said, realising that now the family had all but lost Mark.

Mother and daughter hugged again, both close to tears, and Maria wondered how they could ever get Mark back.

Her mother sniffed, "You never think it'll happen to you. You always think that's the kind of thing that happens to other people, other families."

"Mum, things are going to change soon, and Mark won't be able to stay in those Universes. Do Dad and Martin know?"

"Not yet. Your father will go nuclear."

"Only to start with... But I think we're about to have much worse problems, Mum. And soon, too."

"It's going to be awful, dear. I just can't imagine what it's going to be like."

Maria held her mother, gently kneading the thin flesh around the bony knuckles of her mother's spine. Through the material of her mother's cardigan, the flesh felt withered and old, and a new resolution took shape inside Maria. "I'll tell Dad about Mark, don't worry," she whispered. Maria could feel time advancing and sensed the onrush of futurity. War was coming; a brutal and violent war the like of which Europe had not seen in generations, and it had to be faced without fear. Maria realised abruptly that the time to put aside childish things had arrived, and her parents' generation were ill-equipped to face down the approaching storm.

Her embrace of her mother tightened, and she lied: "Try not to worry, Mum. I'll make sure we'll all be okay, one way or another."

Chapter 50

09.11 Friday 17 February 2062

Corporal Rory Moore looked at Squad Delta Four-Two and tried not to think too hard about what might await them when the invasion began. He brought up the rear on their patrol among the hills of a national park not far from the Spanish coast. In front of him bobbed the heads of Crimble, with the same moustache as Colonel Doyle, who'd seen them off with a rousing speech and smart salute four days earlier. Then came Pratty, with his insufferable indifference which he deliberately used to mask his loyalty to the regiment, and then, just in front of him, Philippa 'Pip' Clarke, who, he suspected, might be tougher than any of the men.

Their patrol was not especially draining. The Spanish commander of the forward base to which they'd been posted had struck Rory as being slightly unsure of what to do with the multinational force that NATO had bestowed on him, so training and patrol rotas had been organised and he and his squad were happy to be occupied.

Rory enjoyed the fresh, mild air and the views the Sierra Nevada Mountains offered. The sky above them shone bright blue and the rocky terrain made him feel as though they traversed the slopes of another planet.

From the front of the line, Crimble called back: "How the hell do we train to defend against an ACA attack anyway?"

Pip answered: "Get underground and stay there?"

"Nah, I'm serious. How, exactly, are we supposed to defend ourselves against those ACAs what the ragheads have got?"

Rory spoke: "Your ability not to pay attention during briefings is amazing, Crimble. We're not here to fight the ACAs; we've got our own machines for that. We're here to fight an invasion, if and when they invade."

"Yeah, but look," Crimble replied. "If those ACAs they've got are so much better than ours, then it's fair to assume all their other kit is gonna be better too, right?"

Rory ignored Crimble's observation and said: "Let's have a slurp on that outcrop. The view will be lovely. We can chin-wag up there. Off you go, Crimble."

Crimble's gangly legs looked like two pistons going underneath his Bergan backpack. Rory twitched an eye muscle to raise the feed from Crimble's Squitch into his own view.

"Getting this, corp.?"

"Yup, looks nice. Anything else going on?"

"Squitch says: 'Nope'."

"Okay. Squad, let's go."

Rory let Pratty and Pip go ahead of him and followed them up to the outcrop. A few minutes later, all of them rested on or next to their packs, canteens in hand.

Crimble stroked his moustache with his thumb and forefinger, pointed and said: "Look, you can see the raghead's lands over there."

Rory joined the others to stare out at the vital landscape. The mountain fell away from the outcrop on which they perched, lower hills continued southwards and disappeared into the Mediterranean, and beyond the turquoise water a mass coloured Aztec gold shimmered distantly.

"So I assume they can see us, then?" Pip said with irony. "Up there, in the sky, all their bloody satellites can see us quite clearly. What's to stop them sending an ACA down to sort us out?"

Rory replied: "Because its approach would trigger a response from our own—"

"But ours are no good against theirs, corp.," Pratty said, scratching his ear. "That is one thing we do definitely, absolutely, comprehensively, fucking know."

"But are you sure?" Crimble asked with a grin.

Rory said: "I have it on good authority that we are currently at no great risk."

Pip whistled through her teeth and said: "Oh, where did you hear that?" She looked at the others. "Our corporal must have been doing some serious brown-nosing."

A wave of chuckles floated around the outcrop, and then Pratty nodded at Rory and asked: "What's the inside info, corp.? Do Brass know what's going on, really?"

Crimble scoffed: "Since when have Brass ever known what's going on?"

Rory decided it wouldn't hurt to share what he knew with his squad: "There's been some intel floating about, but it's unverified so Brass won't include it in briefings—"

"Yeah, and even if it was verified, they wouldn't tell us just to keep us on our toes," Pratty said with cynicism.

Rory went on: "They reckon the invasion will start Sunday morning."

"How sure are they?" Pip asked without humour.

Rory shrugged, "I dunno, for certain. I've heard that it's being treated as pretty solid among the COs and Brass, and I don't think we'd be out on patrols like this if they really thought the shit could kick-off at any minute."

"Yeah," Pratty said, "and we've noticed the absence of our heavy kit. Even if we wanted to be Engineers, it's pretty difficult to engineer anything with all our construction replicators still back in Blighty."

Pip grunted her agreement. "We're out here to be infantry. Like I said, this is Operation Certain Death, guys."

Rory nodded at the landscape and said: "So let's enjoy the view while we still can, then."

"You know what I don't get?" Crimble asked, his forehead creasing in confusion.

Rory swapped amused glances with Pratty and Pip. Pip said: "Go on then, Crimble, what don't you get?"

"How will we know when the invasion starts?"

Pratty said with open sarcasm: "Well, there might be a few clues. What do you think those clues might be, Crimble?"

Crimble thought for a moment and then said: "No, what I mean is, this must be one of the most one-sided face-offs in history. Look, we've always trained for war with the Russians, right?"

"Yeah," Pratty broke in, "one hundred and thirty million alcoholics pretending to be a nation state. Some war that would be."

"But we know what they've got. We know what ACAs they'd attack us with. We'd have a pretty good idea of their order of battle, of the tactics we could expect them to use against us. But now, today, we ain't got no intel at all."

"Crimble's right," Pip said, stretching her arms above her head.

Rory reminded himself not to glance at the swell of her breast under her uniform as she stretched.

Crimble went on: "Here we are without a clue, really. We're preparing for an invasion by an enemy and we have absolutely no idea about them."

310

"Apart from the fact that they're a bunch of right vicious fuckers," Pratty observed.

Rory took a long pull from his canteen and then said: "We can make educated guesses."

"Like what, corp.?" Crimble asked.

Rory was tempted to play on Crimble's lack of intelligence for humour as he would if they were in the UK, but decided not to. "Look, so far they haven't used any surface ships, right?"

Crimble frowned, "Right," he said.

"So it's likely they don't have a navy, or if they do, they're keeping it very secret."

"They don't need one with those bloody ACAs," Pratty said, shaking his head. "Seriously, did you see what those bastard Lapwings did to Israel? How the hell can they get a battlefield-powerful laser on an ACA and fly it around like a fucking smart missile? Totally out-fucking-rageous."

"Maybe they'll keep hitting us only with ACAs, just to keep up the terror attacks like on Athens and Rome?" Pip suggested.

"That's up to them," Rory conceded. "But seeing as the Tosser of Tehran did announce that all Europe was going to be assimilated, I think an invasion is a certainty. And when it comes, I reckon they'll be flying in."

"So I suppose the Spaniards have identified the most likely landing points?" Pratty asked.

Rory nodded.

"Maybe something's changed in the meantime?" Crimble suggested.

"Like what?" Rory said.

"I dunno, maybe there's been a coup? Maybe their forces are too stretched with assimilating Turkey?"

Rory noticed the surprised expressions on the others' faces, along with his own, in reaction to the fact that Crimble should have developed such a grasp of the international dimension.

"Well done, Crimble," Pratty said, giving Crimble a playful slap on the shoulder. "On the other hand, maybe the vicious bastard just wants to make us all sweat. You saw how many refugees are fleeing north to try and escape."

"Yeah," Crimble replied. "I read about it in the media. There was a good column by someone which said that maybe after all the loss of life in Turkey, Israel, Athens and Rome, they hadn't invaded because there'd been a coup."

Pip said: "I wouldn't buy that, Crimble. I reckon the Caliphate is so controlled no one inside knows anything about what's going on outside it, in exactly the same way—"

"The Terror of Tehran must have told his military, for sure. So some of those people know," Rory said.

"Enough to lead to a coup? I doubt it," Pip replied.

"Right," Rory said, getting up. "That's enough of a chinwag. Let's push on for a couple of hours before heading back to barracks."

Pratty said: "Right you are, corp. Only can we move down to lower ground? You know, just in case there's a bored raghead over there who's seen us and fancies sending one of their bloody machines to fry us, you know, just for a giggle, and we don't have a hundred PeaceMakers to take it out, okay?"

The squad heaved their Bergan packs on to their backs. Rory looked at the others, and then spoke to Pratty: "Private Ian Pratt. You make a very strong case for discretion in the face of a potential enemy attack. Your appraisal of our current situation is tactically sound, well done."

A smile spread across Pratty's face which revealed uneven teeth with gaps between most of them. "Why, thank you, corp."

"You're welcome," Rory said. "However, we're going to stay on the high ground because I happen to enjoy the views. Now, shut the fuck up and let's go."

Chapter 51

16.28 Saturday 18 February 2062

Terry Tidbury's adjutant, John Simms, told the door to open and took a step back. "This, Sir Terry, is the new War Room."

Terry strode through the doorway and into the spacious area full of grey steel and black screens. "Squonk," he called. "What's the layout?"

The gender-neutral voice of the super AI spoke in measured tones: "The layout is designed for maximum comms efficiency and takes into account the fundamental limitations of human physicality."

Terry sighed and shook his head: "Let me do the jokes, Squonk," he said.

Light from the ceiling increased over a green, table-height circular surface in the middle of the room. Squonk said: "This area will display the relevant battlespace, expanded or retracted as required, in real time insofar as sufficient data is available."

With a gentle hum, the light close to the walls of the room increased to give greater detail to the control stations with large screens above them. Squonk went on: "Each of these comms stations prioritises contact with various departments, branches and authorities." The lights increased over specific stations as Squonk listed their function: "Here is Home Nations comms, including priority comms to civil defence units, national emergency services and hospitals throughout England and the Home Nations. This station is for British military comms, prioritising comms to army, navy and RAF units and HQs. The station here is Europe comms, for civil defence comms with all at-risk European countries. And here is NATO comms, prioritising comms with SACEUR and all European military command centres."

Terry paced around the room, nodded in satisfaction and said to Simms: "No expense spared, eh?"

Simms replied: "Quite so, Sir Terry."

"And how about the staff?"

Simms tilted his head in acknowledgement and left the room.

Half an hour later, Terry, Prime Minister Napier and her aide, Crispin Webb, and Defence Minister Phillip Gough stood behind the operator seated at the NATO comms station. The operator, a flaxen-haired young woman with a low forehead that gave the impression of permanent concentration, announced: "We're still waiting for a number of participants from—" she stopped as the face of General Joseph E. Jones filled the screen.

"Okay, let's get started, we won't wait for the others. They'll have to catch up when they join."

Terry and Napier swapped curious glances.

Jones continued: "Latest intel shows that the hostile situation remains unchanged. According to diplomatic sources in Beijing, among the higher echelons of politicians and their military, it is accepted as common knowledge that the Caliphate will invade Europe in the early hours of tomorrow morning. Despite the most intense diplomatic efforts by all countries, to give a soldier's opinion, I believe the rest of the world has pretty much shrugged its shoulders. They might care, but not enough to actually do anything.

"Ample Annie and the super artificial intelligence computers of our alliance partners have been running as many simulations as possible, and have come up with probability figures extrapolated from millions of potential attack scenarios. The mostly likely shape any invasion would have, would take place on at least three or four fronts, which I'll show you now."

The image of the general withdrew into a thumbnail in the top left-hand corner of the screen to reveal a map of the Mediterranean basin, with the European countries to the north and Caliphate territory to the south. The general went on: "Ample Annie suggests that the invasion will begin with a massed aerial attack, potentially along the entire southern coast of Europe."

Terry heard a number of gasps from the station operators in the room.

"There's even a high probability that the enemy may be able to deploy many more ACAs than we've seen so far. Now, once the enemy has control of the battlespace above the target area, he will then deploy troops to take physical possession of the territory. Here, the highest probability suggests massive airdrops of troops. This is based on two key factors: one, the enemy has not yet deployed a navy, so the probability that he will is low; and two, our research into the power units in the enemy's ACAs suggests there may be a tonne of other applications, especially in air transportation.

"However, what we cannot disregard entirely are other potential scenarios. The enemy's actual invasion could take any of a number of variations on this multi-point incursion. He could invade at one, two or more points, and might also choose different landing locations. These probabilities are based on assessments of the topography of the target countries, and which areas offer the maximum gain and/or would be the least difficult to secure."

The general reached for something out of view, retrieved what transpired to be a glass of water, and look a long sip.

Terry saw Webb lean and whisper in Napier's ear. She turned and looked back at him in mild shock, giving him a dismissive shake of her head.

"Now," the general continued, "ranged against them we have deployed the following units and formations."

Several indicators appeared in the European countries in varied colours denoting different countries of origin and their regimental and unit specialisation. The general went on: "In each country the bulk of the deployments are made up of that member's armed forces, but you will see here the extent of our multinational effort. For example, we've British and French units in Spain, French and German units in Italy, and Polish and Czech units in Greece, in addition to the comprehensively multinational force that has deployed to Bulgaria, among many others. And I'd like to salute all of our members, both soldiers and support people, who've done such a great job getting us all as prepared as we can be. Now, before I conclude this briefing, any questions?"

One thumbnail in the row of images along the bottom of the screen shimmered and doubled in size. Terry recognised the round, bullish face of Polish General Pakla. In moderately accented English, he asked: "Precisely what are our frontline deployments of SkyWatchers and PeaceMakers?"

General Jones's face remained impassive: "Over two hundred armed SkyWatchers are patrolling at higher altitudes, on rotation from bases in France, Germany and Poland. Each anticipated front will have from seven to nine hundred

PeaceMakers available to repel invasion forces. In addition, each front will deploy from ten to fifteen battlefield-support lasers, along with several batteries of RIM–214 surface-to-air smart missiles."

Silence greeted these numbers. Terry waited and wondered if some of the more passionate military people at the briefing would react, but after a few seconds, all he could sense was the depth of the shock. Terry hoped that for the sake of morale, no one would point out the clearly enfeebled response NATO would be able to mount against the forecast strength of the Caliphate's invasion. The shock on General Pakla's face seemed to stand for the feelings of everyone present, but even the passionate Pole held his counsel.

General Jones said: "Folks, I realise that, on the surface, it doesn't look too good, but I believe if we face this storm together, in unity, we might just be able to turn things around. We gotta remember we have a continent to defend. Right now, we got millions on the move; children, the elderly, the disabled. It's our job to protect them to the best of our ability. And I am convinced that every single member of Operation Defensive Arc will do exactly that." Terry watched as Jones stared out from the screen before concluding: "If there are no changes, I will give an update brief at the same time tomorrow, but by then I'm confident the invasion will have begun. Good luck everyone. That is all."

Terry looked at Napier. He thought he saw her eyes glisten. She said: "My god, we don't stand a chance, do we?"

Terry said: "Until we can find a way to fight back effectively, we must meet the invasion with what we have to hand, and hope for the best."

"Yes," Napier replied, her voice cracking. "Let's hope for the best, then."

Chapter 52

Deputy Grand Vizier Waqas lit a new incense stick and glanced at his brother Saad, who remained motionless. Waqas took a step back to stand next to the third brother, Affan. Waqas threw a confident glance at Affan, who met it with a look of equal assuredness. In front of the two men, Saad stood with his back to them, and Waqas reflected that he and Affan were the only two men in the entire Caliphate whom Saad could trust enough to turn his back on.

Saad turned to face his brothers and a sense of reverence surged inside Waqas. Waqas trusted and relied on Saad's unique sense which allowed him to see things he shouldn't be able to see, to judge others' feelings with unnatural accuracy. Saad had saved them all countless times on the path to domination, from slitting the throats of false allies to sowing just enough doubt and misinformation to wrong-foot opponents and turn them, with a mixture of bribe and threat, into supporters.

A scent of weak jasmine invaded Waqas's nose and coloured his thoughts. His breathing slowed and he sensed

Affan next to him also calm with patience for their older brother. Both knew when to wait on Saad's pleasure. The three brothers enjoyed absolute supremacy over two-hundred-and-sixty million subjects of the Caliphate, and the two younger brothers owed their positions to their older sibling.

Waqas glanced left, past Affan, and looked through the vast window at the mosques, palaces and other luxurious dwellings of Tehran outside. Small coloured lights dotted the view. Tehran had been rebuilt as Saad, the Third Caliph, wished it, with every sign of the previous regimes removed. In his mind's eye, he reviewed the key details of the plan, the plan which had been decades in the making, the plan which, in but a few hours, would see the New Persian Caliphate begin its irresistible rise towards world domination.

Saad turned around, faced them, and spoke. "Brothers, do you realise that today it is twenty years since we joined the First Caliph's forces? Look how far we have come. And this is but the beginning."

Waqas recalled that they'd only been junior officials then, running errands for obese old men whose time would soon pass. The three brothers grasped at once what could be achieved by the technological advancements made in the West. And now, through subterfuge, a little bargaining and a great deal of violence, the oldest brother sat at the summit as the Third Caliph.

It might so easily have never come to pass. It was seldom certain, at least to Waqas, that Saad acceding as Third Caliph was ever assured to happen. So many times their plans might have gone wrong; on so many occasions, they might have been found out and disposed of, disappeared like the thousands of opponents—both suspected and real—of whom Saad had now disposed. But as his brother always said: it did not matter how one fought, as long as one did not lose.

The First Caliph brought the countries and tribes together. There were endless summits and negotiations about which the rest of the world knew nothing. In those years, times were tense but violence infrequent. The First Caliph created the New Persian Caliphate through his appetite and passion to force a resolution to the brutal violence which had plagued the tribes of the Middle East for centuries. The First Caliph had focused on the shame, the endless, unyielding shame of Allah's chosen subjects living and killing each other like pigs. He appealed to the violent ones who took Allah's word in vain, to strive to regain the historical achievements and enlightened education that Muslims had enjoyed in earlier centuries. With some success among his better educated subjects, he drew parallels between how the Christians misinterpreted and abused the words written in the Bible during the time of the Conquistadors, and how the violent Muslims misinterpreted and abused the words of the Qur'an in the twenty-first century.

To bring understanding and unite the many and vastly disparate factions who called themselves Muslim became the First Caliph's life's work, and it went on to cost him his life. With the support of the Chinese and Russian governments, the First Caliph brought peace to areas of the Middle East which had known only the most brutal strife and bloodshed for decades. But this peace came with conditions. The First Caliph closed the new supranational entity off to the outside world. There could be no interference or provocation from outsiders if the Caliphate were to succeed. Anyone could enter the Caliphate if they wished, but no one could leave.

At this time, in the late 2040s, two key technological advances allowed the Caliphate to coalesce and then to consolidate: super artificial intelligence and the construction replicator. On one of those occasions when they were alone together, Saad often discussed with his brothers which of these two inventions made the greater contribution. For Waqas, the closest historical parallel was the formation of the United States of America, and how the steamboat and the railway and the telegraph had facilitated the management of a continent-wide country, the first time in history that a country of such size had been viable as a result of technological advancement. What the railway, steamboat and telegraph were to the USA in the 1840s, artificial intelligence and the construction replicator were to the New Persian Caliphate in the 2040s.

However, the entire project was thrown into serious doubt when the First Caliph died suddenly. Seeing the danger, his closest advisor moved quickly to quell confusion, dissent and anger at suspicion that the First Caliph had been assassinated. For Waqas and his brothers, the question of whether or not the First Caliph's demise had been a natural consequence of his strenuous workload soon became moot when his advisor acceded and became the Second Caliph.

As the 2050s dawned, the impact of the new technologies grew exponentially. The Second Caliph ensured his cities had construction replicators to build schools, hospitals and other infrastructure, and then they built multi-lane highways to link all of the Caliphate's major conurbations. On these new highways ran super-AI controlled vehicles capable of efficiently and reliably moving millions of people during key religious festivals. In a few brief years, super AI coupled with autonomous vehicles ensured the required food and medicines reached all corners of Caliphate territory. Societal development which a mere twenty years earlier would have taken decades, if it could have been accomplished at all, now required only a few years. The Second Caliph's popularity soared. His reputation spread. People in the region flocked to join the Caliphate. More and more countries were subsumed and assimilated, and the old Middle East became the New Persian Caliphate.

But through it all, Waqas and his brothers considered that the Second Caliph's rule lacked ambition. Worse, he neglected defence. At the time, it seemed the rest of the world had other concerns in other regions, in addition to the unfolding, multi-layered disaster of global climate change. The Second Caliph truly believed in peace, but he was also foolish not to see the limitless possibilities of a properly organised and fully armed Caliphate. Waqas' and his brothers' thoughts turned to broader questions of the Caliphate's place in the world. Why should the greatest Caliphate that Allah, in His wisdom, had brought into existence not expand indefinitely? Had not the time now finally arrived for the conversion of all humanity to Allah's will?

Under the Second Caliph, Waqas and his brothers gained promotion in the civil service in Tehran. He smiled when he recalled how the three of them had used their privileges to explore potential options with the assistance of an independent super AI unit. His older brother saw the possibilities in an instant. At length, Waqas realised that Saad had harboured such ambitions for many years, but only with the aid of this technology did he see a way forward, a daring and radical plan to change the course of history.

Waqas expressed his doubts, but his brother's energy and vision and determination infected him. He shivered when he recalled the most dangerous days in 2055, when the three of them decided to move. They'd spent years building a network of supporters who shared their vision, but for a few days the tension became unbearable. Like all such environs, the court of the Second Caliph seethed with rumour and conjecture and lies and backstabbing, and Waqas' brother knew they had to be the best to succeed.

But they did succeed, and after the eradication of potential opponents, Saad secured his position as the Third Caliph. Looking at the night outside, Waqas suddenly realised that he'd almost forgotten the leaders of the other factions who had vied unsuccessfully for the ultimate prize. He mused how soon those who failed were forgotten.

Once his brother was installed and his potential enemies disposed of, the Third Caliph set about realising his plans. Waqas was not scientifically minded, but he could still remember the presentation by a professor from one of the technical universities, about how their super AI had discovered, apparently by accident, a clever and lethal way to exploit a particular type of particle called a muon. He still remembered the excitement in both of his brothers at the realisation that this could give the Caliphate a military advantage which would place it years ahead of its enemies. Within days, the super AI had designed weapons and the facilities to build them.

However, the Third Caliph also insisted that an army of warriors had to be created and trained. The small standing army which the Second Caliph had maintained would act as the concentrate, its contempt of and hatred for all non-Caliphate subjects to spread like the essence of tea in water to infuse the new recruits. Once again, super artificial intelligence used the sum of human knowledge to design and implement the most efficient and effective program, taking rural, uneducated boys from the age of ten, and then drilling them aggressively in martial prowess and religious indoctrination.

Waqas smiled at the richness of the irony: in the past, people had expected the machines to be dumb; dumb like robots which performed menial tasks. No one had thought it would be the machines that would be clever, and the people who would be dumb. Super AI meant that an army of brainwashed, hate-filled young men need have no intelligence other than basic fighting skills and limitless loathing for anyone not like them. Caliphate warriors did not require tactical or strategic thinking ability, for the computers would do this. The warriors only needed to follow orders and kill every thing that had to be killed. Their immediate superiors would be advised by superiors who were advised by the computers. But the lowest Caliphate warrior was only required to be the most basic, brutish creature intent on killing his enemies, nothing more.

Waqas inhaled the scented air deeply. Saad looked at him and then at Affan. He said: "Tonight, my brothers, we begin the next stage of our journey. Europe will be crushed and dominated within weeks, and all the world will tremble at the new, relentless military power which we have created. All of the countries which truly matter: China, India, Brazil, and even Russia, will recoil in shock at the arrival of the newest military superpower.

"With Europe put to the sword and all of its Muslims either absorbed or vaporised, and with the subsequent doubling of our territory, our power will be greater still. And as the infidel country which had tried to attack us with nuclear weapons found out, and suffered total annihilation in result, no other country will dare to attempt to use the same weapons against us. Therefore, we go into this battle already assured of victory."

The Third Caliph turned his back on Waqas and Affan. He said: "Let the invasion commence."

THE END

Coming from Chris James in 2019

The Repulse Chronicles
Book Two

Invasion

For the latest news and releases, follow Chris James on Amazon

In the US, at:
https://www.amazon.com/Chris-James/e/B005ATW34C/

In the UK, at:
https://www.amazon.co.uk/Chris-James/e/B005ATW34C/

You can also follow his blog, at:
https://chrisjamesauthor.wordpress.com/

Printed in Great Britain
by Amazon